Sir John George Bourinot

Bibliography of the Members of the Royal Society of Canada

Sir John George Bourinot

Bibliography of the Members of the Royal Society of Canada

ISBN/EAN: 9783337157616

Printed in Europe, USA, Canada, Australia, Japan

Cover: Foto ©Raphael Reischuk / pixelio.de

More available books at **www.hansebooks.com**

BIBLIOGRAPHY

OF THE MEMBERS OF THE

ROYAL SOCIETY OF CANADA

BY

JOHN GEORGE BOURINOT

EDITOR OF THE TRANSACTIONS AND HONORARY SECRETARY OF THE ROYAL SOCIETY

PRINTED BY ORDER OF THE SOCIETY, MAY 25TH, 1894

PREFATORY NOTE.

Any imperfections in this bibliography must be largely ascribed to the difficulty the editor has experienced, in some cases, in obtaining information from members of the Society, and to his own inability to supply the missing facts in the parliamentary library and other institutions to which he has applied. On the whole, however, the bibliography, which is modelled on that of the *American Historical Association*, now a branch of the Smithsonian Institution at Washington, will be found as accurate as it is possible to make it, in view of the very range it takes for nearly half a century. It will be, probably, of much advantage to scientific and literary students when they wish to obtain all the literature on certain subjects in which many members of the Royal Society have been earnest workers for years. It is proposed to publish each year a similar bibliography of the work of the members of the Royal Society, and to include the publications of deceased members, which have not been available for the present volume.

BIBLIOGRAPHY

OF THE MEMBERS OF THE

ROYAL SOCIETY OF CANADA

Bailey, L. W.

Notes on New Species of Microscopical Organisms
from the Para River, South America.
Boston Journal of Natural History. Vol. VII., No. 3,
July, 1901. Pp. 329-351, with 2 Plates.

Notes on Diatomaceæ from the St. John River.
Canadian Naturalist and Geologist. April, 1863.

Report on the Mines and Minerals of New Brunswick. Fredericton, 1864. Pp. 75.

Mineral Localities of New Brunswick. Extracted
from No. 3.

Observations upon the Geology of Southern New
Brunswick, with a Geological Map. Printed by
the Legislature of New Brunswick. Fredericton, 1865. Pp. 150.

On the Geology of the Island of Grand Manan.
Canadian Naturalist, Vol. VI., No. 1, with Map.

Report on Water Supply to the City of Fredericton. Fredericton : H. A. Cropley, 1867.

The Woods and Minerals of New Brunswick. A
Descriptive Catalogue for Use at the Centennial
Exhibition in Philadelphia. By L. W. Bailey
and Edward Jack, C. E. Fredericton, 1876.
Pp. 51.

The Study of Natural History and Use of Natural
History Museums. An Address at the Encœnia
of the University of New Brunswick. June,
1872. H. Chubb & Co., St. John. Pp. 23.

Remarks on the Age and Relations of the Metamorphic Rocks of New Brunswick and Maine.
Bailey and Matthew.
*Proceedings American Association for Advancement
of Science.* Vol. XVIII., 1869. Pp. 16.

Bailey, L. W.—*Continued.*

On the Diatomaceous Earths of Maine.
*Hitchcock's Report on the Geology and Agriculture
of Maine,* 1862. Pp. 395.

Elementary Natural History. New Brunswick
School Series. St. John : J. & A. McMillan, 1887.
Pp. 94.

Relics of the Stone Age in New Brunswick.
*Bulletin of Natural History Society of New Bruns-
wick.* Vol. VI., 1887. Pp. 16, with 3 Photos.

Notes on the Surface Geology of Southwestern
Nova Scotia.
Transactions of Nova Scotia Institute of Science
Halifax, 1890-91. Pp. 8.

On the Acadian and St. Lawrence Water Shed.
Canadian Record of Science, July, 1888. Pp. 16.

On the Mineral Resources of New Brunswick.
Canadian Mining and Mechanical Review, 1891.

Geology and Geologists in New Brunswick.
Canadian Record of Science, Vol. II., No. 2, 1886.

Desmids and Diatoms.
American Naturalist, Vol. I, pp. 606-607, with Plate.
Salem, 1868.

Fresh-Water Sketches.
Ibid.

In the Reports of the Geological Survey of Canada :

Report on the Geology of Southern New Brunswick. 1870-71. Pp. 228.

Geological Investigations in New Brunswick.
1871-72.

On the Carboniferous System of New Brunswick.
1872-73. (Bailey and Matthew.)

Summary Report of Geological Explorations in
New Brunswick. 1874-75. (Bailey and Matthew.)

Bailey, L. W.—*Continued.*

Report on the Lower Carboniferous Belt of Albert and Westmoreland Counties, New Brunswick, with Section and Geological Map. 1876-77. (Bailey and Ells.)

Report on the Geology of Southern New Brunswick. 1878-79. (Bailey, Matthew and Ells.)

Report of Explorations and Surveys in Portions of York and Carleton Counties, New Brunswick. 1882-84. Pp. 31.

Explorations and Surveys in Portions of the Counties of Carleton, Victoria, York and Northumberland, New Brunswick. New Series, Vol. 1, 1885. Pp. 29, with Map.

Explorations in Portions of the Counties of Victoria, Northumberland and Restigouche, New Brunswick. 1886. (L. W. Bailey and W. McInnes.) Pp. 17.

Explorations and Surveys in Portions of Northern New Brunswick, and Adjacent Areas in Quebec and Maine. 1877-78. (Bailey and McInnes.)

In the Transactions of Royal Society of Canada :

On the Physical and Geological History of the St. John River, New Brunswick. Abstract. Vol. I., Sec. 4, 1882.

On Geological Contacts and Ancient Erosion in Southern and Central New Brunswick. Vol. II., Sec. 4, 1884.

On the Silurian System of Northern Maine, New Brunswick and Quebec. Vol. IV., Sec. 4, 1886.

On the Physiography and Geology of Aroostook County, Maine. Vol V., Sec. 4, 1887.

On the Progress of Geological Investigation in New Brunswick. Presidential Address. Vol. VII., Sec. 4, 1889.

Baillairgé, C.

Conférences Illustrées sur l'Astronomie, l'Optique, la Pneumatique, l'Acoustique, l'Atmosphère, les Vents, les Courants, la Vapeur et la Machine à vapeur, la Mécanique, etc. ; de deux heures chacune en moyenne, dans la Salle des Séances de l'Ancien Parlement du Bas Canada, rues Lamontagne et Fort Dauphin, devant des auditoires de 700 à 800 personnes. Québec : C. Darveau. 1848-50.

Le Calorifère : Chauffage à l'air chaud. Illustré. Québec : Bureau et Marcotte. 1853.
8vo., pp. 23.

Nouveau traité de Géométrie et de Trigonométrie rectiligne et sphérique. Toisé des surfaces et volumes. Tables logarithmiques et sinus, etc., naturels. Ouvrage illustré. Québec : C. Darveau. 1866.
8vo., pp. 83.

Rapport Général de l'Ing. des Ponts et Chaussées de la Ville de Québec, embrassant les départements du Feu, des Marchés et Halles, de la Traverse du Fleuve, de la Police, etc. Québec : C. Darveau. 1868.
8vo., pp. 96.

Baillairgé, C.—*Continued.*

General Report of the City Engineer, Quebec, embracing Roads and Bridges, Markets, Ferry, Health, Fire, and other departments. Quebec : C. Darveau. 1872.
8vo., pp. 120.

Geometry, Mensuration, and the Stereometrical Tableau. Illustrated. Read before the Literary and Historical Society of Quebec. Quebec : C. Darveau. 1873.
8vo., pp. 44.

Géométrie, Toisé, et le Tableau Stéréométrique. Illustrée. Lu devant la Société Littéraire et Historique de Québec. Démonstration et discussion de la formule par l'Abbé Maingui, de l'Université Laval. Québec : C. Darveau. 1873.
8vo., pp. 66.

Clé Synoptique ou abrégée du Tableau Stéréométrique. Illustrée. Québec : C. Darveau. 1874.
8vo., pp. 16.

Abridged Key to Stereometrical Tableau. New System of Measuring all Bodies—Segments, Frusta and Ungulæ of such bodies—by one and the same rule. Illustrated. Quebec : C. Darveau. 1874.
8vo., pp. 16.

Clé du Tableau Stéréométrique illustrée. Précédée du toisé des surfaces, tables, etc. Québec : C. Darveau. 1874.
8vo., pp. 226.

Berthuxabel, ou Le Diable Devenu Cuisinier. Comédie en un acte (épisode de la guerre d'Italie de 1859) jouée par la Cie Maugard à la Salle Jacques-Cartier et deux fois à la Salle de Musique, Québec. Québec : C. Darveau. 1873.
8vo., pp. 20.

Reports on Sections of the then so-called North Shore Railway (now the C.P.R.) between Quebec and Montreal. Quebec : C. Darveau. 1874-5-6. Folio, 10 pp. each.

The Proposed Improvements in the Estuary of the River St. Charles, Quebec. Quebec : C. Darveau. 1873.
8vo., pp. 10.

Toisé des Surfaces illustrée. Québec : C. Darveau. 1875.
8vo., pp. 58.

Supplementary Report on the North Shore Railway (now the C. P. R.) between Quebec and Montreal. Quebec : R. Vincent. 1875.
8vo., pp. 14.

Rapport Supplémentaire de l'Ing. de la Cité de Québec sur le chemin de fer du Nord (aujourd'hui le C. P. R.) entre Québec et Montréal. Québec : E. Vincent. 1875.
8vo., pp. 15.

Report on the Fire-escape Appliances and Facilities of some ninety-six Public Buildings of Quebec and Environs, including Schools, Colleges, Convents, Theatres, Lecture and Music Halls, Manufactories, Hotels, Churches, etc. Folio, pp. 105.

The Proposed Dry Dock in the Mouth of the River St. Charles. Quebec : C. Darveau. 1876.
8vo., pp. 4.

Baillairgé, C.—*Continued.*

Design No. 5 (1000 feet high) of the proposed great Tower for London. Illustrated letter-press, estimates, etc. Illustrated catalogue of the competitive designs sent in. Printed by "Industries," London, 358 Strand. 1890.
Folio, pp. 100.

Homonymes français. Joliette : Révd F. A. Baillairgé. 1891.
12mo., pp. 212.

English Homonyms. Quebec : C. Darveau. 1891.
12mo., pp. 190.

General Report of the City Engineer, Quebec, on Pavements, etc. Quebec : E. Vincent.
8vo., pp. 42.

Etude ayant trait à la solution du problème : Déterminer la hauteur atteinte par un projectile qui en retombant au niveau d'où il est parti, a produit un effet connu. Lue devant la Société Royale du Canada, Sect. III., le 27 mai 1891. Montréal. 1891.

A paper relating to the height to which a missile attained, which, in descending again to the level from which it was projected, produced a known result. Read before Sect. III., Royal Society of Canada, May 27, 1891. Montreal. 1891.

An attempt to deduce the pressure per square inch under which a steam boiler exploded from the effects produced by the explosion. Read before the Royal Society of Canada, Montreal, May, 1891.

Tentative de déduire des effets d'une explosion de chaudière à vapeur, la pression sous la quelle la chaudière a cédé. Lue devant la Sect. III. de la Société Royale du Canada le 27 mai 1891, à Montréal. Québec : C. Darveau. 1891.

The cost of electric lighting in all the principal cities of North America.
Water and Gas Review, New York, 1892.
Folio, pp. 4.

Escape from buildings in case of fire. Illustrated. Read before the Canadian Association of Architects, Montreal, 1892.
Canadian Architect and Builder, Toronto and Montreal, 1892.
Folio, pp. 4.

La ventilation libre des égoûts en rapport avec l'hygiène de l'habitation. Joliette : Révd F. A. Baillairgé. Lue devant la Sect. III., Société Royale du Canada, mai 1892.
8vo., pp. 17.

The free and liberal ventilation of sewers in its relation to the sanitation of our dwellings. Quebec : C. Darveau, Read before the Royal Society of Canada, Sect. III., May, 1892.
Folio, pp. 7.

La Baie d'Hudson. L'exploitation proposée de ses ressources de terre et de mer. Nouvelle colonie. Chemin de fer pour s'y rendre. Joliette : Révd F. A. Baillairgé. 1893.

Conférence faite sous les auspices de la Société de Géographie de Québec à l'Institut Canadien. Joliette : Révd F. A. Baillairgé. 1893.
8vo., pp. 42.

Baillairgé, C.—*Continued.*

The Quebec Land Slide of September 19, 1889. Illustrated and technically explained. Read before the Canadian Association of Civil Engineers, Montreal, and published in the Transactions of the Society, 1883.
8vo., pp. 33.

Retaining Walls. The defects in the new dock walls at the Louise Basin, Quebec.
Canadian Engineering News, Montreal.

✍ Technical Education of the People in Untechnical Language. Read before Section II. of the Royal Society of Canada, Ottawa, May, 1891. Quebec : C. Darveau. 1891.
8vo., pp. 42.

Begin, Monseigneur Louis Nazaire.

La Primauté et l'Infaillibilité des Souverains Pontifes. Leçons d'histoire données à l'Université Laval. Québec : L. H. Huot. 1873.
12mo., pp. 430.

La Sainte Ecriture et la Règle de Foi. Québec : Augustin Côté et Cie. 1874.
12mo., pp. 298.

Le Culte Catholique. Québec : Augustin Côté et Cie. 1875.
12mo., pp. 181.

Chronologie de l'Histoire du Canada. Québec : C. Darveau. 1880.
18mo., pp. 36.

Panégyrique de Saint-Thomas d'Aquin, prononcé à la Cathédrale de St-Hyacinthe, à l'occasion du 6e centenaire de la mort de Saint-Thomas.

✕ Bell, Robert.

In the Publications of the Geological Survey of Canada, viz. :—

The Natural History of the Lower St. Lawrence, the Saguenay and Lake St. John. Report for 1857.

Catalogue, with Notes, of Animals and Plants collected on the Southeast Side of the St. Lawrence, from Quebec to Gaspé. Report for 1858.

Superficial Geology of Canada. General Report on "The Geology of Canada,' 1863, pp. 886-930.

Coloured Map, with Explanations, showing the Distribution of the Superficial Deposits between Lake Superior and Gaspé. Atlas accompanying the last. 1863.

Geology of Grand Manitoulin Island. Report for 1863-06.

Geological and Topographical Map of a portion of the Gaspé Peninsula, from Surveys by Dr. Bell, accompanying a Report on the Occurrence of Petroleum in that Region. Pamphlet published for the Geological Survey in Quebec, 1865.

Geology of the Western Portion of Grand Manitoulin, and of Cockburn, Drummond and St. Joseph's Island. Report for 1863-09.

The Northwest Coast of Lake Superior and the Nipigon District, with a Topographical Map of the Thunder Bay and Lake Nipigon Regions. Report for 1866-09.

Bell, Robert.—*Continued.*

The Country North of Lake Superior, between the Nipigon and Michipicoten Rivers (Pic River, Long Lake, etc.). Report for 1870-71.

The Country between Lake Superior and the Albany River. Report for 1871-72.

The Country between Lake Superior and Lake Winnipeg. Report for 1872-73.

The Country between Red River and the South Saskatchewan, with Notes on the Geology of the Region between Lake Superior and Red River. Contains an Appendix by Mr. Hoffmann on Lignites. Report for 1873-74.

The Country West of Lakes Manitoba and Winnipegosis, with Notes on the Geology of Lake Winnipeg. Report for 1874-75.

Explorations in 1875 between James' Bay and Lakes Superior and Huron. Report for 1875-76.

In Part: Descriptive Catalogue of a Collection of the Economic Minerals of Canada at the Philadelphia International Exhibition, 1876. Special Publication of the Geological Survey.

Geological Researches North of Lake Huron and East of Lake Superior. Report for 1876-77.

An Exploration of the East Coast of Hudson Bay in 1877, with a Map of the East-main Coast, 0 Plates and 3 Illustrations. Report for 1877-78.

Explorations in 1878 in the Country between Lake Winnipeg and Hudson Bay. With Map of Lake Winnipeg, Map of Nelson River and the Boat Route between Lake Winnipeg and Hudson Bay, including an enlarged Plan of the Mouth of Hayes' River and Vicinity of York Factory; also 5 Plates. Report for 1877-78.

Explorations in 1879 on the Churchill and Nelson Rivers and around God's and Island Lakes. With Maps of these Lakes, 6 Plates, and the following Appendices: I. On some Silurian and Devonian Fossils from Manitoba and the Valleys of the Churchill and Nelson Rivers—J. F. Whiteaves. II. List of Plants collected by Dr. Bell around the Shores of Hudson Bay and along the Churchill and Nelson Rivers—J. Macoun. III. List of Fresh-water Mollusca from Manitoba and the Valley of Nelson River—J. F. Whiteaves. IV. List of Lepidoptera from Nelson and Churchill Rivers and the West Coast of Hudson Bay—Herr Geffcken. V. List of Coleoptera collected by Dr. Bell in 1879 on Nelson and Churchill Rivers—J. L. Le Conte. VI. List of Birds from the Region between Norway House and Forts Churchill and York—R. Bell. VII. Variation of the Compass in 21 Localities in the Regions Explored—R. Bell. Report for 1878-79.

Hudson Bay and some of the Lakes and Rivers lying to the west of it; also Log of a Voyage in the "Ocean Nymph" from York Factory to London.

The Northern Limits of the Principal Forest Trees of Canada, east of the Rocky Mountains, with a Map on which they are shown.

Bell, Robert.—*Continued.*

This Report also contains the following Appendices:—I. List of Fossils collected by Dr. Bell in Manitoba in 1880 —J. F. Whiteaves. II. Tabulated List of Plants collected by Dr. Bell west of Hudson Bay—J. Macoun. III. List of Coleoptera collected by Dr. Bell in 1880 in Manitoba and between Lake Winnipeg and Hudson Bay —J. L. Le Conte. IV. List of the Land, Freshwater and Marine Mollusca collected by Dr. Bell—J. F. Whiteaves. V. Analyses of the Waters of Hayes' and Nelson Rivers—Professor Wm. Dittmar, F.R.S. VI. Seasonal and Periodic Events at York Factory—Compiled by Dr. Bell. VII. Tables showing dates of the opening and closing of Hayes' River at York Factory, from Records by Mr. Wm. Woods, Meteorologist, York Factory. VIII. Dates of the arrivals of the vessels of the Hudson's Bay Company at York Factory and of their sailings for 93 years, from 1789 to 1880, both inclusive. IX. Seasonal or Periodic Events at Moose Factory. X. Dates of the arrivals of the vessels of the Hudson's Bay Company at Moose Factory and of their sailings for 147 years, from 1735 to 1880, both inclusive. XI. Statistics of the Weather from Observations taken at York and Moose Factories. Report for 1879-80.

Geology of the Basin of Moose River and adjacent country. With a Geological Map. Report for 1880-81-82.

Geology of Lake of the Woods and Adjacent Country. With a Geological Map. Report for 1880-81-82.

On Part of the Basin of Athabasca River. With a Map of the River from Lac la Biche to Lake Athabasca, one Plate and one Appendix containing a list of Lepidoptera collected by Dr. Bell in the Northwest Territory in 1882. Report for 1882-83-84.

Observations on the Coast of Labrador and on Hudson Strait and Bay, made in 1884. With 2 Steel-plate Engravings and the following Appendices:—I. List of Plants collected by Dr. Bell in Eastern Labrador and on Hudson Strait and Bay—J. Macoun. II. List of Mammals, with Notes Dr. Bell. III. List of Birds, with Notes —Dr. Bell. IV. List of Crustacea collected by Dr. Bell at Port Burwell—S. J. Smith. V. List of Lepidoptera collected by Dr. Bell in Hudson Strait—H. H. Lyman. VI. List of Coleoptera from Fort Churchill. Report for 1882-83-84.

Observations on the Geology, Zoology and Botany of Hudson Strait and Bay, made in 1885. With a Map of the Ottawa Islands, 2 Steel-plate Engravings, 2 Illustrations, and the following Appendices:—I. Lists of Plants collected in Newfoundland and Hudson Strait—J Macoun. II. Partial lists of Insects collected on the Expedition—H. H. Lyman and G. H. Horne. Report for 1885, DD.

Explorations of the Attawapishkat and Albany Rivers. Lonely Lake to James' Bay. With 4 Plates and an Appendix containing a List of

Bell, Robert.—*Continued.*

Lepidoptera from the Southern part of Keewaitin District, by H. H. Lyman and others. Report for 1886.

Geology of the Sudbury Mining District. With a detailed Topographical and Geological Map, 4 Plates, 8 Figures, and the following Appendices:—Notes on the Microscopical Characters of 50 kinds of Rocks, mostly from the Sudbury District—Professor Geo. H. Williams, of Johns Hopkins University. II. Levels of the Lakes of the District above the Sea. List of Elevations on the Canadian Pacific Railway. III. Report, with List, of 73 Species of Lepidoptera collected by Dr. Bell in the Country northward of Lake Huron—H. H. Lyman, of Montreal, Wm. H. Edwards, Professor J. B. Smith, of New Jersey and Rev. Geo. D. Hulst, of Brooklyn. IV. Meanings of Indian Geographical Names in the Country around Sudbury.—Dr. Bell. Report for 1890-91, Part I.

Contributions to 21 Summary Reports from 1870 to 1893, published in the Annual Reports of the Department of the Interior, and reprinted in those of the Geological Survey.

In the Transactions of the Royal Society of Canada :

Notes on the Birds of Hudson Bay. Vol. I., Sec. 4, 1882.

Causes of the Fertility of the Land in the Canadian Northwest. Vol. I., Sec. 4, 1883.

The Geology and Economic Minerals of Hudson Bay and Northern Canada. Vol. II., Sec. 4, 1884.

On Some Points in Reference to Ice Phenomena. Vol. IV., Sec. 3, 1886.

The Petroleum Field of Ontario. Vol. V., Sec. 4, 1887.

The Chickaree, or Red Squirrel. An Appendix to Dr. T. Wesley Mills' Paper on Squirrels. Vol. v., Sec. 4, 1887.

The Huronian System in Canada. Presidential Address to Sec. 4. Vol. v., Sec. 4, 1888.

Glacial Kettle-Holes in Canada. Vol. XII., Sec. 4, 1894.

In the Bulletins of the Geological Society of America, viz. :—

On Glacial Phenomena in Canada. Vol. I., pp. 287-310. April, 1890.

The Nickel and Copper Deposits of Sudbury District, Canada. With an Appendix on the Silicified Glass-Breccia of the District, by Professor George H. Williams, of Johns Hopkins University. Vol. II., pp. 125-140. February, 1891.

Discussion of the Supposed Post-Glacial Outlet of the Great Lakes through Lake Nipissing and the Mattawa River. Vol. IV., pp. 425-6-7. Proceedings of the Ottawa Meeting, December, 1892.

Pre-Palæozoic Decay of Crystalline Rocks North of Lake Huron. With 2 Plates and 3 Figures. Vol. v., pp. 357-366. March, 1894.

Bell, Robert.—*Continued.*

In the Canadian Naturalist and Geologist and (its successor) the Canadian Record of Science, Montreal, viz. :

Natural History of the Gulf of St. Lawrence and the Distribution of the Mollusca in Eastern Canada. Vol. IV., 1859, pp. 241-251.

On the Occurrence of Fresh-water Shells in some of our Post-Tertiary Deposits. Vol. VI., 1861, pp. 42-51.

List (with Notes) of Recent Land and Fresh-water Shells collected around Lakes Superior and Huron in 1859-60. Vol. VI., 1861, pp. 268-270.

Catalogue (with Notes) of Birds collected and observed around Lakes Superior and Huron in 1860. Vol. VI., 1861, pp. 270-275.

Superficial Geology of the Gaspé Peninsula. Vol. VIII., 1863, pp. 175-183.

Roofing Slate as a Source of Wealth in Canada. Vol. VIII., 1863, pp. 358-360.

The Nipigon Territory. Ser. II., Vol. 5, 1870, pp. 118-120.

Mineral Region of Lake Superior. Ser. II., Vol. 7, 1875, pp. 49-51. (Epitomized by J. F. Whiteaves.)

The Forests of Canada. With Map. *Canadian Record of Science,* Vol. II., April, 1886, pp. 63-77.

Biography of the late Alex. Murray, Geologist. With Portrait. *Ibid.,* April, 1892, pp. 77-90.

In the Canadian Journal and (its successor) the Proceedings of the Canadian Institute, Toronto, viz.:

Sketch of the Geology of the Route of the Intercolonial Railway. *Canadian Journal,* Ser. II., Vol. 15, 1878, pp. 381-387.

On the Occurrence of Petroleum in the Northwest Territories, with Notes on New Localities. *Proceedings Canadian Institute,* Ser. III., Vol. 1, 1879-83, pp. 225-230.

The Mode of Occurrence of Apatite in Canada. *Ibid.,* Ser. III., Vol. 3, 1884-85, pp. 294-302. (A Paper by Dr. Bell on the same subject is published in the *Engineering and Mining Journal,* Vol. 39, p. 316, May 9th, 1885.)

Marble Island and the Northwest Coast of Hudson Bay. *Ibid,* Ser. III., Vol. 4, 1885-86, pp. 102-204.

In the Annals of the Botanical Society of Canada :

Catalogue of Plants collected on the South and East Shores of Lake Superior, and on the North Shore of Lake Huron. Kingston, 1861.

The Trees and Shrubs growing around Lakes Superior and Huron. Kingston, 1861.

Miscellaneous Publications :

Annual Reviews of the Progress of Mining in Canada from 1863 to 1877.
Monetary Times, Montreal : *Engineering and Mining Journal,* New York; *Mining Journal,* London, and *Reports* on the Trade and Commerce of Montreal.

The Enniskillen Oil Region. London, England, 1865.

Bell, Robert.—*Continued.*

Notes on the Natural History of the Nipigon Country. A Paper read before the Natural History Society of Montreal, 28th February, 1870.

The Region North of Lake Superior, and the Proposed Pacific Railway. A Lecture before the Mechanics' Institute, Toronto, 17th June, 1870.

The Various Species of Deer inhabiting the Dominion. A Paper read before the Natural History Society of Montreal, 19th December, 1870.

The Wonders of the Glacial Period. Fourth Somerville Lecture, Montreal, 23rd February, 1871.

The Coal-fields of Canada. A Lecture under the auspices of the Grand Trunk Reading-room Association, Point St. Charles, 19th February, 1873.

The Huronian and other Mineral-bearing Rocks of Lake Superior. A Paper read before the Natural History Society of Montreal, 24th February, 1873.

The Fur-bearing Animals of Canada. Fifth Somerville Lecture, Montreal, 27th February, 1873.

A Journey from Montreal to the Saskatchewan in 1873. A Lecture before the St. Gabriel Young Men's Association, 24th February, 1874.

Coal. A Lecture delivered in the Mechanics' Hall, Montreal, on behalf of the Working Men's Mutual Benefit and Widows' and Orphans' Provident Society, March, 1873.

A Summer on the Plains. Third Somerville Lecture, Montreal, 10th February, 1874. Also delivered before the St. Andrew's Church Institute, Ottawa, 8th April, 1890.

The Grasshopper Plague in the Northwest Territory. Third Somerville Lecture, Montreal, 25th March, 1875.

The Uses of a Geological Survey. A Lecture delivered at Prince Arthur's Landing, October, 1875.

Our Great Northwest as a Home for the Emigrant. Second Somerville Lecture, Montreal, 13th February, 1879.

The Glacial Epoch in Canada. A Lecture before the Ottawa Literary and Scientific Society, 20th January, 1881.

Scientific Work in Canada. An Address at Queen's University on receiving the Degree of LL.D., 25th April, 1883.

The Athabasca-Mackenzie Basin. Fifth Somerville Lecture, Montreal, 1st March, 1883.

Notes on Diseases among the Indians. A Paper read before the Bathurst and Rideau Medical Association, Ottawa, January, 1885.

Explorations in Canada by Forest, Sea and Plain. A Lecture before the St. Paul's Young Men's Association, Montreal, 14th December, 1885.

Personal Reminiscences of the late Sir William Logan. A Lecture delivered in St. James' Hall, Ottawa, 10th March, 1885. Also Somerville Lecture, Montreal, 20th March, 1885.

Bell, Robert.—*Continued.*

Hudson Bay. A Lecture before the Young Men's Christian Association of Ottawa, 10th March, 1880.

The Hudson Bay Territories and their Inhabitants. A Lecture before the Ottawa Literary and Scientific Society, 7th January, 1880.

Hudson Bay and the Hudson Bay Route. The Queen's University Lecture of 1880. Delivered in Convocation Hall, Kingston, 20th April, 1880.

Illustrations of our Northern Wilderness. A Lecture delivered in St. George's Church Schoolroom, Ottawa, 7th March, 1888.

North America Furs. A Lecture delivered in St. Bartholemew's Hall, Ottawa, 4th April, 1880, under the auspices of His Excellency the Governor-General.

The Origin of Some Geographical Features in Canada. Read before Sect. IV., Royal Society of Canada, Ottawa, 24th May, 1888.

Some Ojibwé Legends. Read before the Montreal Branch of the American Folk-lore Society, April, 1893.

The Glacial Succession in Canada. A Paper read before the World's Congress of Geologists, Chicago, August, 1893.

Our Forests. An Illustrated Lecture delivered under the auspices of Their Excellencies the Governor-General and the Countess of Aberdeen at Rideau Hall, Ottawa, 20th March, 1894.

Ⅹ Bethune, C. J. S.

The Production of Silk from the Caterpillars of Canadian Moths.
Journal of the Board of Arts and Manufactures for Upper Canada. April, 1861, pp. 85-87.

Description of some species of Nocturnal Lepidoptera found in Canada.
Canadian Journal, Toronto, February, 1863, pp. 1-16.

Nocturnal Lepidoptera found in Canada. Part II.
Ibid., July, 1865, pp. 247-260.

Insect Life in Canada. March and April.
Canadian Monthly Magazine, Toronto, April, 1863.

Description of three new species of Canadian Nocturnal Lepidoptera.
Proceedings of the Entomological Society of Philadelphia, Vol. IV., 1865, pp. 213-5.

Nova Scotian Lepidoptera.
Proceedings of the Nova Scotian Institute of Natural Science, Halifax, Vol. II., Part 3, 1868-9, pp. 78-97.

Insects of the Northern Parts of British America. (From "Kirby's Fauna Boreali-Americana : Insects.")
Reprinted from the *Canadian Entomologist*, Vols. II.-XIII., 1870-1881, pp. 156 + 14.

Insects Injurious to Agriculture.
Toronto Agricultural Commission, Toronto, 1881, Vol. III., pp. 22-51, (Appendix E).

In the Canadian Entomologist and Reports of the Entomological Society of Ontario, viz. :

A Luminous Larva.
Canadian Entomologist, Vol. I., 1868, pp. 2-3 ; 38-39.

---

* In this list the *Entomological Journal* is mentioned by name, and the Reports of the Society only by number, to save repetition.

Bourinot, John George.

The Confederation of the Provinces: A Review of Pamphlet by the Hon. Joseph Howe.
> Series of three articles in *Halifax Evening Reporter*, 1865. (The writer was editor of this paper, 1860-66 and the editorials, for the most part, during those years, were from his pen.) Also in pamphlet form, Halifax, 1866.

Statesmanship and Letters.
> *Stewart's Literary Quarterly*, St. John, N B., 1867.

The Mystery at the Chateau des Ormeaux.
> *Ibid.*, 1868.

British American Union considered in relation to the interests of Cape Breton. A pamphlet, pp. 1-10. Halifax, N.S., 1808.
> Also in *Halifax Colonist*, 1868.

Stories we heard among the Pines.
> *Stewart's Literary Quarterly*, St. John, N.B., 1869.

Gentlemen Adventurers in Acadia: I., Baron de Poutrincourt; II., Charles de la Tour; III., Baron Jean Vincent de Saint Castin.
> *New Dominion Monthly*, Montreal, 1869.

Notes of a Ramble through Cape Breton.
> *New Dominion Monthly*, Montreal, May, 1868. Also, in *Cape Breton News*, Sydney, May 30, 1868.

Resources and Prospects of Cape Breton.
> *Canadian*, Boston, Mass., 1868

Some Stories of a Lost Tribe. (The Red Indians or Boethiks of Newfoundland.)
> *New Dominion Monthly*, Montreal, October and November, 1868.

The State of Affairs in Nova Scotia.
> A series of letters on the Repeal of Confederation movement in Nova Scotia, that appeared in *The Times*, Ottawa, 1868.

The Island of Cape Breton: Its History, Scenery and Resources.
> *Stewart's Literary Quarterly*, St. John, N.B., 1870.

The Maritime Enterprise of British America.
> *Ibid.*, 1870.

Notes from Ottawa.
> *Canadian Monthly*, Toronto, August, 1870.

Marguerite; a tale of Forest Life in the New Dominion.
> *New Dominion Monthly*, Montreal, 1870-71.

Canal Commission. Letter to the Honourable the Secretary of State from the Canal Commissioners respecting the improvement of the Inland Navigation of the Dominion of Canada. Ottawa, 24th February, 1871.
> This report was the author's work *verbatim et literatim*, except from pp. 58-92, which give decision of the Commissioners and the engineer's report. 8vo., pp 328.

The Work of Administration at Ottawa.
> An elaborate essay on the practical working of the government departments at Ottawa, etc, issued as a campaign document by the *Mail*, Toronto, 1872

From the Great Lakes to the Sea.
> *Canadian Monthly*, Toronto, June, 1872. Also in the *New York World*, in abstract, in 1871.

Canadian Materials for History, Poetry and Romance.
> *New Dominion Monthly*, Montreal, 1871.

What happened at Beauvoir one Christmas Eve.
> *Canadian Illustrated News*, Montreal, December, 1872.

Bourinot, John George.—Continued.

The Marine and Fisheries of Canada.
> *Proceedings of the Royal Colonial Institute*, 1872-73, Vol. iv. Also, in *Canadian Monthly*, Toronto, February, 18 3.

The Old Japanese Cabinet.
> *Canadian Monthly*, Toronto, 1874.

Canadian Historic Names.
> *Ibid.*, April, 1875.

The Ottawa Valley: Its History and Resources. A lecture before the Ottawa Literary and Scientific Society.
> In abstract, Ottawa *Citizen*, December 11, 1872. In full, *Canadian Monthly*, Toronto, January, 1875.

Titles in Canada.
> *Canadian Monthly*, Toronto, October, 1877.

Forest Rangers and Voyageurs: I., Gentlemen-Adventurers and Coureurs de Bois; II., Songs of the Forest and River.
> *Rose-Belford Canadian Monthly*. Toronto, April and May, 1877.

The River of the Desert.
> *Belford's Monthly Magazine*, Toronto, February, 1878. Also in *Canadian Monthly*, Toronto, January, 1878, with a few additions and changes, under the title of "Through the Phosphate Country to the Desert."

House of Commons in Session.
> *Canadian Monthly*, Toronto, 1878.

Forms and Usages.
> *Rose-Belford's Canadian Monthly*. Toronto, March, 1879.

Review of the Progress of Literature in Canada.
> *Dominion Annual Register*, Ottawa, 1879, pp 263-297.

Cape Breton; the Long Wharf of the Dominion.
> *Transactions of the Geographical Society of Quebec*. Vol. i., No. 2, 1861. Also in *Canadian Monthly*, Toronto, April, 1882

National Development of Canada.
> *Canadian Monthly*, Toronto, March, 880 Also in *Proceedings of Royal Colonial Institute*, London, Vol. ii.

The Intellectual Development of the Canadian People. An Historical Review.
> *Canadian Monthly*, Toronto, 1880. Also Toronto, 1881. 12 mo., xi + 128.

The Old Forts of Acadia.
> *Canadian Monthly*, Toronto, 1874. Also, in *Transactions of the Royal Society of Canada*, Vol. i., Sec. 2, 1882-83. Also, in *The Current*, Chicago Vol. i., pp. 102, 111.

Canada as a Home.
> *Westminster Review*, London and New York, July, 1882. Also, in pamphlet form, London, 1882. 12mo., pp 30. Also, in French, *Revue Britannique*, Paris, 1882.

Relations between Canada and the United States.
> *The Current*, Chicago. Vol. i., p. 54.

The Progress of the New Dominion.
> *Blackwood's Magazine*, Edinburgh and New York, March, 1883.

Canada: Its Political Development.
> *Scottish Review*, Paisley, London and New York, 1885.

Bourinot, John George.—*Continued.*

The Fishery Question : Its Imperial Importance.
Westminster Review, London and New York, 1886.
Also, in pamphlet, London, 1886.

Canada as a Nation.
La Revue Coloniale-Internationale, Amsterdam, mars 1886.

French Canada.
Scottish Review, Paisley, London, and New York, 1887.

Canada During the Victorian Era : A Short Historical Review. In two parts.
Magazine of American History, New York, 1887.

Canada and the Federation of the Empire.
La Revue Coloniale-Internationale, Amsterdam, juillet, 1887.

Local Government in Canada.
Johns Hopkins University Studies, Baltimore, 1887.
Also, *Transactions of Royal Society of Canada*, Vol. IV., Sec. 2, 1886.

Federal Government in Canada.
A series of four lectures before Trinity University, Toronto. Printed in *Johns Hopkins University Studies*, 1889.

Canada : Its National Development and Destiny.
Quarterly Review, London and New York, July, 1887.
See also *Proceedings of Western Association of Writers*, Richmond, Ind., 1890.

○ The Study of Political Science in Canadian Universities.
Transactions of Royal Society of Canada, Vol. VII., Sec. 2, 1889. Also one of a course of lectures before Trinity University, Toronto.

Federal Government in Canada.
Canadian Law Times, Toronto, 1889.

The National Sentiment in Canada : an Historical Study.
University Quarterly Review, Toronto, 1890.

Canada and the United States.
Scottish Review, Paisley, London and New York, 1890.

Canada and the United States : A Study in Comparative Politics.
A lecture before Harvard University (Sever Hall) and the School of Political Science, Johns Hopkins University, Baltimore, Md. Printed in *Annals of American Academy of Political Science*, Philadelphia, 1890.

The Federal Constitution of Canada.
The Juridical Review, Edinburgh, 1890.

Parliamentary Procedure and Practice in Canada.
With an account of the origin, growth, and operation of Parliamentary Institutions in the Dominion. And an Appendix containing the British North America Act of 1867 and amending Acts, Governor-General's commission, instructions, etc), forms and proceedings in divorce, etc. Montreal : Dawson Bros.
1st edition, 1884, 8vo., pp. xv. + 785. New edition, 1891, 8vo., pp. xx. + 929.

A Manual of the Constitutional History of Canada from the Earliest Period to the Year 1888, including the B. N. A. Act, 1867, and a Digest of Judicial Decisions on Questions of Legislative Jurisdiction. Montreal : Dawson Bros., 1888.
A republication of the first chapter of the author's work foregoing, on Parliamentary Procedure for the use of students. 12mo., pp. xii. + 238.

Bourinot, John George.—*Continued.*

Canada and the United States : Their Past and Present.
Papers of the American Historical Association, Washington. Vol. x.
Also, in *The Quarterly Review*, No. 344, April, 1891, in an abridged form.

Responsible Government in Canada : Its History and Results.
National Club Papers, Toronto, 12mo., 1891.
Also appears in series of papers on *Parliamentary Government in Canada*. See below.

Canadian Studies in Comparative Politics.
I. The English Character of Canadian Institutions. II. Comparison between the Political Systems of Canada and the United States. III. Federal Government in Switzerland compared with that of Canada. Montreal : Dawson Bros., 1891.
First delivered as a series of three lectures before Trinity University and afterwards printed in 4to., pp. 91.
Also in *Transactions of Royal Society of Canada*, Vol. IX., Sec. 2, 1891.

Parliamentary compared with Congressional Government. Continuation of foregoing studies.
Transactions of Royal Society of Canada, Vol. XI., Sec. 2, 1893. Also forms part of series in *Parliamentary Government in Canada*, as below.

Once Famous Louisbourg.
Magazine American History, New York, March, 1892.

The Acadian French in Cape Breton, once Ile Royale.
The Week, Toronto, April, 1892.

Louisbourg in 1891.
Republican Journal, Belfast, Me., January 14, 1892.

Historical and Descriptive Account of the Island of Cape Breton, and of its Memorials of the French Régime ; with historical, bibliographical and general notes.
Large 4to., pp. 177. With illustrations and maps, Montreal, 1892. Also in *Transactions of the Royal Society of Canada*, Vol. IX., Sec. 2, 1891.

Parliamentary Government in Canada. A Constitutional and Historical Study. Washington : Government Printing Office, 1892.
Reprinted from *Annual Report of the American Historical Association* for 1891, pp. 309-407.

The English Character of Canadian Institutions.
Contemporary Review, London and New York, October, 1892.

Alexander Mackenzie's Place in Canadian History.
The Week, Toronto, Nov. 18, 1891.

A Canadian Manual on the Procedure at meetings of municipal councils, shareholders and directors of companies, synods, conventions, societies, and public bodies generally, with an introductory review of the rules and usages of parliament that govern public assemblies in Canada. With an analytical index. Toronto : The Carswell Co., Law Publishers, 1894.
8vo., pp. viii + 444.

A Protest against Historical Hysterics and Plagiarism. A review of "Cape Breton Illustrated."
The Week, Toronto, April 27, 1894.
The foregoing protest against historical pretenders is the first of a series of reviews in the same paper.

3

Bourinot, John George.—*Continued.*

The Constitution of Canada, pp. 7.

Baedeker's Dominion of Canada: a Handbook for Travellers, Leipsic, 1894.

Bovey, Henry T.

Crib Work in Canada.

Proceedings of Institute Civil Engineers (Eng.), No. 1730, 1889.

Applied Mechanics. Two parts. Montreal: J. Lovell & Son, 1882.

Demy, 8vo., pp, 186-150.

An Investigation as to the Maximum Bending Moment at the Points of Support of Continuous Girders of n Spans.

Transactions Royal Society of Canada. Vol. v., Sec. 3, 1887.

The Maximum Shear and Bending Moment produced by a Live Load at different points of Horizontal Girder AB of span l.

Ibid., Vol. vii., Sec. 3, 1889.

The Flexure of Columns.

Ibid, Vol. x., Sec. 3, 1892.

Theory of Structures and Strength of Materials. New York: J. Wiley & Sons, 1893.

8vo., pp. 831.

Hydraulic Motors. Montreal: J. Lovell & Son, 1893.

Results of Experiments on Transverse Strength of Canadian White Pine.

Transactions of Canadian Society Civil Engineers, Montreal, 1893.

Brymner, Douglas.

A large part of his work was editorial, and therefore anonymous. In 1872, he was selected to organize a branch of the Department of Agriculture, Arts and Statistics at Ottawa, for the collection and arrangement of the *Archives of Canada*. For the first nine years, the work of arrangement was carried on so as to have the material which had been collected put in such a condition as would render the works of reference easily accessible to investigators. Reports on the progress of the work can be seen in the *Reports of the Department of Agriculture* for 1872 (No. 29); for 1873 (No. 24). The report for 1874 has also one from the Abbé Verreau (see under proper head in this bibliography).

The first separate report on Canadian Archives was published in 1882, being an account of the proceedings of the previous year (1881). That report was of a general nature, as it included an account of the system of keeping the public records. It contains a sketch of the origin of the present Public Record offices in London and Edinburgh, and a catalogue of the manuscripts in the British Museum relating to Canada. It was regarded as of so much value, that the whole report was published in that of the Public Record Office, London, for 1882.

The report for 1882 (published in 1883) gives details of the work in the branch, a table of the divisions of the Dominion of Canada, commercial tables, and specimens of the system adopted for calendaring the documents.

Brymner, Douglas.—*Continued.*

The report for 1883 contains synopses of papers in the Public Record Office, London, relating to Canada, and the same by Mr. Marmette of papers in the State Departments, Paris; letters on the state of Canada in 1835, by T. Fred. Elliot, secretary of the Gosford commission, and by Hon. A. N. Morin in 1841, in anticipation of the first meeting of the Legislature of United Canada; also, "Transactions relating to Hudson's Bay in 1687."

For 1884, the preliminary report contains a sketch of the capture of Quebec by Kirk in 1629, and its restoration by Charles I. to France in 1631. A very interesting letter written in 1637 by Charles to Wake, the ambassador to France, unearthed by Dr. Brymner in the British Museum, was published in this report, clearing up an obscure historical point. A manuscript account, written in 1673, of the martyrdom of Fathers Brebœuf and L'Allemant is printed in this report, with a translation into English. In the description of Nova Scotia by Lieut.-Col. Morse, in his report dated in 1784, is the first proposal for confederation of the Provinces, the place suggested by Col. Morse for the metropolis being Cape Breton. An abstract of the "Fealty Rolls" of Lower Canada has proved of great value to inquirers respecting the first grants and successions to the seigniories in that Province. The calendar of the Haldimand collection was begun in this volume.

In 1885, the synopsis of papers in the departments at Paris, the abstract of the fealty rolls and the calendar of the Haldimand collection were continued. In the preliminary report a sketch is given of the events, so far as they affected Canada, of the American Revolutionary War, and a hiatus supplied in the letter written by Lord George Germain to Sir Guy Carleton, which, it seems probable, led to the resignation of the latter. The correspondence is given in full in a note (marked D) to the report. A careful outline of the life of an ex-Jesuit named Roubaud is of interest to the investigators of Canadian history.

In 1886 the report on French Archives and the calendar of the Haldimand collection are continued. The preliminary report gives an account of the capture of Louisbourg in 1745, with chart of Gabarus Bay and plan of Louisbourg, showing the position of the fort, etc.; note A giving the proposal of Samuel Waldo for its reduction in 1758. The journal of Legardeur St. Pierre in 1750 to 1752, with Sir Guy Carleton's remarks on Western trade (notes C and D), and the letter-book of Miles Macdonell, reporting his proceedings with the emigrants taken at the expense of Lord Selkirk to settle Rupert's Land, give a view of different parts of the Canadian North-West at different periods. The history of the construction of the first canals on the St. Lawrence in 1799 and 1781, and the discovery that a canal was in existence on the Canadian side of the Sault Ste. Marie from 1747 and a few years onwards, are of interest to engineers. The visit of Capt. Enys to Niagara in 1787, the journal of which is published in full, has been regarded by geologists as of considerable importance.

In 1887, the Report on French Archives and the calendar of the Haldimand papers were continued. In the preliminary report is the sketch of the life of General Haldimand, who became Governor of Canada in succession to Sir Guy Carleton and who continued in command till the close of the Revolutionary war. A letter from M. Tremblay, agent for the Seminary of Quebec, dated in 1695, published in full with a translation, affords reason for a sketch of the ecclesiastical affairs of that Province during the incumbency of the first Bishops, Mgr. de Laval and Mgr. St. Vallière. The account of the capture of Fort Shelby, at Prairie

Brymner, Douglas.—Continued.

du Chien, by Lieut.-Col. McKay, in 1814, taken from the original documents among the Archives gives details of a little known episode in the war of 1812. Fort McKay, so called after the capture, was restored to the United States at the close of the war. Some idea may be formed of the hardships experienced by the early explorers for a route to be used by the Canadian Pacific Railway, by the journal kept by Mr. Hamington of his survey in the Rocky Mountains during the winter of 1874-5.

In 1888, the calendar of the Haldimand collection was continued. The papers published in full as notes to the preliminary report have the titles : The Walker Outrage, 1764 ; General Murray's Recall ; the French Noblesse in Canada after 1760 ; Pierre du Calvet ; the Northwest Trade and French Royalists in Upper Canada. In the preliminary report are sketches of the character, etc., of Walker, the subject of the outrage, and of Pierre du Calvet, whose statements are rigorously weighed in the light of the correspondence. The almost forgotten attempt of French Royalists under the Count de Puisaye to settle in Upper Canada after the Revolutionary party in France had been fully established is clearly shown by the correspondence on the subject, which is published in this report in full, and by the sketches in the preliminary report.

In 1889, the calendar of the Haldimand collection is completed and the diary of Haldimand, containing many curious entries among many that are very trivial, is printed in full with careful translation, the names mentioned being so far as possible identified. The *Bouquet Collection* is also calendared, being begun and completed in this report. Bouquet, it may be mentioned, was a brother soldier with Haldimand, both being foreign officers of the Royal American, afterwards the 60th regiment. In the preliminary report is a reprint of a paper on Archives, read before the American Historical Association, which gives a history of the origin and progress of the department. A sketch of the schools and schoolmasters in Canada is in the body of the preliminary report ; remarks on early explorers in the Northwest ; additional remarks on the forgotten canal at Sault Ste. Marie, with lithographed views of the remains. The general topics dealt with are Northwestern explorations, the journal of La Verandrye of 1738-39 and other twelve documents on the subject being printed in full ; religious, educational and other statistics ; Vermont negotiations ; Before and after the battle of Edge Hill (usually called the battle of Bushy Run), includes the original correspondence published in full ; the Reservation of Indian Lands (after the capture of Canada in 1760 and the treaty of Paris in 1763) ; correspondence respecting the construction of a canal from Lake Champlain to the St. Lawrence in 1785 to 1790.

In 1890, the calendar of the State Papers for the Province of Quebec was begun, the preliminary report giving a summary of the history included in the papers, such as the advances made by Amherst, the first Governor, to give the inhabitants after the surrender in 1760 an opportunity to retrieve their fortunes, the Government and recall of Murray, the first Lieut. Governor ; the accession of Carleton ; the passing of the Constitutional Act of 1774 ; a reference to the Revolutionary war, and a summary of the papers published in full, which are under these heads : Administration of Justice (after the close of the military rule in Quebec ; Correspondence respecting the Constitutional Act of 1791 ; Northwestern exploration ; Internal communication in Canada ; Relations with the United States after the peace of 1783 A lithographed map of one by Peter Pond, an Indian trader,

Brymner, Douglas.—Continued.

hitherto unpublished, illustrates the documents respecting the Northwest in the report for this year.

In 1891, the calendar of the State Papers for Lower and Upper Canada, the Province of Quebec being now divided into two, is begun, and contains lists of the applicants for and grantees of lands, place 1 in alphabetical order at the end of each volume calendared which contains the applications. The preliminary report summarizes the history of the period covered by the calendar from 1792 to 1800 in the case of Lower Canada, and to 1801 in that of Upper Canada. The correspondence is published in full on the subjects of which the titles are : Settlements and surveys ; Division of Upper Canada ; War with France ; French republican designs on Canada ; and the marriage law in Upper Canada. A map of Upper Canada for 1798 shows the extent of settlement at that date.

In 1892, the calendar of State Papers for Lower and Upper Canada from 1400 to 1807 was continued. In the preliminary report the efforts to increase the revenue in Lower Canada are traced, and especially in regard to the St. Maurice Forges ; the settling of lands in both Provinces ; the question of the Jesuit Estates ; a sketch of the services of Mr. Bouchette the Surveyor-General ; the state of religion, and the steps towards building an Anglican cathedral in Quebec ; remarks on the Northwest fur trade. The titles of the subjects, in regard to which the papers are published in full, will serve to show the general nature of the report. These are : Settlements and surveys ; Lower Canada in 1803 ; Ecclesiastical affairs in Lower Canada ; Political state of Upper Canada, 1800 and 1807 ; Courts of justice for the Indian country ; and Proposed general fishery and fur company.

In 1893, owing to the absence of Dr. Brymner in London, making investigations, the report is confined to the calendar of State Papers for Lower and Upper Canada from 1808 to 1813.

⋋**Burgess, T. J. W.**

Polypus of the Heart.
  Canadian Journal of Medical Science, May, 1879, Toronto.

The Beneficent and Toxic Effects of the Various Species of Ithus.
  Ibid., November, 1880, Toronto Also, *Scientific American Supplement,* December, 1880, New York.

Botanical Notes from Canada.
  Botanical Gazette, Vol. vii., Nos. 8 and 9, August and September, 1882, Indianapolis, Ind.

A Botanical Holiday in Nova Scotia.
  Ibid., Vol. ix., N s. 1, 2, 3 and 4, January, February, March and April, 1884, Indianapolis, Ind.

Canadian Filicineæ. By John Macoun, M.A., and T. J. W. Burgess, M.B.
  Transactions of the Royal Society of Canada Vol. II , Sec. 4, 1884.

Aspidium Oreopteris.
  Botanical Gazette. Vol. xi., No. 3, March, 1886, Indianapolis, Ind.

Recent Additions to Canadian Filicineæ, with new stations for some of the species previously recorded.
  Transactions of the Royal Society of Canada. Vol. vi., Sec. 4, 1886.

How to Study Botany.
  Journal and Proceedings of the Hamilton Association Part iv., 1887-8, Hamilton.

Burgess, T. J. W.—*Continued.*

  Orchids.
    Journal and Proceedings of the Hamilton Association.
    Part iv., 1887-8, Hamilton.

  Notes on the Flora of the 49th Parallel from the
  Lake of the Woods to the Rocky Mountains.
    Ibid. Part iv., 1887-8, Hamilton. Also, in *Pioneer
    Press,* September 15, 1888, Saint Paul, Minn.

  The Lake Erie Shore as a Botanizing-ground.
    Journal and Proceedings of the Hamilton Association.
    Part v., 1888-9, Hamilton.

  Art in the Sick-room.
    Times, January 5, 1889, Hamilton.

  Notes on the History of Botany.
    Journal and Proceedings of the Hamilton Association.
    Part vi., 1889-90, Hamilton.

  Ophioglossaceae and Filices.
    Catalogue of Canadian Plants. By John Macoun,
    M.A., F.L.S. Part v., 1890, pp. 253-287.

  Notes on the Genus Rhus.
    Journal and Proceedings of the Hamilton Association.
    Part viii. 1891-2, Hamilton.

Campbell, The Reverend John.

  Affiliation of the Algonquin Languages.
    Proceedings Canadian Institute, New Series, Vol. i.
    1879, Toronto. 8vo , pp. 15-53.

  Asiatic Tribes in North America.
    Ibid., Vol. i., 1881. Toronto. 8vo , pp. 171-206.

  Birthplace of Ancient Religions and Civilization.
  Reprinted from *Canadian Journal,* August,
  1871. Toronto.
    8vo., pp. 29.

  Coptic Element in Languages of the Indo-
  European Family. Reprinted from *Canadian
  Journal,* July and December, 1872. Toronto.
    8vo., pp. 43.

  Culdee Colonies in the North and West.
    British and Foreign Evangelical Review, July, 1881.
    London. 8vo., pp. 455-476.

  Current Unbelief.
    Presbyterian College Journal, December, 1891, Mont-
    real, 8vo., pp. 91-98.

  Descent of Man. *Questions of the Day.* Montreal : Drysdale, 1885.
    8vo., pp. 89-111.

  Eastern Origin of the Celts.
    Canadian Journal, 1876, and January, 1877, reprint.
    Toronto 8vo., pp. 21 and 53.

  Ethnic Relations of the Zimri.
    Transactions Society Biblical Archæology, Vol. vi.,
    1879. London. 8vo., pp. 579-80.

  Etruria Capta.
    Proceedings Canadian Institute, Vol. ii., 1886.
    Toronto. 8vo., pp. 144-266.

  Hittites, their Inscription and their History, 2
  Vols., 1890. Toronto : Williamson & Co.
    8vo., pp. 390 and 310.

  Hittites in America.
    Canadian Naturalist, Vol. ix., 1879. Montreal re-
    print. 8vo., pp. 22 and 23.

  Horites.
    Canadian Journal, May, 1873, reprint, Toronto. 8vo.
    pp. 36.

Campbell, The Rev. John.—*Continued.*

  Hornets of Scripture.
    Presbyterian Quarterly and Princeton Review,
    October, 1876. New York. 8vo., pp. 677-692.

  Inaugural Address, University College Literary
  and Scientific Society, 1885. Toronto : James
  Bain.
    8vo., pp. 31.

  Jabez.
    British and Foreign Evangelical Review, April, 1880.
    London. 8vo., pp. 291-313.

  The Khitan Languages ; the Aztec and its Relations.
    Proceedings Canadian Institute, Vol. ii., Fascic. 2,
    1881, Toronto 8vo., pp. 158-180.

  Monumental Evidence of an Iberian Population
  of the British Islands.
    Transactions Celtic Society of Montreal, 1887. 8vo.
    pp. 1-69.

  Mound Builders Identified.
    Proceedings American Association of Science, 1883.
    Salem, 1884. 8vo., pp. 419-21,

  Origin of Some American Indian Tribes.
    Canadian Naturalist. New Series. Vol. ix., 1879.
    Montreal. 8vo , pp. 65-80 and 193-212.

  Origin of the Aborigines of Canada.
    *Transactions Literary and Historical Society of
    Quebec,* 1881. Quebec. 8vo., pp. 61-95 and i.-xxxiv.

  Origin of the Phoenicians.
    British and Foreign Evangelical Review, July, 1875.
    London. 8vo., pp. 425-448.

  Our Widowed Queen—a Prize Poem. Privately
  printed, 1862. Toronto.
    sm.-4to., pp. 6.

  Pelagianism in Modern Theology.
    Knox College Monthly, December, 1890. Toronto.

  Peopling of Great Britain. Montreal, 1880.
    8vo., pp. 20.

  Perfect Father or the Perfect Book.
    Sunday Afternoon Address, Queen's University.
    Kingston, 1893.

  Personal Revelation.
    Presbyterian College Journal, November, 1890.
    Montreal. 8vo., p . 49-64.

  Pharaoh of the Exodus Identified in the Myth of
  Adonis.
    Canadian Journal, May, 1871, Toronto. Reprint.

  Phili-tines.
    British and Foreign Evangelical Review, July, 1877.
    London. 8vo., pp. 477-511.

  Primitive History of the Ionians.
    Canadian Journal, August, December. 1875. To-
    ronto. Reprint. 8vo., pp. 59.

  Proposed Reading of the Davenport Tablets.
    American Antiquarian, October. 1882, Chicago.

  Scholasticism in Modern Theology.
    Knox College Monthly, December, 1889, Toronto.
    8vo., pp. 61-67.

  Shepherd Kings of Egypt.
    Canadian Journal, April and August, 1874, Toronto.
    Reprint. 8vo., pp. 112.

  Siberian Inscriptions.
    Transactions Canadian Institute, No. 4, 1892, To-
    ronto. 8vo., pp. 261-283.

Campbell, The Rev. John.—Continued.

Some Important Principles of Comparative Grammar as Exemplified in American Aboriginal Languages.
Canada Educational Monthly, March, 1879. Toronto. 8vo., pp. 144-149.

Some Laws of Phonetic Change in the Khitan Languages.
Proceedings Canadian Institute. Vol. i., Fascic. 4, 1889. Toronto. 8vo., pp 282-290.

Some Old Testament Mistranslations.
The Theologue, January, 1892. Halifax. 8vo., pp. 43-48.

Spanish Discovery and Conquest in America. Montreal, 1882.
8vo., pp. 20.

Talks About Books.
Presbyterian College Journal, passim, 1888-93. Montreal.

The Three Foundations.
Canada Presbyterian Church Pulpit. Second Series, Toronto: James Campbell & Son, 1873. 8vo., pp. 245-265.

Traditions of the People of Mexico and Peru Identified with the Mythology of the Old World.
Comptes-rendus du Congrès International des Americanistes. Tome 1, 1876. Nancy. 8vo., pp. 349-376.

Translation of the Oldest Celtic Document Extant, and of its Etruscan Comparison.
Transactions Celtic Society, Montreal, 1887. 8vo, pp. 150-229.

Unity of the Human Race from an American Standpoint.
British and Foreign Evangelical Review, January, 1880. 8vo., pp. 74-001.

The American Indian: Who and Whence?
The Canadian Magazine, February, 1894.

The Great Election. Montreal: Lovell, 1891.

Protest Against the Judgment of the Presbytery of Montreal, and Appeal to the Synod of Montreal and Ottawa. Toronto, May, 1891.

Campbell, William Wilfrid.

Lake Lyrics and other Poems. St. John, N.B.: J. & A. Macmillan, 1889.
12mo., pp. 160.

The Dread Voyage. Toronto: William Briggs, 1893.
12mo., pp. 190.

Ahmet.
Canadian Magazine, 1894.

Casgrain, Abbé H. R.

Légendes Canadiennes. Québec, 1801.
in 12, pp. 425.

Découverte du Tombeau de Champlain. Par MM. les Abbés Laverdière et Casgrain. Québec, 1886. (Avec des cartes, etc.)
8vo., pp. 13.

Vie des Saints. Ottawa, 1807.
4to., pp. 1867.

Casgrain, Abbé H. R.—Continued.

Notice biographique d'Octave Crémazie.
8vo., pp. 94.

Au commencement des Œuvres complètes de O. Crémazie, publiées sous le patronage de l'Institut Canadien de Québec. Montréal: Beauchemin et fils, 1882.

Légendes et Variétés. Montréal: Beauchemin & Valois, 1864.
1 vol., 8vo., pp. 580.

Biographies Canadiennes. Montréal: Beauchemin & Valois, 1885.
1 vol., 8vo., pp. 542.

Histoire de la Vénérable Mère Marie de l'Incarnation. Montréal: Beauchemin & fils, 1886.
1 vol., 8vo., pp. 500. Première ed., Québec, 1864. 8vo., pp. 467.

Le même, traduit en allemand. Regensburg, New York, et Cincinnati, 1872.
1 vol., 12mo., pp. 336.

Histoire de l'Hôtel-Dieu de Québec. Montréal: Beauchemin & fils, 1888.
1 vol., 8vo., pp. 502.

Un Pèlerinage au Pays d'Evangéline. Québec: L. J. Demers et Frère, 1888.
1 vol., 8vo., pp. 544.
Ouvrage couronné par l'Académie française.

Montcalm et Lévis. Québec: L. J. Demers & Frère, 1891.
2 vol., 8vo., pp. 572 et 484.

Dans Le Canada-français, Québec:

Coup d'œil sur l'Acadie avant la dispersion de la colonie française. Tome i., 1888, p. 114.

Eclaircissements sur la question acadienne. *Ibid.* p. 401.

Montcalm peint par lui-même, d'après des pièces inédites. Tome ii., 1890, p. 313.

Dans les Mémoires de la Société royale du Canada:

Notre passé littéraire et nos deux historiens. Tome i., Sec. 1, 1882.

Les quarante dernières années: Le Canada depuis l'union de 1841, par John Charles Dent. Etude critique. Tome ii., sec. 1, 1884.

Biographie de Gérin-Lajoie. Fragment. Tome iii., Sec. 1, 18 4.

Un Pèlerinage au Pays d'Evangéline. Tome iv., Sec. 1, 1886.

Les Acadiens après leur dispersion. Tome v., Sec. 1, 1887.

Eclaircissements sur la question acadienne. Tome vi., Sec. 1, 1888.

Montcalm peint par lui-même, d'après des pièces inédites. Tome vii., Sec. 1, 1889.

Une Seconde Acadie (Ile Saint-Jean, Ile du Prince Edouard sous le régime français). Québec: Demers et Frères, 1894.
1 vol., in 8vo.

Chapman, Edward J.

> Practical Mineralogy. London, 1843.
> > 8vo., pp. 192.
>
> The Characters of Minerals. London, 1844.
> > 12mo., pp. 108.
>
> A Song of Charity. Toronto, 1857, 2nd edition, London, 1858.
> > 12mo., pp. 98.
>
> Examples of the Application of Trigonometry to Crystallographic Calculations, Drawn up for the Use of Students in the University of Toronto. Toronto, 1860.
> > 8vo., pp. 25.
>
> A Popular and Practical Exposition of the Minerals and Geology of Canada. Toronto, 1864.
>
> Contributions to Blow-Pipe Analysis, containing 21 new methods of research. Toronto, 1865.
> > 8vo., pp. 36.
>
> Outline of Geology of Canada. Toronto, 1876.
> > 8vo., pp. 108.
>
> East and West, (a poem). Toronto, 1887.
> > 8vo., pp. 18. Also in the *Canadian Magazine*, April, 1893.
>
> Minerals and Geology of Ontario and Quebec ; 3rd ed., Toronto, 1888.
> > 8vo., pp. 371.
>
> Classification of Trilobites, and other communications in *Transactions Royal Society of Canada*. Vols. 1 to 10.
>
> Practical Instructions for the determination of gold and silver in rocks and ores. 2nd ed. Toronto, 1891.
> > 12mo., pp. 66.
>
> The Mineral Indicator. 2nd ed. Toronto, 1893.
> > 12mo., pp. 121.
>
> Blow-Pipe Practice and Mineral Tables. 2nd ed. Toronto, 1893.
> > 8vo., pp. 308.

In the Transactions of the Canadian Institute, Toronto. Series II., Vols. 1 to 15. 1850 to 1875 :—

> A Review of the Trilobites. (Illustrated.) Series II., Vol. I., pp. 271-80.
>
> New Trilobites from Canadian Rocks. (Illustrated.) Series II., Vol. III., 230-38.
>
> New species of Asaphus. Series II., Vol. IV., pp. 1-4.
>
> Asaphus Megisto-, etc. (Illustrated.) Series II., Vol. IV., pp. 140-2.
>
> New species of Agelacrinites. Series II., Vol. V., pp. 358-65.
>
> Atomic Constitution and Crystalline Form as Classification Characters in Mineralogy. Series II., Vol. II., pp. 435-9.
>
> An outline of the Geology of Ontario. Series II., Vol. XIV., pp. 580-88.
>
> On the Leading Geological Areas of Canada. Series II., Vol. XV., pp. 13-22, 92-121.
>
> Notes on the Drift Deposits of Western Canada, and on the ancient extension of the Lake Area of that region. Series II., Vol. VI., pp. 221-9.

Chapman, Edward J.—*Continued*.

> On the Geology of Belleville and vicinity. (Illustrated.) Series II., Vol. V., pp. 41-48.
>
> On the occurrence of Copper Ore in the Island of Grand Manan. (Illustrated.) Series II., Vol. XIII., pp. 234-0.
>
> On Wolfram from Chief-Island, Lake Couchiching. Series II., Vol. I., pp. 308.
>
> On the Klaprothite or Lazulite of North Carolina. Series II., Vol. VI., pp. 303-8, 155-6.
>
> On the Position of Lievrite in the Mineral Series. Series II., Vol. VII, 42-7.
>
> On the occurrence on Allanite or Orthite in Canadian Rocks. Series II., Vol. IX., pp. 103-5.
>
> On some minerals from Lake Superior. Series II., Vol. X., pp. 400-11.
>
> On the analysis of some Canadian Minerals. Series II., Vol. XII., pp. 205-8, XIII, 507-9.
>
> On some Blow-Pipe Reactions. Series II., Vol. XV., pp. 210-58.
>
> On the Analysis of some Iron Ores and Ankerites from Londonderry, N.S. Series II., Vol. XV., pp. 414-10.
>
> On the Probable Nature of Protichnites. Series II., Vol. XV., pp. 186-90.
>
> Note on the Function of Salt in Sea-Water. Series II., Vol. XV., pp. 329-31.
>
> Note on a Belt of Auriferous Country in the Township of Marmora. Series II., Vol. XIII., pp. 330-34.
>
> On the occurrence of the Genus Cryptocerus in Silurian Rocks. Series I., Vol. II., pp. 204-8.
>
> Note on Stelliform Crystals. (Illustrated.) Series II., Vol. VI., pp. 1-6.
>
> Note on the object of the Salt Condition of the Sea. Series I., Vol. III., pp. 186-7, 227-9.
>
> Note on Phosphorus in Iron Wire. Series II., Vol. IX., pp. 170-4.
>
> On the Silver Locations of Thunder Bay. (Illustrated.) Series II., Vol. XII., pp. 218-26.
>
> Contributions to Blow-Pipe Analysis. (Illustrated.) Series II., Vol. X., pp. 339-55.
>
> A Table for calculating the Weight and Yield per Running Fathom of Mineral Veins. Series II., Vol. XII., 478-79.
>
> Habits of a Small Snake in Captivity. Series II., Vol. XIII., 551-56.
>
> Note on the Cause of Tides. Series II., Vol. XIV., pp. 279-80.

In the Transactions of the Royal Society of Canada:

> Note on Molecular Contraction in Natural Sulphids. Vol. I., Sec. 3, 1882.
>
> Note on Spectroscopic Scales. Vol. I., Sec. 4, 1883.
>
> On the Classification of Crinoids. Vol. I., Sec. 4, 1882.
>
> On some deposits of Titaniferous Iron Ore in the Counties of Haliburton and Hastings, Ont. Vol. II., Sec. 4, 1884.

Chapman, Edward J.—Continued.

On Mimetism in Inorganic Nature. Vol, II.,
Sec. 4, 1884.

On some Iron Ores of Central Ontario. Vol. III.,
Sec. 3, 1885.

On the Wallbridge Hematite Mine, as illustrating
the stock-formed mode of occurrence in certain
ore deposits. Vol. III., Sec. 4, 1885.

On the Colouring Matter of Black Tourmalines.
Vol. IV., Sec. 3, 1886.

On a New Classification of Trilobites. Vol. VII.,
Sec. 4, 1889.

Notes on some Unexplained Anomalies in the
Flame Reactions of certain Minerals and Chemical Bodies. Vol. VII., Sec. 3, 1889.

On the Mexican Type in the Crystallization of the
Topaz. Vol. X., sec. 3, 1892.

On the Corals and Coralliform Types of Palæozoic
Strata. Vol. XI., Sec. 4, 1893.

For early papers of this author see *Transactions of
Royal Society of London, Philosophical Magazine,
Annals of Natural Science,* and *Chemical News.*

Clark, The Reverend William.

The Redeemer : a Series of Sermons on the Person
and Work of our Lord Jesus Christ. London :
Bell & Daldy, 1869.
8vo., pp. 215.

The Comforter : Sermons on the Holy Ghost.
London : Rivingtons, 1864.
8vo., pp. 460.

The Four Temperaments, and Occasional Sermons. London : Hodges, 1874.
Crown 8vo., pp. 174

The Sin of Man and the Love of God. Sermons
on St. Luke xv. London : Wells & Gardner, 1870.
Sm. er. 8vo., pp. 219.

Hefele's History of the Councils. Vol. I. Translated and edited. Edinburgh : T. & T. Clark.
8vo., pp. 500.

Witnesses to Christ. Baldwin Lectures (1887) in
the University of Michigan. Chicago : McClurg,
1888.
Crown 8vo., pp. 300.

Savonarola : His Life and Times. Chicago :
McClurg, 1892.
Crown 8vo., pp 352.

Cuoq, l'Abbe J. A.

N. O. Ancien missionnaire. Etudes philologiques
sur quelques langues sauvages de l'Amérique.
Montréal : J. Lovell, 1866.
8vo., pp 160.

Jugement erroné de M. Ernest Renan sur les
langues sauvages. 2ème edition. Montréal : J.
Lovell, 1869.
8vo., pp. 113.

Lexique de la langue iroquoise. Montréal : J.
Chapleau (1882).
8vo., pp. 216, et avec *additament*, pp. 238.

Lexique de la langue algonquine. Montréal : J.
Chapleau, 1886.
8vo., pp. XII. 446.

Cuoq, l'Abbe J. A.—Continued.

Grammaire de la langue algonquine.
Tomes IX. et X, des *Mémoires de la Société Royale
du Canada,* 1891 et 1892.

Anote-kekon.
Tome XI. des *Mémoires de la Société Royale du
Canada,* 1893.

David, L. O.

Portraits et Biographies. Montréal : Beauchemin
& Valois.
8vo., pp. 300.

Les Patriotes de 1837-1838. Montréal : E. Sénécal
& Fils.
8vo., pp. 298.

Feu P. J. O. Chauveau.
* Dans *Les Mémoires de la Société Royale du Canada.*
Tome IX., Sec. 1, 1891.

Mes Contemporains. Montréal : E. Sénécal & Fils,
1894.
8vo., pp. 285.

Dawson, Very Reverend Æneas McDowell.

The Temporal Sovereignty of the Pope. Ottawa
and London, Eng., 1860.
8vo., pp. 227. The first book printed and published
in Ottawa.

St. Vincent de Paul : a Biography. London,
1865.
8vo., pp. 71.

Seven Letters together with a Lecture on the
Colonies of Great Britain. Ottawa, 1870.

An Essay on the Poets of Canada, Ottawa, 1870.

The late Hon. Thomas D'Arcy McGee, M.P. : a
Funeral Oration. Ottawa, 1870.

Pius IX. and His Time. London, Can., and London, Eng., 1880.
8vo., pp. 440.

The Northwest Territories and British Columbia.
Ottawa, 1881.
8vo., pp. 218.

Canada and its Resources.
Greater Britain, London, Eng.

The Catholics of Scotland. London, Can., and
London, Eng., 1890.
8vo., pp. 678.

Translations.

The Parish Priest and his Parishioners. London,
1846.

Letters of the same author on the Spanish In-
quisition. London, 1848, 61 New Bond St.

Count Joseph de Maistre's celebrated work on
the Pope. London, Eng., 1850, 61 New Bond St.

Philosophical work, "Soirées de St. Petersbourg,"
by the same. London, Eng., 1851.

Poems.

Massacre of Oszniana, a poem in blank verse.
Glasgow, 1844.

Solitude. Ottawa, 1870, 5 pp.

Royalty at Ottawa. Ottawa "Times," May 3,
1860.

Dawson, Very Rev Æneas McD.—*Continued.*

The 12th of July at Ottawa, 1805.

Vision of Burns at Lincluden. Ottawa, 1870, p. 12.

Bombardment of Sonderborg. Ottawa, 1804.

The late Lord Elgin. Elegiac. Ottawa, 1804.

St. Andrew's Day at Ottawa, 1804.

Epistle in verse to a friend descriptive of Canada. Ottawa, 1870, pp. 13.

Calamitous news from Russia, 1805.

Welcome Hon. T. D'Arcy McGee, Minister of Agriculture, to Ottawa, 1817.

Lament for the Rt. Rev. J. Gillis. An elegiac poem. Ottawa, 1864, pp. 14.

The last Defender of Jerusalem. Ottawa, 1882.

The Heroine of Verchères. Ottawa, 1882.

Xenobia,Queen of Palmyra. 108 pp.,8vo. Ottawa, 1882.

Dominion Day. Ottawa, 1880.

Carnetacus. Ottawa, 1880.

Malcolm and Margaret. Ottawa, 1886.

Poem celebrating the Centenary of O'Connell. Read at a dinner given on the occasion, the Hon. John O'Conner, M.P., in the chair.

Te Deum Laudamus.

Dies Iræ.

Stabat Mater.

Psalm, Dominus Regit.

Do., Ecce Quam Bonum.

In Catholic Vesperal. Glasgow, 1835.

O Quot Undis. Hymn.

Præclara Custos. Hymn.

Audiat Mirus. Hymn.

Rex Gloriose. Hymn.

In Belford's Magazine, Toronto.

The Preservation of our Forests. December, 1876.

The Capital of Canada. Illustrated. March, 1877.

Preservation of the Buffalo. October, 1877.

The Heroine of Verchères. A poem. December, 1877.

Papers in The Owl, Ottawa University.

VOLUME IV.

Association of the McDonalds. A Poem.

The Better Age. A Poem.

The Star of Bethlehem. A Poem.

Thyendaga. A Poem.

Ville Marie. A Poem. Read before the Royal Society at the Montreal meeting.

VOLUME V.

Better than Plato. A Poem.

Dominus Regit Me. A Psalm.

Jerusalem ; the old and the new.'

Burns. Reminiscences of the Poet.

Burns : His Travels.

Dawson, Very Rev. Æneas McD.—*Continued.*

France Considered.

It Still Moves.

Burns Further Considered.

Royal Dunfermline and the *Quigrich.*

VOLUME VI.

To the Children of Saint Clare. A Poem.

Fame's Favourites. A Poem.

The Martyr of Mount Athos. A Poem.

A Relic ; Burns and Bishop Geddes.

Attempted Justification.

The Communion of Saints.

Count Joseph de Maistre.

Education Beyond the Grave.

Excavating the Heathen.

Growth of Religion in Scotland.

After the Victory.

Count J. de Maistre's work, "Soirées de St. Petersbourg," reviewed.

Saint Andrew.

VOLUME VII.

King Robert Bruce. A Poem.

Algonquin Park.

Education in the Province of Ontario.

The Georgian Bay.

Kintyre to Glengarry.

May Africa be Civilized ?

The Pope in the Second Century.

Ultramontanism and Modern Civilization.

Pope Honorius.

Dawson, George M.

On Foraminifera from the Gulf and River St. Lawrence.
    Canadian Naturalist, June, 1870, Montreal. 8vo., pp. 172-180.
    (Also separately, pp. 1-8.)
    Also in *Annals and Magazine of Natural History,* February, 1871, 8vo ; pp. 83-90.

The Lignite Formations of the West.
    Canadian Naturalist, April, 1874, Montreal. 8vo., pp 241-252.
    (Also separately, with the next.)

Note on the Occurrence of Foraminifera, Coccoliths, etc., in the Cretaceous Rocks of Manitoba.
    Canadian Naturalist, April, 1874, Montreal, 8vo., pp. 252-257.
    (Also separately, with the foregoing.)

The Fluctuations of the American Lakes and the Development of Sun Spots.
    Nature, April, 1874, London. 4to., pp. 504-506.
    Also in *Canadian Naturalist,* November, 1874, Montreal, 8vo., pp. 310-377.

Report on the Tertiary Lignite Formation in the Vicinity of the Forty-ninth Parallel. (British North American Boundary Commission.) Montreal, 1874.
    8vo., pp. 1-31.

Dawson, George M.—*Continued.*

Report on the Geology and Resources of the Region in the Vicinity of the Forty-ninth Parallel. (British North American Boundary Commission.) Montreal : Dawson Bros., 1875.
8vo., pp. i.-xi.-1-387.

On some Canadian Species of Spongillæ.
Canadian Naturalist, September, 1875, Montreal. 8vo., pp. 1-5.
(Also separately, same pagination.)

On the Superficial Geology of the Central Region of North America.
Quarterly Journal Geological Society, November, 1875, London. 8vo., pp. 603-623.
(Also separately, same pagination.)

Notes on the Locust Invasion of 1874 in Manitoba and the Northwest Territories.
Canadian Naturalist, 1876, Montreal. 8vo., pp. 119-134.
(Also separately, pp. 1-16.)

Note on some of the more recent Changes in Level of the Coast of British Columbia and adjacent regions.
Canadian Naturalist, April, 1877, Montreal. 8vo., pp. 241-248.
(Also separately, pp. 1-8.)

Notes on the Appearance and Migrations of the Locust in Manitoba and the Northwest Territories. Summer of 1875.
Canadian Naturalist, April, 1877. 8vo., pp. 207-228.
(Also separately, pp. 1-20.)

Mesozoic Volcanic Rocks of British Columbia and Chili. Relation of Volcanic and Metamorphic Rocks.
Geological Magazine, July, 1877, London. 8vo., pp. 314-317.
(Also separately, pp. 1-4.)

Report on Explorations in British Columbia.
Report of Progress, Geological Survey of Canada, 1875-76, Montreal, 1877. 8vo., pp. 233-280.

Note on Agriculture and Stock-Raising and extent of Cultivable Land in British Columbia. (Appendix S.)
Report of Surveys, Canadian Pacific Railway, Ottawa, 1877. 8vo., 240-253.

On the Superficial Geology of British Columbia.
Quarterly Journal Geological Society, February, 1878, London. 8vo., pp. 89-123.)
(Also separately, same pagination.)

Travelling Notes on the Surface Geology of the Pacific Coast.
Canadian Naturalist, February, 1878, Montreal. 8vo., pp. 389-399.
(Also separately, pp. 1-11.)

Notes on the Locust in the Northwest in 1876.
Canadian Naturalist, April, 1878, Montreal. 8vo., pp. 411-417.
(Also separately, pp. 1-7.)

Erratics at High Levels in Northwestern America.—Barriers to a Great Ice Sheet.
Geological Magazine, May, 1878, London. 8vo., pp. 209-212.

Report of Explorations in British Columbia, chiefly in the Basins of the Blackwater, Salmon and Ne hacco Rivers and on François Lake.
Report of Progress, Geological Survey of Canada, 1876-77, Montreal, 1878. 8vo., pp. 17-94.

Dawson, George M.—*Continued.*

Report on a Reconnaissance of Leech River and Vicinity.
Report of Progress, Geological Survey of Canada, 1876-77, Montreal, 1878. 8vo., pp. 95-102.

General Note on the Mines and Minerals of Economic Value of British Columbia, with a list of localities.
Report of Progress, Geological Survey of Canada, 1876-77, Montreal, 1878. 8vo., pp. 103-145.
(Also separately, same pagination.)

On a New Species of Loftusia from British Columbia.
Quarterly Journal Geological Society, February, 1879. London. 8vo., pp. 69-75.
(Also separately, same pagination.)

Notes on the Glaciation of British Columbia.
* *Canadian Naturalist,* March, 1879, Montreal. 8vo., pp. 32-39.
(Also separately, pp. 1-8.)

Sketch of the Past and Present Condition of the Indians of Canada.
Canadian Naturalist, July, 1879, Montreal. 8vo., pp. 120-159.
(Also separately, pp. 1-31.)

Note on the Economic Minerals and Mines of British Columbia. First List of Localities in the Province of British Columbia, known to yield Gold, Coal, Iron, Silver, Copper and other Minerals of economic value. (Appendix R.)
Report on Surveys, Canadian Pacific Railway, Ottawa, 1877. 8vo., pp. 218-245.

Memorandum on the Queen Charlotte Islands, British Columbia. (Appendix No. 0.)
Report Canadian Pacific Railway, Ottawa, 1880. 8vo., pp. 139-143.

Preliminary Report on the Physical and Geological Features of the Southern Portion of the Interior of British Columbia.
Report of Progress, Geological Survey of Canada, 1877-78, Montreal, 1879. 8vo., pp. 1a-187a.

Notes on the Distribution of Some of the More Important Trees of British Columbia.
Canadian Naturalist, August, 1880, Montreal. 8vo., pp. 321-331.
(Also, separately, pp. 1-11.)
Reprinted as an Appendix to Report on an Exploration from Fort Simpson, etc. *Report of Progress,* Geological Survey of Canada, 1879-80.

Report on the Climate and Agricultural Value, General Geological Features and Minerals of Economic Importance of part of the Northern Portion of British Columbia and of the Peace River Country. (Appendix 7.)
Report Canadian Pacific Railway, 1880, Ottawa. 8vo., pp. 107-131.

Report on the Queen Charlotte Islands. With Appendices A to G.
Report of Progress, Geological Survey of Canada, 1878-79, Montreal, 1880. 8vo., pp. 1a-239a.
(Also separately, same pagination.)

Note on the Geology of the Peace River Region.
Canadian Naturalist, April, 1881, Montreal. 8vo., pp. 20-22.
Also in *American Journal of Science,* May, 1881, New Haven. 8vo., pp. 391-394.

4

Dawson, George M.—*Continued.*

Additional Observations on the Superficial Geology of British Columbia and Adjacent Regions.
Quarterly Journal Geological Society, May, 1881, London. 8vo., pp. 272-299.
(Also separately, same pagination.)

Sketch of the Geology of British Columbia.
Geological Magazine, April and May, 1881, London. 8vo., pp. 156-172, 214-227.
(Also separately, pp. 1-19.)

Report on an Exploration from Fort Simpson, on the Pacific Coast, to Edmonton, on the Saskatchewan, embracing a portion of the northern part of British Columbia and the Peace River Country.
Report of Progress, Geological Survey of Canada, 1879-80. Montreal, 1881. 8vo., pp. 1a-177a.

The Haidas.
Harper's Magazine. Vol. xlv., August, 1882, New York, 8vo., pp. 401-408.

Descriptive Note on a General Section from the Laurentian Axis to the Rocky Mountains north of the 49th Parallel.
Transactions Royal Society of Canada. Vol. i., Sec. 4, 4to., pp. 39-41.
(Also separately, same pagination.)

Notes on the More Important Coal-seams of the Bow and Belly River Districts.
Canadian Naturalist, March, 1883, Montreal. 8vo., pp. 423-435.

Note on the Triassic of the Rocky Mountains and British Columbia.
Transactions Royal Society of Canada. Vol. i., Sec. 4, 1883. 4to., pp. 143-145.
(Also separately, same pagination.)

Preliminary Report on the Geology of the Bow and Belly River Region, Northwest Territory, With special reference to the Coal Deposits.
Report of Progress, Geological Survey of Canada, 1880-82. Montreal, 1883. 8vo., pp. 1a-23a.

On the Occurrence of Phosphates in Nature.
Transactions Ottawa Field Naturalists' Club, February, 1884, Ottawa. 8vo., pp. 91-98.

and Selwyn, A. R. C. Descriptive Sketch of the Physical Geography and Geology of the Dominion of Canada. Montreal, 1884.
8vo., pp. 1-55.

and Tolmie, W. F. Comparative Vocabularies of the Indian Tribes of British Columbia. With a map illustrating distribution. Montreal, 1884.
8vo., pp. 1-131.

Notes on the Coals and Lignites of the Canadian Northwest. Montreal Printing and Publishing Co., 1884.
8vo., pp. 1-21.

On the Microscopic Structure of certain Boulder Clays and the Organisms contained in them.
Bulletin Chicago Academy of Science, June, 1885, Chicago. 8vo., pp. 59-80.
(Also separately, same pagination.)

The Dominion of Canada. (Part thus entitled in *An American Geological Railway Guide.*) D. Appleton & Co., New York, June, 1885.
8vo., pp. 51-83.
(Also separately, same pagination.)

Dawson, George M.—*Continued.*

Report on the Region in the Vicinity of Bow and Belly Rivers, N.W.T.
Report of Progress, Geological Survey of Canada, 1882-84. Montreal, 1885. 8vo. pp. 1c-169c.

On the Superficial Deposits and Glaciation of the District in the vicinity of the Bow and Belly Rivers. (Reprinted from the *Report of Progress,* Geological Survey of Canada, 1882-84.)
8vo., pp. 1-14.

On Certain Borings in Manitoba and the Northwest Territory.
Transactions Royal Society of Canada. Vol. iv., Sec. 4, 1886. 4to., pp. 85-99.
(Also separately, same pagination.)

Preliminary Report on the Physical and Geological Features of that portion of the Rocky Mountains between Latitudes 49° and 51° 30'.
Annual Report, Geological Survey of Canada. (N. S.) Vol. i. Montreal, 1886. 8vo., pp. 1a-169a.
(Also separately, same pagination.)

On the Canadian Rocky Mountains, etc.
Canadian Record of Science, April, 1887, Montreal. 8vo., pp. 285-300.
(Also separately, pp. 1-16.)

Note on the Occurrence of Jade in British Columbia, and its Employment by the Natives. With extracts from a paper of Prof. Meyer.
Canadian Record of Science, April, 1887, Montreal. 8vo., pp. 361-378.
(Also separately, pp. 1-15.)

Notes and Observations on the Kwakiool People of Vancouver Island.
Transactions Royal Society of Canada. Vol. iv, Sec. 2, 1887. 4to., pp. 1-36.
(Also separately, same pagination.)

Report on a Geological Examination of the Northern Part of Vancouver Island and Adjacent Coasts.
Annual Report, Geological Survey of Canada. (N. S.) Vol. ii. Montreal, 1887. 8vo., pp. 1a-129a.
(Also separately, same pagination.)

Notes to accompany a Geological Map of the Northern Part of the Dominion of Canada east of the Rocky Mountains.
Annual Report, Geological Survey of Canada. (N. S.) Vol. ii. Montreal, 1887. 8vo., pp. 1a-62a.
(Also separately, same pagination.)

Recent Observations on the Glaciation of British Columbia and Adjacent Regions.
Geological Magazine, August, 1888, London. 8vo., pp. 347-350.
(Also separately, same pagination.)

Report on an Exploration in the Yukon District, N.W.T., and adjacent Northern Portion of British Columbia.
Annual Report, Geological Survey of Canada. (N. S.) Vol. iii. Montreal, 1888. 8vo., pp. 1a-277a.
(Also separately, same pagination.)

Notes on the Indian Tribes of the Yukon District and adjacent Northern Portion of British Columbia. (Reprinted from the *Annual Report,* Geological Survey of Canada, 1887.)
8vo., pp. 1-21.

Dawson, George M.—Continued.

The Mineral Wealth of British Columbia with
annotated list of localities of Minerals of
Economic Value.
 Annual Report, Geological Survey of Canada.
 (N. S.) Vol. III. 8vo., pp. 1a-163a.
 (Also separately, same pagination.)

Glaciation of High Points in the Southern Interior of British Columbia.
 Geological Magazine, August, 1889, London. 8vo.,
 pp. 350-352.
 (Also separately, same pagination.)

On the Earlier Cretaceous Rocks of the North-
western Portion of the Dominion of Canada.
 American Journal of Science, August, 1889, New
 Haven. 8vo., pp. 120-127.
 (Also separately, same pagination.)

Notes on the Ore deposit of the Treadwell Mine,
Alaska.
 American Geologist, August, 1889, Minneapolis,
 8vo., pp. 84-83.
 (Also separately, same pagination.)

Notes on the Cretaceous of the British Colum-
bian region. The Nanaimo Group.
 American Journal of Science, March, 1890, New
 Haven. 8vo., pp. 180-183.
 (Also separately, same pagination.)

On some of the Larger Unexplored Regions of
Canada.
 Ottawa Naturalist, May, 1890, Ottawa. 8vo., pp.
 29-19.
 (Also separately, pp. 1-12.)

Also printed in Appendix to Pike's Barren Ground
 of Northern Canada, 1892. London : Macmillan &
 Co. 8vo., pp. 277-290.

On the Glaciation of the Northern part of the
Cordillera, with an attempt to correlate the
events of the Glacial Period in the Cordillera
and Great Plains
 American Geologist, September, 1890, Minneapolis.
 8vo., pp. 153-162.
 (Also separately, same pagination.)

On the later Physiographical Geology of the
Rocky Mountain Region in Canada, with spe-
cial reference to Changes in Elevation and the
history of the Glacial Period.
 Transactions Royal Society of Canada. Vol. VIII.,
 Sec. 4. 1890. 4to., pp. 3-74.
 (Also separately, same pagination.)

Report on a portion of the West Kootanie Dis-
trict, British Columbia.
 Annual Report, Geological Survey of Canada.
 (N. S.) Vol. IV. Montreal, 1890. 8vo., pp. 1a-65a.
 (Also separately, same pagination.)

Note on the Geological Structure of the Selkirk
Range.
 Bulletin Geological Society of America, February,
 1891, Rochester. 8vo., pp. 149-170.
 (Also separately, same pagination.)

Notes on the Shuswap People of British
Columbia.
 Transactions Royal Society of Canada. Vol. IX.,
 Sec. 2. 4to., pp. 3-44.
 (Also separately, same pagination.)

and Alex. Sutherland. Geography of the British
Colonies. London : Macmillan & Co., 1892.
 8vo., pp. I-XIII., 1-290.

Dawson, George M.—Continued.

and Baden Powell, Sir G. Report of the British
Behring Sea Commissioners, London, Government, June, 1892.
 pp. I-VII., 1-381.

Notes on the Geology of Middleton Island,
Alaska.
 Bulletin Geological Society of America. Vol. IV.,
 1892, Rochester. 8vo., pp. 427-431.

Mineral Wealth of British Columbia.
 Proceedings of the Royal Colonial Institute. Vol.
 XXIV., 1893. 8vo., pp. 270-284.

Geographical and Geological Sketch of Canada
with Notes on Minerals, Climate, Immigration
and Native Races.
 Burdekin's Dominion of Canada Hand Book,
 Leipsic, 1894. 12mo., pp. XXIII-XLVIII.

Notes on the Occurrence of Mammoth Remains in
the Yukon District of Canada and in Alaska.
 Quarterly Journal Geological Society, February,
 1894. London. 8vo., pp. 1-9.
 (Also separately, same pagination.)

Geological Notes on some of the Coasts and
Islands of Behring Sea and vicinity.
 Bulletin Geological Society of America, February,
 1894. Rochester. 8vo., pp. 117-146.
 (Also separately, same pagination.)

Dawson, Sir J. W.

Species of *Meriones* in Nova Scotia.
 Edinburgh Philosophical Journal. (Illustrated.) 1841.

A Geological Excursion in Prince Edward Island.
 Barnard's Gazette. 1842.

The Lower Carboniferous Formation of Nova
Scotia.
 Journal Geological Society of London. (Sections.) 1843.

The Newer Coal Formation of the Eastern Part
of Nova Scotia.
 Ibid. (Map and Sections.) 1844.

Fossils from the Coal Formation of Nova Scotia.
 Ibid. (Illustrated.) 1845.

Report on the Coal Fields of Carribou Cove and
River Inhabitants.
 Journals of Nova Scotia Legislature, 1845.

The Reproduction of Forests Destroyed by Fire.
 Edinburgh Philosophical Journal. 1847.

The Boulder Formation of Nova Scotia.
 Proceedings Royal Society of Edinburgh, 1847.

The Mode of Occurrence of Gypsum in Nova
Scotia.
 Ibid, 1847.

The New Red Sandstone of Nova Scotia.
 Journal Geological Society of London. (Map and
 Sections.) 1847.

The Colouring Matter of Red Sandstones.
 Ibid, 1847.

The Gypsum of Plaister Cove, Cape Breton.
 Ibid, 1847.

*Hand-book of the Geography and Natural His-
tory of Nova Scotia.* (Map.) Pictou and Edinburgh, 1848, and 3rd edition, 1852.

Metamorphic and Metalliferous Rocks of Eastern
Nova Scotia.
 Journal Geological Society of London. (Map and
 Sections.) 1848.

Dawson, Sir J. W.—*Continued.*

The Mode of Occurrence of Erect Calamites near Pictou, Nova Scotia.
Journal Geological Society of London, 1848.

Additional Notes on the Red Sandstone of Nova Scotia.
Ibid., 1849.

Remains of a Reptile and Land Shell in an Erect Tree in the Carboniferous of Nova Scotia. (Lyell, Dawson, Wyman and Owen.)
Ibid. (Illustrated,) 1852.

The Albert Mine, New Brunswick.
Ibid. (Illustrated.) 1852.

The Structure of the Albion Mines Coal-field. (Dawson and Poole.)
Ibid, 1852.

Scientific Agriculture in Nova Scotia. Halifax, 1852, and enlarged edition 1857.

Notice of the Discovery of Baphetes planiceps. (Dawson and Owen.)
Ibid., 1854.

The Coal Measures of the South Joggins.
Ibid. (Figures and Sections.) 1853.

Modern Submerged Forest at Fort Lawrence.
Ibid. (Section.) 1854.

Acadian Geology. 1st edition, 1855; now in 4th edition, 1891. (Illustrations and Map.)

The Fossils known as Sternbergia.
Canadian Naturalist. (Illustrated.) 1857.

Pleistocene Fossils of Montreal and vicinity.
Canadian Naturalist. (Illustrated.) 1857. And additional papers in subsequent volumes.

Archaia, or Studies of the Narrative of the Creation in Genesis. Montreal, 1857.

The Copper-bearing Deposits of Maimanse, Lake Superior.
Canadian Naturalist. 1857.

The Lower Carboniferous Coal Measures of British North America.
Journal of Geological Society. (Illustrated.) 1858.

The Vegetable Structures in Coal.
Ibid. (Illustrated.) 1859.

The Tubicolous Worms of the Gulf of St. Lawrence.
Canadian Naturalist. (Illustrated.) 1859.

Fossil Plants from the Devonian of Canada.
Ibid. (Illustrated.) 1859.

A Terrestrial Mollusk, a Millipede, and new Reptiles from the Coal Formation of Nova Scotia.
Journal Geological Society. (Illustrated.) 1860.

A New Fossil Fern.
Ibid., 1860.

The Silurian and Devonian Rocks of Nova Scotia and their Fossils. (Dawson and Hall.)
Canadian Naturalist. (Illustrated.) 1860.

Arctic and Alpine Plants and their Geological History.
Canadian Naturalist. 1861.

Additional Reptilian Remains from the Coal of Nova Scotia.
Journal Geological Society. (Illustrated.) 1861.

Carpolite and Erect Sigillaria.
Ibid. (Illustrated.) 1861.

Dawson, Sir J. W.—*Continued.*

Preliminary Notice of the Pre-Carboniferous Flora of New Brunswick, Maine and Eastern Canada.
Canadian Naturalist. (Illustrated.) 1861.

The Recent Discoveries of Gold in Nova Scotia.
Ibid., 1861.

The Flora of the Devonian Period in North America.
Journal Geological Society. (Illustrated.) 1861.

Farther Observations on Devonian Plants from Maine, Gaspé and New York.
Ibid. (Illustrated.) 1862.

A New Species of Dendrerpeton and on Dermal Coverings of Fossil Batrachians.
Ibid. (Illustrated.) 1862.

Footprints of a Reptile from the Carboniferous of Cape Breton.
Canadian Naturalist. (Illustrated.) 1863.

Synopsis of the Carboniferous Flora of Nova Scotia.
Ibid., 1863.

Fossils of the Genus Rusophycus (*Rusichnites*).
Ibid. (Illustrated.) 1864.

The Air-breathers of the Coal Period.
Ibid. (Plates.) 1863. And issued as a separate volume.

Agriculture for Schools. Montreal, 1864.

Eozoon Canadense. (Logan, Dawson, Hunt and Carpenter.)
Ibid. (Plates.) 1865.

The Conditions of Accumulation of Coal, and the Coal Flora of Nova Scotia and New Brunswick.
Journal Geological Society. (Plates.) 1867.

Notes on Laurentian Fossils. (Dawson and Carpenter.)
Ibid., 1867.

A New Land Snail from the Carboniferous. (Dawson and P. P. Carpenter.)
Ibid., 1868.

Structure of Calamites and Calamodendron.
Ibid., 1870.

Report on the Geology of Prince Edward Island. (Map and Plates.) (Dawson and Harrington.) Montreal, 1871.

Hand-book of Canadian Zoology. Montreal, 1871.

Report on the Flora of the Upper Silurian and Devonian of Canada.
Geological Survey of Canada. (Plates.) 1871.

Report on the Flora of the Lower Carboniferous and Millstone Grit of Canada.
Ibid. (Plates.) 1872.

Notes on the Post-pliocene of Canada.
Republished from Papers in the *Canadian Naturalist.* (Plates, Cuts and Maps.) Montreal, 1872.

Footprints of Sauropus ungulfer.
London Geological Magazine. (Illustrated.) Vol. IX. 1872.

The Story of the Earth and Man. (Illustrated.) London, 1872.

Impressions and Footprints of Animals on Carboniferous Rocks.
American Journal of Science. (Illustrated.) 1873.

Dawson, Sir J. W.—*Continued.*

Sigillaria, Calamites and Lepidodendron.
Journal Geological Society, 1873.

Relation of the Upper Coal Measures of Nova
Scotia to the Permian.
Ibid. (Sections.) 1874.

Nature and the Bible. New York, 1875.

Life's Dawn on Earth. A summary of facts as
to Eozoon. (Map and Illustrations.) London,
1875.

Phosphates of the Laurentian Rocks.
Journal Geological Society, 1875.

On the Occurrence of Eozoon Canadense at Cote
St. Pierre.
Ibid. (Illustrated.) 1876.

New Carboniferous Batrachians.
American Journal of Science, 1876.

The Origin of the World. London and New
York, 1878.

Carboniferous Fishes from New Brunswick.
Canadian Naturalist. (Illustrated.) 1878.

Canadian Earthquakes.
Ibid., 1878, and subsequent years.

Phoca Greenlandica from Pleistocene.
Ibid., 1878.

New Facts Relating to Eozoon.
Ibid., 1878.

Supplement to Acadian Geology. (Illustrated.)
London, 1878.

Devonian Plants of Scotland.
Transactions Edinburgh Geological Society, 1879.

Fossils Injected with Silicates and Forms of
Stromatopora.
Journal Geological Society. (Plates.) 1879.

Recent Controversies Respecting Eozoon.
Canadian Naturalist, 1879.

Mohlus on Eozoon Canadense.
American Journal of Science. 1879.

Remarks on Recent Papers on the Geology of
Nova Scotia.
Canadian Naturalist, 1879.

Geological Relations and Fossils of the Silurian
Iron Ores of Nova Scotia.
Ibid., 1880.

Fossil Men, and their American Analogues.
(Illustrated.) London, 1880.

Revision of the Land Snails of the Palæozoic
Period.
American Journal of Science. (Illustrated.) 1880.

New Erian Plants.
Journal Geological Society. (Illustrated.) 1881.

The Chain of Life in Geological Time. (Illustrated.) London, 1881.

Results of Recent Explorations of Erect Trees
containing Reptilian Remains in the Coal Formation of Nova Scotia.
Transactions Royal Society of London. (Plates.) 1882.

Second Report on Fossil Plants of the Upper
Silurian and Erian of Canada.
Geological Survey of Canada. (Plates.) 1882.

Cretaceous and Tertiary Floras of British Columbia.
Transactions Royal Society of Canada. (Plates.) 1882.

Dawson, Sir J. W.—*Continued.*

New Fossils from the Lower Carboniferous of
Nova Scotia.
Memoirs Peter Redpath Museum, 1883.

Unsolved Problems in Geology. Presidential
Address.
American Association for Advancement of Science,
Minneapolis, 1883.

X Geology of the Canadian Northwest.
Journal Geological Society, 1883.

Relations of Geological Work in Canada and the
Old World.
Transactions Royal Society of Canada, 1884.

Résumé of Pleistocene Geology of Canada.
London Geological Magazine, 1884.

Mesozoic Floras of the Rocky Mountain Region.
  *   *Transactions Royal Society of Canada*, 1885.

Address on Canadian and Scottish Geology.
Transactions Edinburgh Geological Society, 1885.

Fossils Collected by Mr. Bain in Prince Edward
Island.
Canadian Naturalist. (Illustrated.) 1885.

Papers on Geology of Egypt and Palestine.
London Geological Magazine. (Sections.) 1885.

Points in which American Geological Science is
Indebted to Canada.
Address to Section IV. Royal Society of Canada, 1886.

Fossil Plants of the Laramie.
Transactions Royal Society of Canada. (Plates.) 1886.

The Geological History of the North Atlantic.
Presidential Address.
British Association, Birmingham, 1886.

Rhizocarps in the Upper Erian Formation.
Transactions Chicago Academy. (Illustrated.) 1887.

Fossil Woods of the Cretaceous and Laramie.
Transactions Royal Society of Canada, 1887.

The Geological History of Plants. (Illustrated.)
London and New York, 1888.

New Facts Relating to Eozoon.
Geological Magazine, 1888.

Specimens of Eozoon Canadense in the Peter
Redpath Museum.
Memoirs Peter Redpath Museum, 1888.*

Eozoic and Palæozoic Rocks of the Atlantic Coast
of Canada, in comparison with those of Western
Europe and the Interior of America.
Journal of Geological Society, 1888.

Modern Science in Bible Lands. (Map and Illustrations.) London and New York, 1888.

Hand-book of Canadian Geology. (Maps and
Illustrations.) Montreal, 1889.

New Cambro - Silurian Sponges from Little
Metis.
Transactions Royal Society of Canada. (Plates.)
1889.

Fossil Plants from the Laramie of Mackenzie and
Bow Rivers.
Ibid. (Plates.) 1889.

New Plants from the Erian and Carboniferous.
Memoirs Peter Redpath Museum, 1890.

---

* Contains reference to various minor notes and papers not
in this list.

Dawson, Sir J. W.—*Continued.*

Burrows and Tracks of Invertebrate Animals in Palæozoic Rocks.
Journal Geological Society, 1890.

Modern Ideas of Evolution. London, 1890.

Tertiary Plants of Similkameen River.
Transactions Royal Society of Canada. (Plates.) 1890.

Dendrerpeton Acadianum and Hylonomus Lyelli.
Geological Magazine. (Illustrated.) 1891.

Fossil Plants from the Carboniferous of New-foundland.
Bulletin Geological Society of America. (Illustrated) 1891.

Notes on Trees Cultivated on the Grounds of McGill University.
Canadian Record of Science, 1891.

Pleistocene Plants of Canada. (Dawson and Pen-hallow.)
Transactions American Geological Society. (Illus-trated.) 1892.

Parka decipiens. (Penhallow and Dawson.)
Transactions Royal Society of Canada, 1892.

The Relation of Early Cretaceous Floras in Canada and the United States.
Ibid. (Illustrated.) 1892.

New Cretaceous Plants from Vancouver Island.
Ibid. (Plates.) 1893.

Some Salient Points in the Science of the Earth. (Illustrated.) London and New York, 1893.

The Ice Age in Canada. (Illustrated.) Montreal, 1894.

The Meeting-Place of Geology and History.
Religious Tract Society, London, 1894.

Our Record of Canadian Earthquakes.
Canadian Record of Science, 1894.

Preliminary Note on Recent Discoveries of Fossil Batrachians.
Ibid., 1894.

Note on the Genus Naiadites (Dawson and Wheel-ton-Hind).
Journal Geological Society, 1894.

Revision of Bivalve Mollusks of the Coal Forma-tion of Nova Scotia.
Canadian Record of Science, 1894.

Dawson, Samuel E.

The Birthday of Modern Chemistry.
Gazette, Montreal, 1874.

Prof. Tyndall's Belfast Address.
Ibid., 1874.

Church and State in Quebec.
Canadian Monthly, Toronto, 1875.

Colonial Copyright.
Gazette, Montreal, 1875.

Sir Arthur Helps, Life and Works of.
Ibid., 1875.

The Geological Survey, Utility of.
Ibid., 1875.

Protestant Education in Quebec.
Ibid., 1876.

Rationale of the Ridsdale Judgment.
Ibid., 1877.

Dawson, Samuel E.—*Continued.*

Prerogatives of the Crown. A Series of Papers on the Quebec (Letellier) Crisis.
Spectator, Montreal, 1879.

The Chemistry of Cooking.
Witness, Montreal, 1878.

Specific Duties on Books.
American Publishers' Weekly, 1880.

Montreal in the Days of James McGill.
Gazette, Montreal, 1882.

Old Times in Montreal—1703 to 1830. With illus-trations of old buildings.
Star, Montreal, Carnival Number, 1885.

The Jesuits' Estates. Three papers.
Gazette, Montreal, 1888.

The Parliament Buildings of Canada from the Conquest to Confederation. With Illustrations.
Star, Montreal, Carnival Number, 1886.

Christmas in Canada.
Ibid., Montreal, Christmas Number, 1888.

The English Minority in Quebec. A series of seven papers on the Parish Law of Lower Can-ada.
The Week, Toronto, 1890.

The Chace Copyright Bill.
Nation, New York, 1890.

Problems of Greater Britain. Three papers on Sir Charles Dilke's book.
The Week, Toronto, 1890.

The Constitutional Question.
Gazette, Montreal, 1873.

Scientism. A paper read before the Athenæum Club of Montreal.
Belford's Monthly, Toronto, December, 1877.

Nineteenth Century Progress. A paper read be-fore the Athenæum Club of Montreal.
New Dominion Monthly, Montreal, January, 1878.

Prayer and Modern Science.
Canadian Monthly, Toronto, December, 1875.

The Massacre of the Cedars. An inquiry into the question of the employment of Indians during the Revolutionary War; a chapter of local his-tory in 1776-7 on the frontier from the Cedars to St. Anne's.
Ibid., April, 1874.

Champlain. A Poem. Montreal, 1890.
12mo., pp. 8.
Republished in the Ottawa *Owl,* 1892.

Report on the relative positions of Bishop and Rector in Christ-Church, as Cathedral and Par-ish Church, under the Laws of England and Canada. Montreal, 1875.
8vo., pp. 100.

Copyright in Books. An inquiry into its origin and an account of the present state of the Law in Canada. Montreal, 1882.
8vo., pp. 40.

Episcopal Elections: Ancient and Modern. Mont-real, 1877.
8vo., pp. 54.

Yea or Nay. The Railway Crisis in Montreal in 1872.

The Montreal Board of Trade. A Commercial History of the City from 1842 to 1892, with

Dawson, Samuel E.—*Continued.*

    tables of the statistics of trade for fifty years. Montreal, 1892.

    Old Colonial Currencies. An inquiry into the origin of the Par of Exchange.
        Canadian Monthly, Toronto, April, 1872.
        Canadian Antiquarian, Montreal, July, 1872.
        Banker's Magazine, New York, February, 1874.

    The Argument for Bi-metallism.
        The Week, Toronto, February 3, 1893.
        8vo., pp. 6.

    Handbook for the City of Montreal, prepared for the Meeting of the American Association for the Advancement of Science at Montreal in 1882. Montreal, 1882.
        12mo., pp. 167.

    Handbook for the Dominion of Canada, prepared for the British Association for the Advancement of Science at 1 a meeting in Montreal in 1884. Montreal, 1884.
        12mo , pp. xiii. + 315.

    A Study; with Critical and Explanatory Notes of Lord Tennyson's poem, *The Princess.* 1st ed., Montreal, 1882. 2nd ed., with a letter from Lord Tennyson, Montreal, 1884.
        12mo., 2nd ed., pp. xv. + 120.

Denison, George T.

    The National Defences: or observations on the best defensive force for Canada. Toronto, 1861.
        8vo., pp. 32.

    Canada: Is she Prepared for War: or a few remarks on the State of her Defences. By a Native Canadian. Toronto, 1861.
        8vo , pp. 24.

    A Review of the Militia Policy of the Present Administration. By Junius, jr. Hamilton, 1863.
        8vo., pp. 18.

    Manual of Outpost Duties. Toronto: Rollo & Adam, 1866.
        12mo , pp. 61.

    The Fenian Raid at Fort Erie. Toronto: Rollo & Adam. 1866.
        8vo., pp. 92.

    Cavalry Charges at Sedan.
        Canadian Monthly, January, 1872.

    A Visit to General Robert E. Lee.
        Ibid, March, 1872.

    Modern Cavalry. London: Bosworth, 1868. In German, Munich, 1869. In Russian, St. Petersburg, 1872. In Hungarian, Buda-Pesth, 1881.

    A History of Cavalry. (Awarded the Emperor of Russia's First Prize). London: Macmillan & Co., 1877. Berlin, 1879.

DeCelles, Alfred D.

    Persécutions et réparations.
        Revue Canadienne, Montréal, 1881.

    Une paroisse Canadienne au dix-septième siècle.
        Ibid., 1882.

    Notre avenir.
        Le Canada Français, Québec, 1887.

    Oscar Dunn. Biographie.
        Mémoires de la Société royale du Canada. Tome iv., Sec. I., 1886.

DeCelles, Alfred D.—*Continued.*

    La crise du régime parlementaire. Montréal. Imprimérie générale.
        8vo., pp. 31.

    A la Conquête de la liberté en France et au Canada.
        Mémoires de la Société royale du Canada. Tome ix., Sec. I., 1891.

    L'honorable Juge Routhier. Biographie.
        Les hommes du Jour, Ottawa, 1890.

    Sir Alexandre Lacoste.
        Ibid., Montréal, 1891.

    L'honorable S. H. Molson, C.P. Biographie.
        Ibid., Montréal, 1891.

Deville, E.

    Examples of Astronomic and Geodetic Calculations for the use of Land Surveyors. Quebec, 1878.

    Photographic Surveying, including the elements of Descriptive Geometry and Perspective. Ottawa, 1889.

    In the Transactions of the Royal Society of Canada:
    Sur la mesure des distances terrestres par des observations astronomiques. Tome I., Sec. 3, 1883.

    Du choix d'une projection pour la carte du Canada. Tome iv., Sec. 3, 1886.

    Determination of Time by Transits across the vertical of Polaris. Vol. vi., Sec. 3, 1888.

    Lever topographique des Montagnes Rocheuses, exécuté par la photographie. Tome xi., Sec. 3, 1893.

Dionne, N.-E.

    Le Tombeau de Champlain. Québec: Brousseau, 1880.
        12mo., pp. 92.

    Les Cercles agricoles dans la Province de Québec. Québec: Brousseau, 1881.
        12mo., pp. 66.

    Etats-Unis, Manitoba et Nord-ouest. Notes de voyage. Québec: Brousseau, 1882.
        16mo., pp. 184.

    Fête nationale des Canadiens-Français à Windsor, Ont. Québec: Brousseau, 1883.
        16mo., pp. 152.

    Historique de l'église de Notre-Dame des Victoires—Deuxième centenaire. Québec: Brousseau, 1888.
        16mo., pp. 83.

    Des figures oubliées de notre histoire.
        Revue Canadienne, pp. 382 à 392.

    Jacques Cartier. Québec: Brousseau, 1889.
        12mo., pp. 350.

    Les Lieutenant-Gouverneurs de Gaspé.
        Revue Canadienne, 1889, pp. 100 à 112.

    Le nud de terre.
        Ibid., pp. 505 à 215.

    Miscou. Hommes de mer et hommes de Dieu.
        Canada-Français, 1889. Tome iii., pp. 433 à 443, et 514 à 532.

    La traite des pelleteries sous Champlain.
        Ibid., 1890-91. Tomes iii., iv., pp. 556-572, et 675-692—5-26.

Dionne, N.-E.—*Continued.*

Le Séminaire de Notre-Dame des Anges. Montréal, 1890.
8vo., pp. 38.

Le plus grand des Souriquois.
Revue Canadienne, 1891, pp. 577-587.

Les Indiens en France.
Ibid., pp. 641-659.

Français et Sauvages.
Ibid., pp. 705-719.

La Nouvelle France—De Cartier à Champlain.
Québec ; Darveau, 1891.
8vo., pp. 400.

Samuel Champlain : Sa vie et ses œuvres. 1er volume. Québec : Côté, 1891.
8vo., pp. xviii., 450.

C.-F. Painchaud, fondateur du Collège de Sainte-Anne. Translation de ses restes mortels. Québec : Brousseau, 1891.
12mo., pp 192.

Etude archéologique. Le fort Jacques-Cartier et la Petite-Hermine. Montréal, 1891.
8vo., pp. 84.

La monnaie de cartes sous le régime français.
Revue Canadienne, 1893, pp. 30-33, 72-84.

Chouart et Radisson.
Mémoires de la Société royale du Canada. Tome xi., Sec. 1, 1893, et Tome xii., Sec. 1, 1894.

Vie de C.-F. Painchaud, prête, missionnaire et fondateur du Collège de Sainte-Anne de la Pocatière. Québec : Brousseau, 1891.
8vo., pp. xii., 440.

✗ **Dupuis, N. F.**

Elements of Geometrical Optics. Kingston, 1868.
8vo., pp. 111.

Junior Algebra. Kingston, 1882.
8vo., pp. 120.

University Matriculation in Ontario.
Educational Monthly, Toronto, December, 1884.

Synthetic Geometry of the point, line, and circle in the plane, London : Macmillan & Co., 1889.
8vo., pp. 294.

Principles of Elementary Algebra. New York : Macmillan & Co., 1893.
8vo., pp. 336.

Synthetic Solid Geometry. New York : Macmillan & Co., December, 1893.
8vo., pp. 230.

In the Transactions of the Royal Society of Canada :

On the means of making a sidereal clock show mean time. Vol. 1., Sec. 3, 1883.

Elementary means of expanding the functions a , sin. θ, cos. θ, tan. θ. Vol. vii., Sec. 3, 1889.

Development of general Bernoullian number as a combinatorial determinant. Vol. vii., Sec. 3, 1889.

On the graphic projection of Occultations and Eclipses. Vol. vii., Sec. 3, 1889.

On the use of a symbolic form of Demoivre's theorem. Vol. ix., Sec. 3, 1891.

Ellis, R. W.

In the Reports of the Geological Survey of Canada :

On Operations in Boring for Coal at Newcastle Creek, N.B. 1872, pp. 231-237.

On Boring Operations at Newcastle Creek, N.D. 1874-75, pp. 90-95.

On Iron Ore Deposits of Ca le on County, N.B. 1874-75, pp. 97-104.

On Boring Operations in Northwest Territories. 1875-76, pp. 282-291.

On the Lower Carboniferous Belt of Albert and Westmoreland Counties, N.B., including the "Albert Shales." 1876-77, pp. 351-401.

On the Pre-Silurian Rocks of Albert, King's and St. John counties, N.B. 1877-78, pp. 1-13n.

On the Geology of Southern New Brunswick, in Charlotte, Sunbury, Queens, St. John and Albert counties, 1878-79, pp. 1-26n.

On the Geology of Northern New Brunswick, 1879-80, pp. 1-47D.

On the Geology of Northern and Eastern New Brunswick and North Sid · of Bay des Chaleurs. 1880-81, pp. 1-24D.

On the Geology of the Gaspé Peninsula. 1881-82, pp. 1-32Dn.

On the Geology of Gaspé and Prince Edward Island. 1882-83, pp. 1-34E.

On the Geology of Eastern Albert and Westmoreland counties, N.B., and of portion of Cumberland and Colchester counties, N.S. 1885, pp. 1-71E.

On the Geology of the Eastern Townships of Québec, counties of Compton, Stanstead, Beauce, Richmond and Wolfe. 1886, pp. 1-70J.

On the Geology of Megantic, Beauce, Dorchester, Lévis, Bellechasse and Montmagny. 1887-88, pp. 1-120K.

On the Mineral Resources of the Province of Quebec. 1888-89, pp. 1-150K.

A History of New Brunswick Geology. Government Printing Office.
8vo., pp. 1-64.

Notes on the Geological Relations and Mode of Occurrence of some of the more Economic Minerals of Eastern Quebec.
Ottawa Naturalist, Vol. III., 1889, pp. 45-57.

Geological Progress in Canada.
Ibid., Vol. III., 1889, pp. 119-145.

Asbestos : Its History, Mode of Occurrence and Uses.
Ibid., Vol. IV., March, 1891, pp. 201-225.

The Work of the Geological Survey of Canada.
Ibid., Vol. v., January, 1892, pp. 161-179.

The Stratigraphy of the Quebec Group.
Bulletin Geological Society of America, 1890, pp. 453-467.

The Geology of Quebec, south of the St. Lawrence.
Transactions Royal Society of Canada. Vol. ix., Sec. 4, 1891, pp. 105-126.

The Mining Industries of the Province of Quebec.
Transactions Institute American Mining Engineers, 1889, pp. 316-334.

Fleming, Sandford.—*Continued.*

Canada and its undeveloped interior.
Proceedings of Royal Colonial Institute, London, 1878, pp. 55.

Canadian Pacific Railway. Report on Location and Harbours in the Pacific. Ottawa, 1878. pp. 104.

Temps Terrestre. Paris, 1878.
8vo., pp. 35.

North Shore Railway. Report on Route Maskinongé to Montreal, 1878, pp. 12.

Canadian Pacific Railway.
Report of Progress, Ottawa, 1879, pp. 142.

Chemin de Fer Canadien du Pacifique. 1877-1879, Montréal.
8vo., pp. 508.

Time-Reckoning.
Transactions Canadian Institute. Toronto, 1879, pp. 51.

Selection of a Prime Meridian.
Ibid., Toronto, 1879, pp. 19.

Daily Prayers for Busy Households. Montreal: Dawson Bros, 1879, pp. 70.

Canadian Pacific Railway. Memo. for Parliament. Ottawa, 1880, pp. 17.

Canadian Pacific Railway. Report on Construction. Ottawa, 1880, pp. 373.

Canadian Pacific Railway. Farewell Address to Staff. Ottawa, 1880, pp. 7.

Chancellor's Inaugural Address. Queen's University.
Queen's College Journal.
4to., pp. 10.

Uniform Standard Time.
American Society Civil Engineers, Montreal Convention, 1881, pp. 6.

Adoption of a Prime Meridian.
The International Congress, Venice, Italy, 1881, pp. 16.

Cosmopolitan Scheme for Reckoning Time.
Transactions American Meteorological Society. New York, 1881, pp. 10.

Standard Time for United States, Canada and Mexico.
American Society Civil Engineers. New York, 1881, pp. 34.

Chancellor's Address, Queen's University.
Queen's College Journal, Vol. IX., 1882.

A Cable Across the Pacific. (Pamphlet.) London, 1882 pp. 25.

Standard Time.
American Society Civil Engineers. Washington Convention, 1882.

Canadian Pacific Railway. Review of the Report and Conclusion of Royal Commission. Ottawa, 1882.

Letter on Standard Time.
American Society for Advancement of Science, Montreal, 1882, pp. 129.

Standard Time for the World.
The International Standard. Cleveland, Ohio, 1883. pp. 4.

Time Reform and a Prime Meridian.
American Meteorological Society. New York, 1883, pp. 5.

Fleming, Sandford.—*Continued.*

Second Installation Address as Chancellor of Queen's University.
Queen's College Journal, 1883. 4to., pp. 7.

Standard Time at the St. Paul Convention.
Transactions American Society of Civil Engineers, 1883, pp. 7.

Uniform Standard Time.
Ibid., New York, 1884, pp. 11.

The Prime Meridian Question.
International Standard, Cleveland, Ohio, 1884. pp. 8.

England and Canada. Old to New Westminster.
Montreal : Dawson Bros., 1884, pp. 449.

Standard Time at the Buffalo Convention.
Transactions American Society of Civil Engineers, 1884, pp. 7.

Chancellor's Report on Confederating Universities.
Queen's University Endowment Association, 1885, pp. 5.

The Time Reform Movement.
Transactions American Society of Civil Engineers, New York, 1884, pp. 11.

A Prime Meridian and Time zero—at the International Prime Meridian Conference, Washington, 1884, pp. 12.

Chancellor's Address. Queen's University.
Queen's College Journal, 1885, pp. 14.

Universal Time Reckoning.
Transactions Canadian Institute, Toronto, 1885, pp. 101.

Uniform Standard Time.
Transactions American Society of Civil Engineers, New York, 1885, pp. 4.

The new Time Reckoning.
Smithsonian Report, 1886, Washington, D.C., pp. 22.

Third Installation Address as Chancellor of Queen's University.
Queen's College Journal, 1886, 4to., pp. 4.

Proposed Telegraph between Australia, Canada and Great Britain. London, 1886, pp. 28.

Time Reckoning for the 20th Century.
Transactions Royal Society of Canada, Vol. IV., Sec. 3, 1886. 4to., pp. 13.

The Canadian Route to the East.
Remarks at the Colonial Conference, London, 1887, pp. 21.

Telegraph to Australia and India via Canada.
Speech at Colonial Conference, London, 1887, pp. 13.

Benefactors and Benefactions. Address at Queen's University.
Queen's College Journal, 1888.

Treatise on Time for the Use of Schools. Ottawa, 1888, pp. 20.

Presidential Address, Royal Society of Canada.
Transactions Royal Society of Canada, Vol. VII., 1889. 4to., pp. 11.

Expeditions to the Pacific.
Ibid., Vol. VII., Sec. 2, 1889. 4to., pp. 53.

A Problem in Political Science.
Ibid., Vol. VII., Sec. 3, 1889, pp. 6.

Fourth Installation Address as Chancellor of Queen's University.
Queen's College Journal, 1889, 4to., pp. 2.

X Fletcher, James.—*Continued.*

In the Canadian Entomologist (London, Ont.):
The Calosomas. 1890, pp. 32-35.
Notes on the Preparatory Stages of *Carterocephalus Mandan.* 1880, pp. 113-116.
The Northern Mole-cricket. 1892, pp. 23-25.

In the Transactions of the Ottawa Field-Naturalists' Club:
Inaugural Address as President. 1879, I., pp. 12-22; 1880, II., pp. 8-21; 1881, III., pp. 11-19; 1882, IV., pp. 11-21.
Flora Ottawaensis. 1879, I., pp. 48-61.

In the Ottawa Naturalist (Ottawa, Ont.):
Short Instructions for Collectors Away from Home. III., 1889, pp. 8-9.
Educational Value of Botanic Gardens. V., 1891-92, pp. 105-113.
Fall Web-worm. VI., 1892-93, pp. 70-71.
Flora Ottawaensis, 2nd Edition (not yet complete). pp. 1-08.

The Report of the Dominion Entomologist for 1894. pp. 1-7.

The Report of the Dominion Entomologist for 1895. pp. 1-56.

In the Annual Report of the Experimental Farms:
Report of the Entomologist and Botanist, 1887, pp. 8-41; 1888, pp. 47-77; 1889, pp. 50-92; 1890, pp. 154-205; 1891, pp. 100-220; 1892, pp. 144-167; 1893, pp. 157-193.

In Insect Life (Washington, U. S.):
Preliminary Note upon *Chionobas Macounii.* II., 1889, pp. 45-46.

In the Farmer's Advocate (London, Ont.):
The Clover-root Borer. 1891, p. 387.
Articles on Injurious Insects (I.-XI.). 1892, pp. 18, 68, 147, 198, 231, 308, 348, 305, 430, 479; 1893, pp. 10, 50.
Clothes Moths. 1893, p. 140.
Does Wheat turn to Chess? 1893, p. 167.
Granary Weevils. 1893, p. 423.
Injurious Insects. 1894, p. 157.

In "Instructions to Canadian Pacific Railway Land Examiners" (Winnipeg, Man.), 12mo.:
Botanical Collections. pp. 24-27.

In The Nor'-West Farmer (Winnipeg):
Collecting Botanical Specimens. 1892, p. 100.

In the Reports of Geological Survey of Canada:
List of Diurnal Lepidoptera of Yukon District, Northern British Columbia and Mackenzie River. 1887, pp. 229-231B.

Foville, de, P.
M. Léon Hubert, docteur en médecine, séminariste et prêtre de St-Sulpice. Notice biographique. Paris : Jules Vic, 1878.
12mo., pp. XI. 315.
Les Etudes naturelles et la Bible (Naturforschung und Bibel, von Dr. Carl Güttler).
Revue des Questions Scientifiques. Paris et Bruxelles. 1er article, (tome VII., avril 1890, 8mo., pp. 582-596; 2ème article, tome VIII., juillet 1880, 8mo., pp. 235-259.

Foville, de, P.—*Continued.*
Les Jours de la Semaine et les Œuvres de la Création.
Revue des Questions Scientifiques, tome XI., janvier 1882. 8mo., pp. 33-84.
La Bible et la Science.
Ibid., 1er article, tome XII., octobre 1882, 6mo., pp. 504-534; 2ème article, tome XIII., janvier 1883, 8mo., pp. 118-166.
Encore les Jours de la Création.
Ibid., tome XV., avril 1884. 8mo., 380-426.
Das Antlitz der Erde von Eduard Suess—die Sintfluth.
Ibid., tome XV., avril 1881. 8mo., pp. 591-605.
Du Rôle de la Faculté des Arts.
Canada Français, Québec, tome I., janvier 1888. 8mo., 79-91.
L'Astronomie et la Vie de l'Humanité.
Ibid., 1er article, t. I., juillet 1883, 8mo., pp. 343-379; 2ème article, t. II., juillet 1886, 8mo., pp. 404-432.

Fowler, James.
A plea for the Study of Natural History.
Stewart's Quarterly, vol. 4, No. 1, April, 1870, St. John, N.B.
8vo., pp. 11.
Arctic Plants Growing in New Brunswick, with notes on their Distribution.
Transactions Royal Society of Canada, vol. V., sec. 4, 1887.

Fréchette, Louis.
En Vers.
Mes Loisirs. Québec : Léger Brousseau, 1863.
8vo., pp. 204.
La Voix d'un exilé. Première année, 1800; seconde année, 1868. s.l.n.d.
Pêle Mêle. Montréal : Lovell, 1877.
12mo., pp. 274.
Les Fleurs Boréales. Les Oiseaux de Neige, Poésies couronnées par l'Académie Française. Québec, 1880.
2me édition, Paris : E. Rouveyre, Eu. Terquem, 1881. 12mo., pp. 264.
8me edition, 1886, Québec, 12mo., pp. 278.
La Légende d'un Peuple. Paris: Librairie Illustrée, 1887.
8vo., pp. 347.
Les Fouilles Volantes. Montréal : Granger & Frères, 1891.
12mo., pp. 222.
En Prose:
Lettres à Basile. Québec : Hector Fabre, 1871.
8vo., pp. 81.
Originaux et détraqués. Montréal : Louis Patenaude, 1803.
12mo., pp. 300.
Lettres à M. l'abbé Baillairgé. Montréal, 1893.
Imprimerie Desaulniers. 8vo., pp. 91.
Traductions:
Une rencontre fortuite (W. D. Howells).
Revue de Montréal, vol. III. and IV. 1879-80.
Une rencontre, roman de Deux Touristes sur le Saint-Laurent, Québec et le Saguenay (W. D. Howells). Montréal, 1893.
8vo.

Gilpin, E., Jr.—*Continued.*

The Geological Relations of the Principal Nova Minerals.
Transactions American Institute of Mining Engineers, 1887.

The Distinctive Features of the Nova Scotia Coal Fields.
Transactions British Association, Montreal, 1884.

Results of Past Experience in Gold-mining in Nova Scotia.
Ibid.

Coal-mining in Nova Scotia.
Transactions Canadian Society of Civil Engineers, 1888.

The Geology of Cape Breton Island.
Quarterly Journal of the Geological Society, November, 1888.

Notes on Nova Scotia Gold Veins.
Transactions Royal Society of Canada, vol. vi., Sec. 4, 1888.

The Carboniferous of Cape Breton.
Transactions Nova Scotia Institute of Natural Science, 1888.

The Minerals of the Carboniferous in Cape Breton.
Ibid., 1889.

Geological Writings of Rev. Dr. Honeyman.
Ibid., vol. vii., part 4, 1889.

Notes on Some Explosions in Nova Scotia Coal Mines.
Ibid., vol. vii., part 4, 1889.

The Devonian of Cape Breton.
Ibid., 1890.

The Iron Ores of Nova Scotia.
Transactions Canadian Society of Civil Engineers, 1891.

The Silurian of Cape Breton.
Transactions Nova Scotia Institute of Natural Science, 1892.

The Use of Safe Explosives in Coal Mines. Part I.
Transactions Canadian Society of Civil Engineers, 1892.

The Geological Relation of Nova Scotia Iron Ores.
Transactions Nova Scotia Mining Institute, 1892.

The Use of Safe Explosives in Coal Mines. Part II.
Transactions Canadian Society of Civil Engineers, 1893.

Note on an Occurrence of Zinc and Manganese Ore in Nova Scotia.
Transactions Nova Scotia Mining Institute, 1893.

Nova Scotia—its Economic Minerals.
Report to the Government of Nova Scotia, 1893.

Annual Reports on the Progress of the Mines and Mineral Development of Nova Scotia to the Government of Nova Scotia. Years 1870 to 1894.

Note on the Sydney Coal Field.
Ser. 2, Vol. 1, 1893-1894.

Mineral Development of Nova Scotia.
Federated Institute Mining Engineers' Annual Meeting, 1894.

Explosions in Nova Scotia Coal Mines.
Ibid.

Goodwin, W. L.

On the Nature of Solution. Part I.—On the Solubility of Chlorine in Water and in Aqueous Solutions of Soluble Chlorides.
Transactions Royal Society of Edinburgh, Vol. xxx., Part iii. 4to, pp. 597-619.

and G. Carr Robinson. On Some New Bases of the Leucoline Series.
Ibid., Vol. xxix., 1879. 4to, pp. 265-279.

Ueber die Natur der Lœsungen. Berlin.
Berichte der Deutschen Chem. Gesellsch, 1882.

The Nature of Solution.
Report as Secretary of Committee of the British Association, 1885.

and Ramsay, Tilden, and Marshall. Report of Committee appointed for the purpose of investigating certain Physical Constants of Solution.
Reports of the British Association for the Advancement of Science, 1886. London. 8vo, pp. 207-213.

and Ramsay, Tilden, and Marshall. Third Report.
Ibid., 1887. London. 8vo., pp. 48-55.

Invaporation.
Canadian Record of Science, vol. ii., No. 4, October, 1886.

Invaporation.
Ibid., vol. ii., No. 8, October, 1887.

Text-book of Chemistry. Toronto: The Copp-Clark Co., 1887.
8vo., pp. 416.

"Ringed" Trees.
Canadian Record of Science, October, 1888.

The High School Curriculum in Science.
Canada Educational Monthly, March, 1891.

The Water Supply of the City of Kingston.
Canadian Record of Science, April, 1892.

Notes on an old Indian Encampment.
Ibid., January, 1893.

Reclaiming Bog in Westmoreland Co., N.B.
Ibid., April, 1893.

(Communicated by.) On a Highly Nickeliferous Pyrite.
Ibid., April, 1893.

Chemical Laws. Toronto: The Copp-Clark Co., 1893.
8vo., pp. 37.

Gosselin, Abbé Auguste.

Vie de Mgr de Laval, premier évêque de Québec et apôtre du Canada. Québec: L. J. Demers & Frère, 1890.
2 vols., 8vo., pp. 1375.

Le Vénérable François de Laval. Sa vie et ses vertus. Québec : L. J. Demers & Frère, 1890.
12mo., pp. 84.

Les Normands au Canada. Jean Bourdon. Evreux, Imprimerie de l'Eure, 1892.
8vo., pp. 31.

Les Normands au Canada. Jean Nicolet. Evreux: Imprimerie de l'Eure, 1893.
8vo., pp. 56.

Les Normands au Canada. Jean Le Sueur, ancien curé de Saint-Sauveur de Thury, premier prêtre séculier du Canada. Evreux : Imprimerie de l'Eure, 1894.
8vo., pp. 52.

Gosselin, Abbe Auguste.—*Continued.*

Jubilé Sacerdotal de S. E. le Cardinal Taschereau : Noces d'Or de la Société Saint-Jean-Baptiste. Québec : Leger Brousseau, 1892.
Roy. 8vo., pp. 291. Avec un portrait du cardinal.

- Un Historien Canadien Oublié, le Docteur Jacques Labrie.
Mémoires de la Société royale du Canada, tome xi., Sec. 1, 1893.

Dans Le Canada-Français, Québec :

Rôle politique de Mgr de Laval. Tome i., 1888, pp. 43.

La Basilique de Saint-Etienne à Jérusalem. Tome ii., 1889, p. 608.

Just de Bretenières. Un martyr au XIXe siècle. Tome iii., 1890, pp. 52, 200.

Dans La Revue Canadienne, Montréal :

Augustin Cochin. Tome xii., 1875, pp. 22.
Jacques Cartier. Tome xxix., 1893, pp. 8.

Dans La Revue Catholique de Normandie, Evreux :

Le mouvement catholique en Canada. Tome i., 1892, pp. 10.

Le mouvement catholique aux Etats-Unis. Tome iv., 1891, pp. 12.

Grant, George M.

New Year Sermons. Halifax : James Bowes & Sons, 1865, 1866.

Sermon to the Synod of Nova Scotia and Prince Edward Island. Halifax : James Bowes & Sons, 1866.

"Reformers of the Nineteenth Century," A Lecture. Halifax : James Bowes & Sons, 1867.

"Ocean to Ocean," or Sandford Fleming's Expedition Across Canada in 1872. Toronto : James Campbell & Son ; England : Sampson, Low, Marston, Low & Searle, 1873.

"Picturesque Canada," written in part by the Editor. Toronto : Belden Bros., 1882.

"Our Five Foreign Missions." Kingston: Printed by the *British Whig*, 1887.

Advantages of Imperial Federation. The Case for Canada, Nos. 1 and 2. Published by Edward Arnold, 18 Warwick Sq., Paternoster Row, London, E.C., 1890, 1891.

Sermons in "Sunday Afternoon Addresses." The Publishing Committee of Queen's University Students, 1891-2-3-4.

"Current Events."
Queen's Quarterly, July and October, 1893, January, July and October, 1894, and January, 1895.

Christianity and Modern Thought.
Canadian Monthly, Toronto, December, 1875.

The Late Hon. Joseph Howe. Parts i. to iv.
Ibid., May to August, 1875.

Education and Co-Education.
Rose-Belford's Canadian Monthly, November, 1879.

The Dominion of Canada. Parts i. to iv.
Scribner's Monthly, May to August, 1880.

The British Association at Montreal.
The Contemporary Review, August, 1884.

Grant, George M.—*Continued.*

Progress and Poverty.
The Presbyterian Review (Quarterly), April, 1888.

The New Empire.
Westminster Review, October, 1891.

Our National Objects and Aims. Published in "Maple Leaves" by the National Club. Toronto : R. G. McLean, 1890-91.

The Birth of a Sister Dominion, Vice Presidential Address to the Royal Society of Canada, 1890.
Transactions Royal Society of Canada, vol. viii., pp. xx.-xxiv.

Presidential Address to the Royal Society of Canada, 1891.
Ibid., vol. ix. pp. xxxiii.-2.

Presbyterian Reunion and Reformation Principles.
Queen's Quarterly, January, 1891.

New Zealand.
Harper's Magazine, August, 1891.

The Religions of the World in Relation to Christianity. London : Adam & Charles Black ; Toronto : William Briggs, 1894.

Grant, Sir James A.

In the Medical Chronicle, Montreal :

Punctured Wound, anterior lobe of Brain, 1856.
Compound Comminuted Fracture of Femur and Ligature Femoral Artery, 1857.
Punctural Wound of Pleura ; Pleuritic Effusion ; Iodine Injection.
Carcinoma Medullare, 1859.
Notes of Cases of Poisoning, 1859.
Twins with Single Placenta, 1859.

In the British Medical Journal :

Notes of Surgical Cases. 1860.
Unique Anchylosis of Knee Joint, forward at a right angle, 1861.
Tetanus and Poisoning by Strychnine Contrasted, 1861.
Obstruction of the Bowels, Appendix Concretion, 1861.
Notes of Surgical Cases, 1862.
Treatment of Rheumatism by Boletus Laricis Canadensis, 1862.
Notes of Obstetrical Cases, 1862.

In the Medical Times and Gazette, London :

Treatment of Skin Diseases, 1863.
Disease termed "Black Leg," as observed amongst Ottawa Lumbermen, 1864.
Excision of the Knee Joint, 1865.
Tetanus treated by Acupuncturation.

In the Canada Medical Journal, Montreal :

Puerperal Mania, 1865.
Protracted Uterine Gestation, 1865.
Dermold Cyst of the Ovary, 1870.
Cancer of the Breast in its relation to Paget's Disease of the Breast, 1882.
Aneurism of the Thoracic Aorta, 1885.
Urethral Stricture and Perineal Section, 1880.

Grant, Sir James A.—Continued.

Elevation of the Pelvis as a means of relieving Vomiting of Pregnancy, 1891.

In the Canada Lancet :

Retrospect of the Year 1876.

Addresses delivered before the Bathurst and Rideau Medical Association, 1876, 1877, 1878 and 1879.

Gymnastics of the Brain—Canadian Medical Association, 1880.

Uterine Fibrous Polypus, 1881.

Aphasia or Alalia, 1881.

Address on Medicine—Medico-Chirurgical Society, Ottawa, 1885.

Epidemic Zymotic Diseases of Animals, and how they are communicated to man.

Superficial Geology of the Valley of the Ottawa and the Wakefield Cave.
Canadian Naturalist, 1868.

Presidential Address to the Canada Medical Association, St. John, N.B., August 6, 1873.

Cystidian Life.
Transactions Ottawa Field-Naturalists' Club, January, 1880.

On a Specimen of the Inferior Maxilla of Phoca Groenlandica.
Transactions Royal Society of Canada, vol. i., Sec. 4, 1882.

Cheyne Stokes's Respiration and Renal Calculus—Canada Medical Association, Hamilton, September, 1887.

Introductory Lecture, McGill University, November, 1887.

Peri-Urethral Cellulitis and Urethral Fistula—Canada Medical Association, Toronto, September, 1890.

Address before Queen's University on Medical Education, October 14, 1892.

Rare Forms of Gout and Rheumatism. Address in New York City, October 11, 1893, before the State of New York Medical Association.

Hamel, Monsignor Thos. E.

Eloge funèbre de M. Lucien Turcotte.
Annuaire de l'Université Laval, 1874-5, p. 52.

Oraison funèbre de Son Excellence l'honorable R.-E. Caron, prononcée à ses funérailles, déc. 1876, à la Basilique de Québec.
Journaux du temps.

Notice biographique sur M. James-George Colston et M. l'abbé Ovide Brunet.
Annuaire de l'Université Laval, 1877-78, p. 43.

Discours d'ouverture des Cours à Québec, le 8 octobre 1877. Québec : A. Côté et Cie.
8vo., p. 9, 1877.

Oraison funèbre de Pie IX., prononcée dans la Basilique de Québec le 14 février 1878.
Annuaire de l'Université Laval, 1878-79, p. 67.

Translation des restes de Mgr. de Laval à la Chapelle du Séminaire de Québec. Québec : A. Côté et Cie.
8vo., 110 pages, 1878.

Hamel, Monsignor Thomas E.—Continued.

Discours prononcé à l'inauguration de la Faculté de Droit de l'Université Laval à Montréal, le 1er octobre 1878. Montréal : J. Chapleau et Fils. 1878.
8vo., p. 6.

Discours à l'occasion de la collation du grade de Docteur à Lord Dufferin.
Annuaire de l'Université Laval, 1879-80, p. 52

Discours à l'ouverture des Cours de l'Université Laval à Montréal, le 1er octobre 1879. Montréal : Chapleau et Lavigne, 1880.
8vo., p. 1.

Questions sur la Succursale de l'Université Laval à Montréal. Québec : A. Côté et Cie.
8vo., 44 pages, 1881.

Plaidoyers de MM. Hamel et Lacoste devant le Comité des bills privés en faveur de l'Université Laval, les 20, 21, 27 et 28 mai 1881. Québec : A. Côté et Cie.
8vo., 138 pages, 1881.

Discours à l'occasion de la démonstration solennelle faite à l'Université Laval contre la spoliation des biens de la Propagande, le 30 avril 1884. Québec : P.-G. Delisle, 1884.
8vo., pp. 9 et 56.

Le premier Cardinal Canadien. Québec : A. Côté et Cie, 1886.
8vo : 302 pages.

Discours d'ouverture des Cours à Québec et à Montréal, 1885.
Annuaire de l'Université Laval, 1886-87, p. 57.

Oraison funèbre de Mgr Dominique Racine, premier Evêque de Chicoutimi, prononcée le 1er février 1888 dans la cathédrale de Chicoutimi.
Feuille détachée du Progrès du Saguenay, 1888.

Démonstration en faveur du pouvoir temporel du Pape, à l'Université Laval, le 28 avril 1889. Discours d'introduction. Québec : A. Côté et Cie, 1889.
8vo., pp. 7, 39.

Eloge funèbre de Mgr C.-E. Legaré, prononcé à ses funérailles, le 25 janvier 1890.
Annuaire de l'Université Laval, 1891-92, p. 106.

Notice sur Mgr Méthot.
Ibid., 1892-93, p. 41.

Notice sur Joseph-Charles Taché.
Ibid., 1894-95, p. 98.

Harrington, Bernard J.

Catalogue des Minéraux du Canada, avec Notes, Descriptives et Explicatives, Londres : Eyre et Spottiswoo e, 1878.
This volume was prepared to accompany the Geological Collections sent by the Geological Survey of Canada to the Paris Exposition of 1876, and contains a series of Articles on the Economic Minerals of Canada.

Life of Sir William Logan, Kt., First Director of the Geological Survey of Canada. Montreal : Dawson Bros., and London : Sampson, Low & Co., 1883.
8 vo. pp. 432.

In the Reports of the Geological Survey of Canada :

The Coals of the West Coast, 1872-73.

Harrington, W. Hague.—_Continued._

Causes of Rarity in Some Species of Insects.
Canadian Sportsman and Naturalist, April, 1883, vol. III., pp. 225, 226.

Additions to Canadian Lists of Coleoptera.
Canadian Entomologist, 1884, vol. XVI., pp. 44, 47, (March); pp. 70, 73, (April); pp. 96, 98, (May); pp. 117, 119, (June).

Entomology for Beginners. Notes of a June Ramble.
Ibid., June, 1884, Vol. XVI., pp. 101, 103.
Fifteenth Annual Report of the Entomological Society of Ontario, 1884, pp. 30, 31. (Reprint).

Saw-flies—Tenthredinidæ.
Ibid., 1884, pp. 64-72.

List of Ottawa Coleoptera.
Ottawa Field-Naturalists' Club Transactions, No. v., 1884, pp. 67, 85.

Xyloryctes satyrus. (Correspondence.)
Canadian Entomologist, March, 1885, vol. XVII., p. 54.

Hymenoptera Aculeata—Ants, Wasps and Bees.
Sixteenth Annual Report of the Entomological Society of Ontario, 1885, pp. 48, 54.

Are Curculio Larvæ Lignivorous?
Entomologica Americana, April, 1885, vol. I., pp. 18, 19.

Notes on our Saw-flies and Horn-tails.
Ottawa Field-Naturalists' Club Transactions, No. IV., 1885, pp. 241, 247.

Note on Oryssus Sayi.
Canadian Entomologist, February, 1886, vol. XVIII., p. 20.

Tenthredo delta, Prov.
Ibid., February, 1886, vol. XVIII., pp. 32, 33.

Notes on Tenthredinidæ, 1885.
Ibid., February, 1886, vol. XVIII., pp. 38, 40.

Notes on Xiphydria Albicornis.
Ibid., March, 1886, vol. XVIII., pp. 45, 46.

Insects Infesting Maple Trees.
Seventeenth Annual Report of the Entomological Society of Ontario, 1886, pp. 22, 23.

President's Inaugural Address.
Ottawa Field-Naturalists' Club Transactions, No. VII., 1886, pp. 294. 305.

Oryssus Sayi.
Canadian Entomologist, May, 1887, vol. XIX., pp. 81, 86.

Hints on Collecting Hymenoptera.
Ibid., June, 1887, vol. XIX., pp. 115, 116.
Eighteenth Annual Report of the Entomological Society of Ontario, 1887, pp. 43, 44. (Reprint.)

The Nuptials of Thalessa.
Canadian Entomologist, November, 1887, vol. XIX., pp. 206, 209.
Eighteenth Annual Report of the Entomological Society of Ontario, 1887, pp. 25, 27. (Reprint).

Further Observations on Oryssus Sayi.
Canadian Entomologist, December, 1887, vol. XIX., pp. 239, 240.

Note on Flour and Grain Beetles.
Ottawa Naturalist, 1887-88, vol. I., pp. 133, 134.

New Species of Canadian Tenthredinidæ.
Canadian Entomologist, May, 1889, vol. XXI., pp. 95, 99.

Thalia maculipennis, Haldeman.
Ibid., August, 1889, vol. XXI., pp. 141, 145.

Harrington, W. Hague.—_Continued._

Insects Infesting Willows.
Twentieth Annual Report of the Entomolgical Society of Ontario, 1889, pp. 41, 55.

Harpiphorus maculatus, Norton.
Insect Life, January and February, 1890, vol. II., pp. 227, 229.

Tenthredinidæ Collected at Ottawa, 1889.
Canadian Entomologist, February, 1890, vol. XXII., pp. 23, 25.

The Corn Saw-fly.
Ibid., April, 1890, vol. XXII., p. 40.

Two Interesting Monstrosities.
Ibid., June, 1890, vol. XXII., p. 124.

On the Lists of Coleoptera published by the Geological Survey of Canada, 1842-1888.
Ibid., 1890, vol. XXII., pp. 135, 140, (July); pp. 135, 160, (August); pp. 164, 197, (September.)

Hymenoptera Parasitica.
Twenty-first Annual Report of the Entomological Society of Ontario, 1890, pp. 61, 73.

Notes on a Few Canadian Rhyncophora.
Canadian Entomologist, February, 1891, vol. XXIII., pp. 21, 27.

Platynus New to Canada.
Ibid., May, 1891, vol. XXIII., p. 115.

Canadian Rhyncophora.
Ibid., May, 1891, vol. XXIII., p. 114.

Two New Species of Canadian Pimplinæ.
Ibid., June, 1891, vol. XXIII., pp. 132 135.

Note on Amblyopone pallipes, Hald.
Ibid., June, 1891, vol. XXIII., pp. 138, 139.

Notes on Japanese Insects.
Twenty second Annual Report of the Entomological Society of Ontario, 1891, pp. 94, 96.

Notes of Travel in Japan.
Ottawa Naturalist, February, 1892, vol. v., pp. 181, 191.

The Japanese Glass-rope Sponge.
Ibid., February, 1892, vol. v., pp. 191, 192.

The Microscope in Entomology.
Ibid., March, 1892, vol. v., pp. 206, 208.

Additional Note on Amblyopone pallipes, Hald.
Canadian Entomologist, March, 1892, vol. XXIV., p. 76.

Canadian Hymenoptera. No. 1.
Ibid., April, 1892, vol. XXIV., pp. 98, 99.

Two Distinguished Settlers.
Ibid., May, 1892, vol. XXIV., p. 112.

The Abbé Provancher. (Obituary.)
Ibid., May, 1892, vol. XXIV., pp. 130, 131.
Twenty-third Annual Report of the Entomological Society of Ontario, 1892, p. 88. (Reprint.)

A New Ischalia from Vancouver Island.
Canadian Entomologist, May, 1892, vol. XXIV., p. 132.

Fauna Ottawaensis—Hemiptera.
Ottawa Naturalist, June, 1892, vol. VI., pp. 25, 32.

Entomology. (Notes on Ottawa Insects.)
Ibid., September, 1892, vol. VI., pp. 81, 86.

List of Coleoptera collected in 1883-84 by Mr. T. C. Weston on, and in the vicinity of, the Cypress Hills, N.W.T.
Ibid., January, 1893, vol. VI., p. 149.

Entomology. (Notes on Ottawa Insects.)
Ibid., January, 1893, vol. VI., pp. 150, 151.

Harvey, Arthur.

Year Book for British North America, 1867, and for Canada, 1868 and 1869. Montreal : Gazette office.

The Grain Trade of the Lake Regions.
Transactions Literary and Historical Society of Quebec, 1863.

Miscellaneous Statistics of Canada.
Government Blue Books, 1865-1870.

The Reciprocity Treaty, First Prize Essay. Quebec : Hunter, Rose & Co., 1864.

Valuators' Tables for the use of Building Societies. Toronto : Hunter, Rose & Co., 1873.

The appearance and decline of malarious disease in the valley of the Grand River. Hamilton Association, 1858.
Canadian Journal, January, 1859.

The Census of Canada.
Canadian Monthly, 1893.

The discovery of Lake Superior.
Magazine of American History, June, 1885.

Champlain's Endeavour to reach Hudson Bay by the Ottawa in 1613.
Ibid., March, 1886.

The Cruel Plant (*Physianthus albens*). Natural History Society, Toronto (Biological section, Canadian Institute).
Transactions Canadian Institute, 1889.

Outlines of the Geology of Northwest Lake Superior.
Ibid., April, 1890.

L'État de la Population d'Origine Française du Canada.
Compte-Rendu du Congrès de Philologie Romane, Montpellier (France), 1890.

Celtic, Roman and Greek Types, still existent in France, with notes on the Langue d'Oc.
Transactions Canadian Institute, 1890-91.

Bone Caves.
Ibid., October, 1891.

The Enterprise of Christopher Columbus.
Magazine of American History, January and February, 1842.

The Pythagorean Philosophy.
Transactions Astronomical and Physical Society of Toronto, 1891.

The Height of an Auroral Arch.
Ibid., 1893.

The Antarctic Regions of the Earth and of Mars.
Ibid., 1894.

A Physical Catastrophe to America.
Canadian Magazine, April, 1891.

Hay, Geo. U.

Life and Work of Professor C. Fred. Hartt.
Natural History Society Proceedings, 1882, St. John, N. B.

New Brunswick Flora, chiefly of the River St. John and its Tributaries.
Ibid., 1883-1891, St. John, N. B.

The Botany of Northern New Brunswick.
Proceedings American Association for Advancement of Science, 1886.

Hay, Geo. U.—*Continued.*

Marine Algæ of New Brunswick.
Transactions Royal Society of Canada, vol. v., sec. 4., 1887.

History of Botany in New Brunswick.
Ibid., vol. x., sec. 4, 1892.

Ideal School Discipline, and How to Secure it.
Proceedings Dominion Educational Association, Montreal, 1892.

Various papers on Education and Natural Science.
Educational Review, vols. i-vii., St. John, N. B.

Hoffmann, G. Christian.

The Eucalypts of Australia (on the essential oils, kino and manna, etc., obtained therefrom, and suitability of the bark of certain species of the same for paper-making), with an appendix on the essential oils of certain species of the genus Melaleuca, and other indigenous Victorian plants. A paper read before the Montreal College of Pharmacy, February 6, 1873. Mitchell and Wilson, Montreal. 1873.
8vo., p. 39, 2 plates.

In the Reports of the Geological Survey of Canada :

Chemical Contributions to the Geology of Canada, Report of Progress, 1874-75, pp. 313-319 ; *ibid.*, 1875-76, pp. 410-432 ; *ibid.*, 1878-79, pp. 1-25H ; *ibid.*, 1879-80, pp. 1-21H ; *ibid.*, 1880-81-82, pp. 1-16H ; *ibid.*, 1882-83-84, pp. pp. 1-10MM. Annual Reports (New Series) vol. I., 1885, pp. 1-20M ; *ibid.*, vol. II., 1886, pp. 1-42T ; *ibid.*, vol. III., 1887-88, pp. 1-58T ; *ibid.*, vol. IV., 1889-90, pp. 1-08R ; *ibid.*, vol. v., 1880-90-91, pp. 1-72R.

On Canadian Graphite, Report of Progress, 1876-77, pp. 489-512.

On Canadian Apatite, Report of Progress, 1877-78, pp. 1-14H.

On the Coals and Lignites of the Northwest Territory, Report of Progress, 1882-83-84, pp. 1-44M.

Catalogue of Section 1 of the Museum of the Geological Survey of Canada. Embracing the systematic collection of minerals, and the collections of economic minerals and rocks and specimens illustrative of structural geology. Ottawa : S. E. Dawson, Queen's Printer, 1893.
8vo., pp. 256, with folding plan of room.

In the Transactions of the Royal Society of Canada :

On a specimen of Canadian Native Platinum. Vol. v., sec. 3, 1887.

On the Hygroscopicity of Certain Canadian Fossil Fuels. Vol. vII., sec. 3, 1889.

Annotated List of the Minerals occurring in Canada. Vol. vII., sec. 3, 1889.

On a peculiar form of Metallic Iron found on St. Joseph's Island, Lake Huron, Ontario. Vol. vIII., sec. 3, 1890.

Hale, Horatio.

United States Exploring Expedition during the Years 1838 to 1842, under the command of Charles Wilkes, U. S. N. Vol. vII. Ethnography and Philology. Philadelphia : Lea & Blanchard, 1846.
4to., pp. 673.
The author was philologist to the expedition,

Hale, Horatio.—*Continued*.

Hiawatha and the Iroquois Confederation. A paper read at the annual meeting of the American Association for the Advancement of Science in August, 1881, under the title of "A Lawgiver of the Stone Age."
Proceedings of the American Association, 1881. Reprinted in pamphlet form. The Salem Press, 1881. 8vo. pp. 20.

Indian Migrations as Evidenced by Language. Read at the Montreal meeting of the American Association in August, 1882.
The American Antiquarian for January and April, 1883. Reprinted in pamphlet, Chicago: Jameson & Morse, 8vo., pp. 27.

The Tutelo Tribe and Language.
Reprinted in pamphlet from the *Proceedings of the American Philosophical Society*, Philadelphia, March, 1883. 8vo., pp. 47.

The Iroquois Book of Rites. With an introduction on the history, customs and language of the Huron-Iroquois nations.
Volume No. 2 of *Brinton's Library of Aboriginal American Literature*. Philadelphia, D. G. Brinton, 1883. 8vo., pp. 220.

On Some Doubtful or Intermediate Articulations.
Journal of the Anthropological Institute of Great Britain and Ireland, February, 1885. 8vo., pp. 12.

Chief George H. M. Johnson—Onwanonsyshon : His Life and Work among the Six Nations. With portraits and other illustrations.
Magazine of American History, February, 1886. 8vo., pp. 12.

Report on the Blackfoot Tribes. Prepared for the British Association for the Advancement of Science as the First Report of a Committee on the Northwestern Tribes of Canada.
Proceedings of the Association for 1885. Reprinted in *Nature*, and (with some omissions) in the *Popular Science Monthly* for June, 1886. 8vo pp. 12.

The Iroquois Sacrifice of the White Dog.
American Antiquarian for January, 1885. 8vo., p. 6.

The Origin of Wampum. A paper read at the Montreal meeting of the British Association in 1884.
Popular Science Monthly for January, 1890, under the title of "The Origin of Primitive Money." 8vo., pp. 11.

The Origin of Languages and the Antiquity of Speaking Man. An address delivered before the Section of Anthropology of the American Association for the Advancement of Science in August, 1886.
Proceedings of the Association of 1886, and in pamphlet, Cambridge, Mass. : John Wilson & Son, 1886. 8vo., pp. 47.

Language as a Political Force.
Andover Review for August, 1896. 8vo., pp. 11.

Notes by the Editor of the Third Report of the British Association on the Northwestern Tribes of Canada.
Proceedings of the Association for 1887. 8vo., pp. 4.

Notes by the Editor of the Fourth Report of the above Committee.
Ibid., 1888. 8vo., pp. 3.

Hale, Horatio.—*Continued*.

Huron Folk-lore. No. 1. Cosmogonic Myths. The Good and Evil Minds.
Journal of American Folk-lore for October and December, 1888.

An International Language.
Proceedings of the American Association for the Advancement of Science, 1888. 8vo., pp. 5.

The Development of Language. A paper read before the Canadian Institute, Toronto, April, 1888.
Proceedings of the Canadian Institute, and reprinted in pamphlet by the Copp-Clark Co., Toronto, 1888. 8vo., pp. 45.

Race and Language. Read at the annual meeting of the American Association in 1887, under the title of "The True Basis of Ethnology."
Popular Science Monthly, January, 1888.

The Aryans in Science and History. Read at the annual meeting of the American Association in 1888.
Ibid., March, 1889. 8vo., pp. 15.

Remarks on North American Ethnology : introductory to the Fifth Report of the Committee of the British Association on the Northwestern Tribes of Canada.
Proceedings of the Association for 1889. 8vo., pp. 5.

Huron Folk-lore. No. 2. The Story of Tijaiha, the Sorcerer.
Journal of American Folk-lore, October and December, 1889. 8vo., pp. 6.

An International Idiom : A Manual of the Oregon Trade-language or Chinook Jargon. London : Whittaker & Co., 1890. 12mo., pp. 63.

Was America Peopled from Polynesia ? A Study in Comparative Philology.
Proceedings of the International Congress of Americanists, Berlin, October, 1888. Reprinted in pamphlet, Berlin : H.C. Hermann, 1890 8vo., pp. 15.

"Above" and "Below" : A Mythological Disease of Language.
Journal of American Folk-lore, July and September, 1890. 8vo., pp. 13.

Remarks on the Ethnology of British Columbia : Introductory to the Fifth Report of the Committee of the British Association on the Northwestern Tribes of Canada.
Proceedings of the Association, 1890. 8vo., pp 10.

Huron Folk-lore. No. 3. The Legend of the Thunderers.
Journal of American Folk-lore, October and December, 1891. 8vo., pp. 6.

Language as a Test of Mental Capacity; being an attempt to demonstrate the True Basis of Anthropology.
Pamphlet reprinted from the *Transactions of the Royal Society of Canada*, vol. ix., Sec. 2, 18 1. Republished in the *Journal of the Anthropological Institute of Great Britain and Ireland* for May, 1891. Also (under the title of 'Man and Language") in the *American Antiquarian* for January, March, May and July, 1893. 4to., pp. 30.

Hale, Horatio.—Continued.

Remarks on Linguistic Ethnology : Introductory
to the Eighth Report of the Committee of the
British Association on the Northwestern Tribes
of America.
Proceedings of the Association for 1892. 8vo., pp. 5.

The Klamath Nation.
Science for January 1, 8, and 15, 1892.

The Fall of Hochelaga : A Study of Popular
Tradition. A paper prepared for the International Congress of Anthropology, held at the
" World's Columbian Exposition," at Chicago,
in 1893.
Memoirs of the Congress, Chicago : The Schulte Publishing Co., and in the *Journal of American Folk-lore*
for March, 1894, pp. 15.

An International Scientific Catalogue and Congress.
Science for March, 1895.

Johnson, Alexander.

In the Transactions of the Royal Society of Canada:

Symmetrical Investigation of the Curvature of
Surfaces. Vol. I., Sec. 3, 1882.

Report on the Preparations at Montreal for Ob-
serving the Transit of Venus of December 6,
1882. Vol. I., Sec. 3, 1883.

Presidential Address to the Third Section of the
Society. Vol. III., Sec. 3, 1885.

Tidal Observations in Canadian Waters. *Ibid.*

On the same subject. Vol. VIII., Sec. 3, 1890.

Newton's use of the Slit and Lens in forming a
Pure Spectrum. Vol. IX., Sec. 3, 1891.

On the need of a " Coast Survey " for the Dominion of Canada. Vol. XI., Sec. 3, 1893.

*In the Reports of the British Association for the
Advancement of Science, viz. :*

On the Importance of Tidal Observations in the
Gulf of St. Lawrence and on the Atlantic Coast
of the Dominion. 1894.

Also six reports as Chairman of a Committee
appointed by the Association to promote Tidal
Observations in Canada. 1885 to 1890 inclusive.

University of McGill Addresses :

Science and Religion. 1870.

The Faculty of Arts—the heart of a University.
1891.

A Professor's Vacation. 1892.

Keefer, T. C.

Reports as Division Engineer Welland Canal,
1840-1845. Board of Works.

Reports as Chief Engineer on Ottawa River
Works, 1845-1848. Board of Works.

Philosophy of Railways. Montreal, 1840, Jno.
Lovell.
8vo., pp. 40.

Canals of Canada. (Prize Essay.) Toronto, 1850,
Lovell.
8vo., pp. 111.

Keefer, T. C.—Continued.

Report on Temiscouata Route for Railway and
Canal, 1850. Board of Works.

Report on Improvement of the Rapids, River St.
Lawrence. Board of Works.

Report on Canadian Commerce and Transporta-
tion, for Andrews's first Report on Reciprocity
between Canada and the United States, 1850.

Report on Kingston and Toronto Section Grand
Trunk Railway, 1851.

Report on Montreal and Kingston Section Grand
Trunk Railway, 1851.

Report on Montreal Water Works, 1852.

Report on Canadian Commerce, etc., for Andrews's
second Report on Reciprocity between Canada
and the United States, 1852.

Report on Victoria Bridge across the St. Lawrence
at Montreal, 1853.

Lecture delivered before Mechanics Institute on
" Montreal," 1853.

Report on St. Lawrence and Ottawa Grand Junc-
tion Railway, 1853.

Report on Toronto Water Works, as Referee,
1854.

Lecture before Mechanics' Institute, Montreal,
on "The Ottawa," 1854.

Report on Hamilton Water Works, 1855.

Report on Dredging in Lake St. Peter and Harbour of Montreal, as Harbour Engineer, 1855.

Report on Halifax Water Works.

Report on Water Supply for the City of Toronto,
1857.

Report on Harbour, St. John, N.B., 1860.

Report on Water Works, Quebec, 1860.

Report on Harbour, Richibucto, N.B.

Report on Water Works, Dartmouth, N.S.

Report on Water Works, Ottawa, 1860.

Ten letters in favour of " all rail " versus " water
stretches " for the Canadian Pacific Railway,
1860-1870.

Report on Water Works, London, Ont.

Report on Water Works, St. Catharines, Ont.

Handbook for Canadian Commission, Paris Exhibition, 1878.

Report as Executive Commissioner for Paris Exhibition of 1878-1879.

Report as Chairman Flood Commission, Montreal, 1886-88,

Address as President Canadian Society Civil
Engineers, Montreal, 1887.

Address as President American Society Civil
Engineers, Milwaukee, 1888.

Paper on Canadian Waterways to the Atlantic,
read before World's Water Commerce Congress
at Chicago, 1893.

The Canals of Canada.
Transactions Royal Society of Canada, Vol. IX.,
Sec. 3, 1893.

Kirby, William.

Counter Manifesto to the Annexationists of Montreal.
Published in pamphlet form by the Government of Canada. Niagara, 29th October, 1849.

W. Kirby and J. B. Plumb, The Broadside and Welland Electors Companion. (Political Squibs). Niagara, June 15th, 1863.

The U. E. A Tale of Upper Canada, A Poem in XII. Cantos. Niagara : W. Kirby, 1859. 12mo., pp. 174.

Miss Rye's Emigrant Children. London, England. Leisure Hour, May, 1873.

Acadia. Toronto : J. Briggs, July, 1878.

The United Empire Loyalists.
Canadian Methodist Magazine, Toronto, April and May, 1881.

The Golden Dog. A Legend of Quebec, New York and Montreal. Lovel, Adam, Wesson & Co., 1877.
8vo., pp. 678.

Le Chien d'or.
French Translation of above by Pamphile Le May. Montréal : Imprimerie de l'Etendard, 1884.

Memoirs of Servos Family. Toronto : W. Briggs, 1884.

Canadian Idyls.
Published separately in Pamphlet form.
A Second Edition in 1894, 8vo., pp. 175, Welland,Ont.

The Sparrows. Niagara, December, 1870.

Dead Sea Roses. Toronto : W. Briggs, 1878.

The Hungry Year. Toronto : W. Briggs, 1870.

Stony Creek. Toronto : W. Briggs, 1880.

Queen's Birthday and Spina Christi. Toronto, Rose-Belford Co., 1881.

The Bells of Kirby Wiske and The Lord's Supper in the Wilderness. Toronto, Rose-Belford Co., 1882.

The Harvest Moon. Toronto, Rose-Belford Co., 1883.

Pontiac, A.D. 1763. Niagara : W. Kirby, 1887.

Bushy Run, A.D., 1763. Niagara : W. Kirby, 1887.

Address, U. E. Loyalist Centennial at Niagara, August 14th, 1884. Toronto : Rose Publishing Co., 1885.
Also in 2nd Edition of Canadian Idyls, 1894.

Memoir of Hon. J. B. Plumb in Representative Canadians. Toronto : Rose Publishing Co., 1880.

Monody on the Sickness and Retirement of His Excellency Lord Metcalf from the Government of Canada, November, 1845.
Niagara Chronicle, 31st December, 1845.

The Wreck of the Hungarian, 10th February, 1860.
Niagara Mail.

Stuart's Raid. An Incident in the Siege of Richmond, 12th June, 1862.
Niagara Mail, 1862.

Titles of Published Sonnets, viz :

The Wax Wing.

On The Jubilee of Her Majesty's Reign.

Spencer Grange.

Winter Roses on the Children's Faces.

Kirby, William.—Continued.

Portrait of Mrs. Hope Sewell, Quebec.

A Night Vision. Vidi Coelum Apertum.

On a Child of Two Summers.

On Her Majesty's Providential Escape from Assassination, March 2nd, 1882.

To James M. LeMoine, Quebec.

On General Gordon's Death.

Et Arborum folia, sic dies nostri.

"For the Hairs of your Head are all Numbered."

On the Visit of the Marquis of Lorne to the North-west.

On the Departure of His Excellency The Marquis of Lorne and the Princess Louise, October 27th, 1883.

Montmorency.

On a photograph, Mrs. M. LeMoine, Quebec.

Brock's Seat.

Lundy's Lane.

National Song, Canadians Forever, 1867.

Laflamme, Mgr. J. C. K.

Age de la chute Montmorency.
Annuaire de l'Institut Canadien, No. 5, 1878.

Eléments de Minéralogie et de Géologie. Edité par M. P.-G. Delisle, 1881.

Le Canada d'autrefois. Esquisse géologique.
Annuaire de l'Institut Canadien, No. 9, 1882.

Note sur la géologie du lac St-Jean.
Mémoires de la Société royale, Tome I., Sec. 4, 1883.

Note sur les dépots auriféres de la Beauce.
Ibid., Tome II., Sec. 4, 1884.

Note sur un gisement d'émeraude au Saguenay.
Ibid., Tome II., Sec. 4, 1891.

Eléments de Minéralogie, de Géologie et de Botanique. Edité par J.-A. Langlais. 1885.

Le Saguenay. Essai de géographie physique.
Bulletin de la Société de Géographie de Québec, Tome I., 1885.

Note sur les contacts des formations paléozoïques et archéennes de la Province de Québec.
Mémoires de la Société royale, Tome IV., Sec. 4, 1886.

Michel Sarrazin. Sa biographie, ses travaux scientifiques.
Ibid., Tome V., Sec. 4, 1887.

Le gaz naturel de la Province de Québec.
Ibid., Tome VI., Sec. 4, 1888.

Travail sur les cours dits d'extension universitaire.
Ibid., Tome IX., Sec. 4, 1891.

Etude sur le Dr T.-S. Hunt.
Ibid., Tome X., pp. XLVII.-LII.
Reproduite avec additions dans l'Annuaire de l'Université Laval, No. 36.

Métallurgie électrique.
Canada-Français, Tome I.

Chroniques scientifiques.
Ibid., Tomes II., III. et IV.

La poésie chez les plantes. Dans le volume intitulé : A la mémoire de A. Lusignan. Montréal : Desaulniers et Leblanc, 1892.

Notions sur l'électricité et le magnétisme. Québec : A. Côté et Cie, 1893.

Laflamme, Mgr. J. C. K.—*Continued.*

L'Eboulis de St-Alban.
Canadian Engineer.
De plus, un grand nombre d'articles scientifiques publiés à diverses reprises dans les journaux quotidiens.

Lawson, George.

On the Arracacha of Brazil. With letter from M. Decaisne of Paris.
Proceedings Dundee Naturalists' Association, 1848.

On the Occurrence of Mimulus luteus in Forfarshire.
Phytologist, Vol. II., p. 889, 1848.

Stray Thoughts on Botanical Rambles and Visits, suggested by Mr. Hewett Cottrell Watson's remarks on the usefulness of a Periodical devoted to British Botany.
Ibid., Vol. II., pp. 417-419, 1846.

Note on Mimulus luteus.
Ibid., Vol. II., p. 450, 1846.

On the Occurrence of Pyrola rotundifolia, Alchemilla alpina, and Viola lutea γ, on Sidlaw Hills, Forfarshire.
Ibid., Vol. II., p. 578, 1846.

On a Monstrosity of Cardamine pratensis.
Ibid., Vol. II., p. 379, 1846.

Occurrence of a New Variety of Silene inflata in Fifeshire.
Ibid., Vol. II., p. 789, 1846.

A New Locality in Scotland for Ruscus aculeatus.
Ibid., Vol. II., p. 653, 1846.

On Viola odorata, and its occurrence in Fifeshire.
Ibid., Vol. II., p. 863, 1846.

On a White-flowered Variety of Epilobium montanum.
Ibid., Vol. II., p. 823, 1846.

On Silybum Marianum.
Ibid., Vol. II., p. 416, 1846.

On Salvia verbenaca, Linn.
Ibid., Vol. II., p. 416, 1846.

* Notes on Viola odorata and its occurrence in Fifeshire, etc.
Ibid., Vol. II., pp. 863, 1846.

Notice of a Black Swan (Cygnus niger) shot in the Valley of Eden, Fife, in 1840.
Zoologist, 1847.

List of the Rarer Flowering Plants observed during a residence in Fifeshire in 1846-47.
Phytologist, Vol. III., pp. 128-130, 1848.

* Notes on the Periods of Flowering of Wild Plants.
Ibid., Vol. III., pp. 292-293, 1848.

* Remarks on the Naturalization of Plants in Britain.
Ibid., Vol. III., pp. 292-293, 1848.

* Remarks on the Naturalization of Plants in Britain.
Ibid., Vol. III., pp. 294-299, 1848.

* On the occurrence of Euphorbia salicifolia as a naturalized plant in Forfarshire.
Ibid., Vol. III., pp. 314-315, 1848.

* Titles marked with an asterisk (*) are included in the (London) *Royal Society's Catalogue of Scientific Papers*, Vol. III., pp. 895-896, published in 1869.

Lawson, George.—*Continued.*

Observations on the Floral Changes of the Present Day in relation to Past Changes of the Earth's Flora. Presidential Address to the Geological Society of Edinburgh, 17th April, 1851.
The Naturalist (London), Vol. I. pp. 75-81.

* Note on the effects of Cultivation upon Plantago lanceolata γ, sphærostachya (W. & G. of *Brit. Manual.*)
Henfrey's Botanical Gazette, Vol. I, pp. 35-36, 1849.

The Royal Water-Lily of South America (Victoria regia) and the Water-Lilies of our own Land. Edinburgh: Hogg. 1849. Pp. 100, 2 coloured plates.

On Plants collected on Wandsworth Common in 1851 (now either to England or to the London district), Melilotus parviflora, Scorpiurus subvillosus, Trifolium ochroleucum, Anacharis alsinastrum (Udora Canadensis), etc.
Proceedings Botanical Society of Edinburgh, 1851.

On the occurrence of "Cinchonaceous Glands" in Galiaceæ, and on the relations of that Order to Cinchonaceæ.
Annals of Natural History, Vol. XIV., pp. 161-168, plate, 1854.
Transactions of Botanical Society of Edinburgh, Vol. V., pp. 3-10, plate II.

* On the Stipular Glands of Rubiaceæ.
British Association Report, 1854, Part II., p. 99.

* On Rotation in the Cells of Plants.
Journal of Microscopical Science, Vol. II., pp. 54-55, 1851. Resumé in *English Cyclopædia*, Natural History Division, Vol. I. "Cyclosis."

* Report on the Musci and Desmideæ collected during the trip of the Edinburgh University Botanical Class to Falkland and the Lomond Hills, Fife, June, 1855.
Proceedings Botanical Society of Edinburgh, 1855, pp. 75-81.

On Species of Bryum, viz., B. calophyllum, Marratti, Warneum, and on Didymodon.
Ibid., 1855, pp. 2-3.

* On the Microscopical Structure of the Victoria Regia, Lindl.
Proceedings Botanical Society of Edinburgh, 1855, pp. 119-121. Also *Journal of Microscopical Science*, Vol. IV., pp. 163-165, 1856.

On Orthotrichum phyllanthum, Brachythecium micropus and B. glaciulis.
Proceedings Botanical Society of Edinburgh, 1856, p. 33.

* Remarks on Dust Showers, with notice of a shower of mud that occurred at Corfu on 21st March, 1857.
Ibid., Vol. V., pp. 179-181, 1858. (A translation in modern Greek printed at Corfu, 1858.)

On the Application of Botany to Ornamental Art (with special reference to examples in wood-carving).
Ibid., Vol. V., pp. 177-179, 1857.

Remarks on Certain Glandular Structures in Plants (controverting Dr. Carpenter's view as to absence of true secretion in plants, and pointing out homology of secreting cells with epidermal cells).
Ibid., Vol. V., pp. 212-214, 1857.

Lawson, George.—*Continued.*

On Diatomaceæ of Braemar (with Dr. R. K. Greville and Prof. J. Hutton Balfour).
Ibid., Vol. v., pp. 45-54, 1857.

Catalogue of the Library of the Royal Society of Edinburgh, (with Preface by Prof. J. D. Forbes, secretary). Edinburgh : Printed for the Society, 1857.

Notice of the Occurrence of Hypnum rugulosum, Web. et Mohr, on Demyat, Ochils.
Transactions Botanical Society of Edinburgh, Vol. vi., p. 26, 1857.

British Agriculture, illustrated by the actual accounts of the tenant of a Midlothian farm, for a series of years, abstracted so as to show expense of cultivation of, and revenue or loss from, every crop, etc. Edinburgh : Edmonston & Douglas, 1858.

The British Mosses, illustrated by the Nature-printing Process.
(When the printing of this work was nearly completed, in the year 1858, its issue was prevented by the sudden death of a member of the publishing firm that had acquired the copyright, and consequently the book has not been published.)

Note on Cryphæa (Daltonia) Lamyana, Montagne.
Transactions Botanical Society of Edinburgh, Vol. vi., p. 30, 1858.

Remarks on the Distribution of Plants in the Northern States, Canada, and the Hudson's Bay Company's Territories.
Ibid., Vol. vi., p. 41, 1858.

Notice of the Produce of the Olive Crop in the Island of Corfu during the past season (1857).
Ibid., Vol. vi., p. 42, 1858.

Notice of Plants collected in the Isle of Skye by Drs. Smith and Gilchrist.
Ibid., Vol. vi., p. 44, 1858.

On Mollugo Cerviana.
Ibid., Vol. vi., p. 45, 1858.

* Remarks on Lepas anatifera, Linn.
Annals of Natural History, Vol. ii., pp. 172-175, 1858.

* Further Observations on Dust Showers.
Transactions Botanical Society of Edinburgh, Vol. v., pp. 206-207, 1858.

List of Plants found at Tayport, Fife, in September, 1858.
Ibid., Vol. vi., pp. 217-218.

Notice of a few Plants collected in the vicinity of Stirling (Scotland).
Ibid., Vol. vi., pp. 73-74, 1858.

Remarks on M. Montagne's specimen of Cryphæa Lamyana, Mont.
Ibid., Vol. vi., p. 117, 1858.

* Remarks on the Microscopical Structure of Cotton Fibre with reference to Mr. Gilbert J. French's proposed improvements in Spinning.
Ibid., Vol. vi., pp. 8-14, 1857.

* Contributions to Microscopical Analysis No. 1. Tobacco.
Ibid., Vol. vi., pp. 24-26, 1857.

Lawson, George.—*Continued.*

* Contributions to Microscopical Analysis No. 2. Celastrus scandens, Linn., with Remarks on the Colouring Matters of Plants.
Transactions Botanical Society of Edinburgh, Vol. vi., pp. 362-363, 1860.
Also in *Edinburgh New Philosophical Journal,* Vol. xii., pp. 52-58, 1860.

Bailey's Circular ; Monthly Treatises on the Field Crops of Britain. Edinburgh, 1857-58.

* On Macadamia, Müller, a new genus of Proteaceæ.
Transactions Botanical Society of Edinburgh, Vol. vi., pp. 36-37, 1858.

Address at opening of Agricultural Exhibition in Crystal Palace. Kingston, September, 1859.
Canadian Agriculturist, 1859.

On a New Dye (resembling cochineal) obtained from the black spruce Aphis.
Annals of the Botanical Society of Canada, 1860.

On Raphanus caudatus, description with figure.
Horticulturist, New York, 1860.

* On the Structure and Development of Botrydium granulatum.
Transactions Botanical Society of Edinburgh, Vol. vi., pp. 424-431, plate xii.
New Philosophical Journal, Edinburgh, Vol. xii., pp. 206-213, 1860.

On Aphis Avenæ.
Canadian Naturalist, Vol. vii., pp. 264-277, 1862.

* Some account of Plants collected in the Counties of Leeds and Grenville, Upper Canada, in July, 1862.
Transactions Botanical Society of Edinburgh, Vol. vii., pp. 463-470, 1863.
Edinburgh New Philosophical Journal, Vol. xvii., pp. 197-208, 1863.

* Note on Lemania variegata, Agardh.
Transactions Botanical Society of Edinburgh, Vol. vii., pp. 521-524, 1863.
Edinburgh New Philosophical Journal, Vol. xvii., pp. 30-34, 1863.

* Synopsis of the Canadian Species of Equisetum.
Transactions Botanical Society of Edinburgh, Vol. vii., pp. 558-564, 1863.

' Botanical Science—Record of Progress.
Canadian Naturalist, New Series, Vol. i., Article i., 1864.

Diatomaceæ of the District of Braemar, (with Prof. J. H. Balfour and Dr. R. K. Greville).
Transactions Botanical Society of Edinburgh, Vol. v., pp. 45-54.

On the Applications of Botany to Ornamental Art.
Ibid., Vol. v., p. 177.

Notice of the Occurrence of Hypnum rugulosum, Web. et Mohr, on Demyat, Ochils.
Ibid., Vol. vi., p. 26.

Note on Cryphæa (Daltonia) Lamyana, Montagne.
Ibid., Vol. vi., p. 30.

Synopsis of the Canadian Species of Equisetum.
Ibid., Vol. vii., pp. 558-564.

Remarks on some Fibrous Plants of Canada, with Letters from Lord Lyons and Lord Monck in reference to the use of the Silk-cotton of Asclepias in spinning.
Ibid., Vol. vii., pp. 375-378.

Lawson, George.—*Continued.*

* Synopsis of Canadian Ferns and Filicoid Plants.
  Transactions Botanical Society of Edinburgh. Vol. viii., pp. 20-50, 1864. Also in *Edinburgh New Philosophical Journal,* New Series, Vol xix., pp. 102-116 and pp. 273-291. Reprinted in *Canadian Naturalist,* New Series, Vol. i., pp. 262-380.

Notice of the Occurrence of Woodsia alpina (hyperborea) in Gaspé, Canada East.
  Transactions Botanical Society of Edinburgh, Vol. viii., p. 109, 1864.

Remarks on Myrica cerifera, or Candleberry Myrtle.
  Ibid., Vol. viii., pp. 166-103, 1864.

Note on the Leaves [trifoliate] of Ulex Europæus, (Whin).
  Ibid., Vol. viii., p. 109, 1864.

Translation of Paper by M. J. Personne on the Chemical and Natural History of Lupuline, with Introductory Note.
  Ibid., Vol. viii., pp. 131-144, Plate ii., 1864.

On the Flora of Canada: a Synopsis of all the Flowering Plants and Ferns observed in Canada, with habitats in detail. (Abstract; the List [in bound volume] not printed.)
  Transactions Nova Scotian Institute of Natural Science, Vol. i., Part ii., pp. 75-77, 1864.

Notice of the Occurrence of Heather at St. Ann's Bay, Cape Breton Island.
  Ibid., Vol. i., Part iii., pp. 30-35, 1864.

Note [additional] on Lemania variegata of Agardh.
  Ibid., Vol. i., Part iii., pp. 35-36, 1864.

On Calluna vulgaris.
  Transactions Botanical Society of Edinburgh, Vol. viii., pp. 324-327, 1865.

On some Recent Improvements in the Amalgamation Process for Extracting Gold from Quartz.
  Transactions Nova Scotian Institute of Natural Science, Vol. i. Part iv., pp. 71-76 1866. *Chemical News,* 1866.

Notes of Analyses of Gold Coins of Columbia, New Grenada, Chili, and Bolivia. With some account of the operations of gold-mining in Nova Scotia, Dominion of Canada.
  Chemical News, Vol. xvi., pp. 145-   , 1867.

On Trichina spiralis in the Human Body and Tænia pectinata in the Porcupine.
  Transactions Nova Scotian Institute of Natural Science, Vol. ii., Part i., p. 48, 1867.

Monograph of Ranunculaceæ of the Dominion of Canada, and adjacent parts of British America.
  Ibid., Vol. ii., Part iv., pp. 17-51, 1869. Reprinted in *Canadian Naturalist,* New Series, Vol. iv., pp. 407-421.

On the Laminariaceæ of the Dominion of Canada and adjacent parts of British America.
  Transactions Nova Scotian Institute of Natural Science, Vol. ii., Part iv., pp. 109-111, 1870. Reprinted in *Canadian Naturalist,* N. S., Vol. v., pp. 99-101.

Description of the Canadian Species of Myosotis, with Notes on other Plants of the Natural Order Borraginaceæ.
  Canadian Naturalist, New Series, Vol. iv., Art. 27.

On the Botany of the Dominion of Canada and adjacent parts of British America, Ranunculaceæ.
  Transactions Botanical Society of Edinburgh. Vol. x., pp. 345-348, 1870.

Lawson, George.—*Continued.*

Monograph of Ericaceæ of the Dominion of Canada and adjacent parts of British America.
  Transactions Nova Scotian Institute of Natural Science, Vol. iii., p. 74, 1871.

On the Geographical Range of the Species and Varieties of Canadian Rubi over the Continents of America, Asia and Europe, as indicating Possible Regions of Primitive Distribution.
  Ibid., Vol. iii., pp. 361-360, 1874. Also *Transactions Botanical Society of Edinburgh.* Vol. xii., pp. 111-113, 1874.

Chemical Relations of Heat.
  Transactions Nova Scotian Institute of Natural Science, Vol. iii., pp. 436-438, 1874. Also in *Chemical News,* Vol. xxxi.

Botanical Descriptions accompanying Mrs. Miller's Drawings of the Wild Flowers of Nova Scotia, 2nd and 3rd Series. London: L. Reeve & Co.

Notes on some Nova Scotian Plants: Calluna vulgaris, Sarothamnus Scoparius, Rhododendron maximum.
  Transactions Nova Scotian Institute of Natural Science, Vol. iv., pp. 167-179, 1876.

The Journal of Agriculture, Nova Scotia, Vol. i., March, 1865, to March, 1872, p. 728. Vol. ii., April, 1872, to February, 1877.

Report on Cattle Pastures and Well, Pond, and Brook Waters of Picton County, (in connection with Dr. McEachran's investigation of disease in Cattle).
  Sessional Papers of Dominion Parliament. Reprinted in *Annual Report of Secretary for Agriculture of Nova Scotia.*

Introduction to Professor How's Paper on the East Indian Herbarium of King's College, Windsor, N.S.
  Transactions Nova Scotian Institute of Natural Science, Vol. iv., pp. 369-379, 1878.

On Diatomaceous Deposits in the Lakes of the Halifax Water Works.
  Ibid., Vol. v., p. 114, 1879.

Report, with Analyses, on the Water Supply of the City of Halifax.
  Annual Report of Halifax Corporation, 1879.

On the British American species of the genus Viola.
  Transactions Botanical Society of Edinburgh, Vol. xiv., pp. 64-66, 1880. Also *Bot. Centralblatt,* 1880.

On Native Species of Viola of Nova Scotia.
  Transactions Nova Scotian Institute of Natural Science, Vol. v., p. 115, 1880.

Notice of New and Rare Plants.
  Ibid., Vol. vi., p. 64, 1882.

On the Northern Limit of Wild Grape Vines.
  Ibid., Vol. vi., pp. 101-109, 1884.

Revision of the Canadian Ranunculaceæ.
  Transactions Royal Society of Canada, Vol. ii., Section 4, 1884, pp. 15-90.

On the Canadian species of the genus Melilotus.
  Transactions Nova Scotian Institute of Natural Science, Vol. vi., pp. 180-190, 1885.

Remarks on the Flora of the Northern Shores of America; With tabulated observations made by Mr. F. F. Paine on the seasonal development

Lawson, George.—*Continued.*

of plants at Cape Prince of Wales, Hudson
Strait, during the growing season of 1886,
Transactions Royal Society of Canada, Vol. v., Sec.
4, 1887, pp. 207-212.

Vice-President's Address to the Royal Society of
Canada, May 25th, 1887.
Ibid., Vol. v., 1887, pp. xxii-xxv.

President's Address to Royal Society of Canada,
May 23rd, 1888.
Ibid., Vol. vi., 1888, pp. xvii-xxx.

On the first principles of Chemistry and the system of Chemical Nomenclature ; an Introduction to Tanner's First Principles of Agriculture.
Halifax : A. & W. Mackinlay, 1887.

The Fern Flora of Canada. Halifax : A. & W.
Mackinlay.

On the Canadian Species of Picea.
Canadian Record of Science, 1888.

On the Nymphæaceæ. Part i., Structure of Vic-
toria Regia, Lindl. Part ii., Nomenclature of
Nymphæaceæ. Part iii., Synopsis of Species.
Transactions Royal Society of Canada Vol. vi.,
Section 4, 1888, pp. 97-125.

Notes for a Flora of Nova Scotia.
*Transactions Nova Scotian Institute of Natural
Science*, New Series, Vol. i., pp. 84-110, 1891.

On the Present State of Botany in Canada.
Transactions Royal Society of Canada, Vol. ix.,
Section 4, 1891, pp. 17-20.

Nova Scotia Register of Thoroughbred Cattle, including Bulls, Cows and Heifers of the following
breeds : Short Horn, Devon, Ayrshire, Polled
Angus, Jersey, Holstein, Guernsey, Hereford,
Galloway. Prepared and published by author-
ity of the Government of Nova Scotia. Halifax :
Queen's Printer, 1892.

Annual Reports of the Secretary for Agricultural
of Nova Scotia. From 1864 to 1894. Halifax :
Queen's Printer.

Crop Reports of Nova Scotia. From 1888 to 1894.
Halifax : Queen's Printer.
[The above list does not include anonymous articles
in reviews and other periodicals, cyclopædias, etc.]

LeMay, L. Pamphile.

L'épreuve (nouvelle). *Le Journal de Québec*,
nov. 1863.

Essais poétiques. Québec : G. E. Desbarats, 1865.
8vo., pp. 329.

Evangéline (traduction). Québec : P.-G. Delisle,
1870.
12mo., pp. 200.

Poèmes couronnés. Québec : P.-G. Delisle, 1870.
12mo., pp. 239.

Les " Vengeances" (poème). Québec : C. Darveau,
1875.
8vo., pp. 323.

Le Pèlerin de Sainte-Anne (roman). Québec : C.
Darveau, 1877.
2 vol., 12mo., pp. 651.

Quelques poètes illettrés de Lotbinière.
La Revue de Montréal. 1877.
8vo., pp. 10.

Picounac-le-maudit (roman). Québec : C. Darveau, 1878.
2 vol., 12mo., pp. 667.

LeMay, L. Pamphile.—*Continued.*

Une perle, (poésies). Québec : C. Darveau, 1879.
12mo., pp. 232.

Fables canadiennes. Québec : C. Darveau, 1881.
12mo., pp. 351.

Petits poèmes. Québec : C. Darveau, 1883.
12mo., pp. 264.

Le chien d'or (traduction), (roman). Montreal :
L'Etendard, 1884.
2 vol., 8vo., pp. 777.

L'affaire Sougraine (roman). Québec : C. Darveau, 1884.
12mo., pp. 458.

Tonkouron, (édition corrigée de " Les Vengeances"). Québec : C. Darveau, 1888.
12mo., pp. 295.

Rouge et bleu (comédies). Québec : C. Darveau,
1891.
12mo., pp. 288.

Fables (édition corrigée). Québec : C. Darveau,
1891.
11mo., pp. 287.

Dans les Mémoires de la Société royale du Canada :
Le bien pour le mal. Tome i., Sec. 1, 1882.

Les derniers seront les premiers. Hommage à
Son Honneur Rodrigue Masson, lieutenant-
gouverneur de la province de Québec. Tome iii.,
Sec. 1, 1885.

Hosanna. Tome v., Sec. 1, 1887.

Par droit chemin. Tome vi., Sec. 1, 1888.

Les Souffrants. Tome vi., Sec. 1, 1888.

Agar et Ismaël. Tome x., Sec. 1, 1892.

Legendre, Napoleon.

Sabre et Scalpel. Roman. Montréal : 1872.

Albani. Biographie. Québec : 1874.

A mes Enfants. Québec : 1875.

Echos de Québec. Québec : 1877.

Notre Constitution et nos Institutions. Montréal : 1878.

Les perce-neige premières. Poésies. Québec :
1886.

Dans les Mémoires de la Société royale du Canada :
La province de Québec et la langue française.
Tome ii., Sec. 1, 1884.

Les Races Indigènes de l'Amérique devant l'histoire. *Ibid.*

La Race Française en Amérique. Tome iii., Sec.
1, 1885.

Autrefois et Maintenant. *Ibid.*

L'Anatomie des Mots. *Ibid.*

La Cloche. Tome v., 1887.

La langue que nous parlons. *Ibid.*

Réalistes et Décadents. Tome viii., Sec. 1, 1890.

La Femme dans la Société moderne. *Ibid.*

Dans le Canada-français, Québec :
Le réalisme en littérature. Tome i., 1888, p. 143.

La légende d'un peuple. Par Louis Fréchette.
Ibid., p. 304.

Pèlerinage au pays de l'Evangéline. Par l'abbé
H.-R. Casgrain. *Ibid.*, p. 317.

Legendre, Napoleon.—*Continued.*

Le poète. Poésie. Tome II., 1889, p. 213.

Noël. Poésie. Tome III., 1800, p. 5.

Annibal. Nouvelle Canadienne. *Ibid.,* pp. 138, 288, 408, 572.

Revue étrangère. *Ibid.,* pp. 350, 478, 599, 723.

LeMoine, James MacPherson.

L'Ornithologie du Canada. Québec: Le Canadien, 1860-1861.
2 vol., 12mo., pp. 400.

Etude sur Sir Walter Scott, comme poète, romancier, historien.
Opinion Publique, Montréal, 1862, pp. 61.

Navigateurs Arctiques: Franklin, McClure, Kane, McClintock.
Journal de Québec, 1863, pp. 40.

Les Pêcheries du Canada.
Le Canadien, Québec, 1863, pp. 150,

Tableau Synoptique de l'Ornithologie du Canada, 1864.
pp. 6.

Mémoire de Montcalm vengée.
Le Canadien, Québec, 1865, pp. 100.

L'Album Canadien, Québec, 1871.
pp. 128.

L'Album du Touriste. Québec: A. Côté et Cie, 1872.
pp. 384.

Notes historiques sur les rues de Québec.
Le Canadien, Québec, 1875.

Coup-d'œil général sur l'Ornithologie de l'Amérique du Nord. Etude lue devant l'Institut Canadien à Québec.
Annuaire de l'Institut, 1875.

Etude sur le chant des oiseaux, leurs mœurs, leurs migrations.
Opinion Publique, Montréal, 1876.

Grand Tableau synoptique des oiseaux du Canada à l'usage des écoles, 1877.

Notes sur l'Archéologie ; l'histoire du Canada.
Revue Canadienne, Montréal. *Soirées Canadiennes,* Québec, 1862.

Dans les Mémoires de la Société royale du Canada :

Nos Historiens Modernes—Bibaud, Garneau, Ferland, Faillon. Tome I., Sec. 1, pp. 12, 1882.

Les Archives du Canada. Tome I., Sec. 1, pp. 6, 1883.

Les Aborigènes du Canada ; leurs rites mortuaires. Tome II., Sec. 1, pp. 22, 1884.

Les Pages Sombres de l'Histoire. Tome IV., Sec. 1, pp. 13, 1886.

The last Decade of French Rule at Quebec. Vol. II., Sec. 2, pp. 10, 1888.

Le général Sir Frederick Haldimand à Québec, (1778-84). 1889.

Parallèle historique entre le comte de la Gallsonnière (1748-40), et le comte de Dufferin (1872-78). Tome VII., Sec. 1, pp. 18, 1880.

Le général Murray, le premier gouverneur Anglais, à Québec. Tome VIII., Sec. 1, pp. 18, 1890.

LeMoine, James MacPherson.—*Continued.*

Etude Ethnographique des éléments qui constituent la population de la province de Québec. Tome X., Sec. 1, pp. 12, 1892.

L'Administration de Lord Elgin. pp. 10, 1893.

Legendary Lore of the Lower St. Lawrence. Quebec : Geo. T. Cary, 1862.
12mo., pp. 34.

Maple Leaves—History, Archæology, 1st series. Quebec : Hunter, Rose & Co., 1863.
8vo., pp. 104.

Maple Leaves—History, Archæology, 2nd series. Quebec : Hunter, Rose & Co., 1864.
8vo., 224.

Maple Leaves—History, Archæology, 3rd series. Quebec : Hunter, Rose & Co., 1865.
8vo., pp. 137.

The Tourist's Note Book, 1st edition. Quebec : Middleton & Dawson, 1870.
12mo., pp. 128.

Jottings from Canadian History, 1871.
Stewart's Quarterly Magazine, St. John, N.B.

The Sword of Brigadier-General R. Montgomery. Quebec : Middleton & Dawson, 1870.
12mo., pp. 36.

Trifles from my Portfolio, 1872.
Dominion Monthly, Montreal.

Quebec Past and Present. Quebec : A. Côté et Cie, 1870.
8vo., pp. 465.

The Tourist's Note Book, 2nd edition. Quebec : F. X. Garant et Cie, 1870.
pp. 60.

The Chronicles of the St. Lawrence. Montreal : J. W. Lovell. Dawson Bros., 1870.
8vo., pp. 386.

The Scot in New France. Inaugural address to Literary and Historical Society, Quebec, 1879.
pp. 42.

Glimpses of Quebec (1740-59). Inaugural address to Literary and Historical Society, Quebec, 1880.
8vo , pp. 42.

Edinburg, Rouen, York. Inaugural address to Literary and Historical Society, Quebec, 1881.
pp. 88.

Picturesque Quebec. A Cyclopedia of Canadian History. Montreal : Dawson Bros., 1882.
8vo., pp. 535.

Brighton, the Queen of the English Watering Places. Scarborough, the Northern Empress of the Seaside. Versailles, the Lion Mount of Waterloo. Inaugural address to Literary and Historical Society of Quebec, 1882.
pp. 11.

Our Wild Flowers. Quebec : Morning Chronicle, 1885.
12mo., pp. 34.

The Tourist's Note Book, 3rd edition. Quebec : C. Darveau, 1887.
12mo. pp. 60.

Canadian Heroines, Madame de Champlain, Madame de la Tour, Mlle de Verchères. Address read before the Canadian Club, in New York. Nap. Thompson & Co., 1887.
Canadian Leaves, pp. 27.

LeMoine, James MacPherson.—*Continued.*

The Tourist's Note Book, 4th edition. Quebec:
C. Darveau, 1880.
pp. 68.

Maple Leaves, 5th series. L. P. Demers & Co.,
1880.

The Tourist's Note Book, 5th edition. Quebec:
C. Darveau, 1890.
pp. 150.

The Sword of Brigadier-General Richard Montgomery, 2nd edition. Quebec: Daily Telegraph,
1891.
12mo. pp. 36.

The Birds of Quebec. A popular lecture, delivered before the Natural History Society, at Montreal, 1801.

"The Land we Live In." Address, as Chairman
of the Citizen's Committee, at Quebec, to President and members of American Forestry
Association, 1891.
pp. 4.

X **Loudon, James.**

On Trilinear Co-ordinates.
Canadian Journal, May, 1871, pp. 82-85.

On the Stability of Floating Bodies.
Ibid., August, 1871, p. 135.

Notes on Statics.
Ibid., February, 1872, pp. 231-237; May, 1873, pp.
546-550.

Loan Tables. By Cherriman and Loudon. Toronto, 1873.

Algebra. Part I. Toronto, 1873.

Notes on Mechanics.
Canadian Journal, March, 1875, pp. 354-355.

Algebra for Beginners. Toronto: Copp, Clark &
Co., 1876.

Note on Ventilation.
Canadian Journal, January, 1878, p. 645.

Notes on Relative Motion.
Ibid., 1881, pp. 231-235.

Euler's Equations of Motion.
Ibid., 1881, pp. 95-96.

Notes on Relative Motion.
American Journal of Mathematics, Vol. III., pp.
174-178.

Geometrical Methods chiefly in the Theory of
Thick Lenses.
Proceedings Canadian Institute, March, 1885, pp.
7-16.

Geometrical Methods in the Theory of Refraction
at one or more Spherical Surfaces.
Philosophical Magazine, 1884, pp. 455-494.

Notes on Mathematical Physics.
Transactions Royal Society of Canada, Vol. VII.,
Sec. 3, 1889, pp. 7-9.

A National Standard of Pitch.
Ibid., pp. 11-12.

MacCabe, John A.

English Grammar for the use of Schools. Halifax: A. & W. Mackinlay, 1874.
12mo., pp. 175.

MacCabe, John A.—*Continued.*

Practical Lessons in English. (Canadian Edition. Toronto: Gage & Co., 1883.
12mo., pp. 200.

Hints for Language Lessons and Plans for Grammar Lessons. Boston: Ginn & Co., 1892.
12mo., pp. 60.

X **Macoun, John.**

On the Physical Character of the East Riding of
Northumberland County, Ont., with a list of
plants found therein.
Annals of Kingston Botanical Society, 1863.

Catalogue of Carices collected in the vicinity of
Belleville, Ont.
Canadian Naturalist, Vol. III. (2nd Series), 1866,
pp. 56-66.

Report on the Botany of the Canadian Interior
from Lake Superior to the Pacific Ocean.
Report, Canadian Pacific Railway, 1874, pp. 56-99.

Geographical and Topographical Notes on the
Lower Peace and Athabasca rivers.
Report, Geological Survey of Canada, 1876, pp. 87-96.

Report on the Botanical Features of the Country
from Victoria, Vancouver Island, to Carlton
House on the Saskatchewan, by the Fraser
and Peace rivers to Lake Athabasca.
Ibid., 1876, pp. 110-233.

Synopsis of the Flora of the St. Lawrence Valley
and Great Lakes, with descriptions of the rarer
plants.
Canadian Journal, Vol. xv., 1876, pp. 51-66; 161-176; 340-361; 429-435; 546-556.

Sketch of that portion of Canada between Lake
Superior and the Rocky Mountains, with special
reference to its agricultural capabilities.
Report, Canadian Pacific Railway, 1877.

Catalogue of the Phænogamous and Cryptogamus
Plants of the Dominion of Canada. Belleville,
Ont., 1876, pp. 52.

Notes on the Physical Phenomena of Manitoba
and the North-West Territories.
Canadian Journal (3rd Series), 1879, Vol. I, pp.
151-160.

List of Plants collected by Dr. G. M. Dawson on
Queen Charlotte Islands.
Report, Geological Survey of Canada, 1878-79, pp.
219-231.

List of Plants collected by Dr. Robert Bell around
the shores of Hudson Bay and along the
Churchill and Nelson rivers in 1877 and 1879.
Ibid., 1878-79, pp. 53-50.

Extract from a Report of Exploration in the
Northwest Territories.
Report of Department of Interior (Part I.), 1880,
pp. 3-40.

General Remarks on the Land, Wood and Water
of the Northwest Territories from the 102nd to
115th meridian and between the 51st and 53rd
parallels of latitude.
Report, Canadian Pacific Railway, 1880, pp. 235-246.

List of Plants collected in the Northern Part of
British Columbia and the Peace River Country
by Dr. G. M. Dawson in 1879.
Report, Geological Survey of Canada, 1879-80, pp.
B143-B147.

Macoun, John.—Continued.

List of Plants collected north of Lake Winnipeg by Dr. R. Bell in 1880, with notes on their distribution.
Ibid., 1879-80, pp. C59-C69.

Report of an Exploration of the Country on the Western Slopes of Duck and Porcupine mountains and on the Swan and Red Deer rivers.
Report, Department of Interior (Part i.), 1881, pp. 67-88.

Catalogue of the Plants collected by Dr. R. Bell along the Michipicoten River and in the southern part of the basin of Moose River.
Report, Geological Survey of Canada, 1880-81-82, pp. C17-C29.

Manitoba and the Great Northwest. Guelph, Ont.: World Publishing Co., 1882.
8vo., pp. 687.

Catalogue of Canadian Plants. Part I. Polypetalæ.
Geological and Natural History Survey of Canada, 1883, pp. 192.

Notes on the Distribution of Northern, Southern and Saline Plants in Canada.
Transactions Royal Society of Canada, Vol. I., Sec. 4, 1882, pp. 45-49.

On the Flora of the Gaspé Peninsula.
Ibid., Vol. I., Sec. 4, 1883, pp. 127-137.

Notes on Canadian Polypetalæ.
Ibid., Vol. I., Sec. 4, 1883, pp. 151-157.

Catalogue of the Plants collected by Dr. R. Bell on the Coasts of Labrador, Hudson Strait and Bay.
Report, Geological Survey of Canada, 1882-84, pp. DD38-DD47.

Catalogue of Canadian Plants. Part II. Gamopetalæ.
Geological and Natural History Survey of Canada, 1884, pp. 193-394.

and T. W. Burgess. Canadian Filicineæ.
Transactions Royal Society of Canada, Vol. II., Sec. 4, 1884, pp. 163-227.

List of Plants collected by Dr. Robert Bell in Newfoundland in 1885.
Report Geological Survey of Canada, 1885, pp. DD21-DD25.

Catalogue of Canadian Plants. Part III. Apetalæ.
Geological and Natural History Survey of Canada, 1886, pp. 394-628.

List of Plants obtained by Dr. G. M. Dawson on Vancouver Island and adjacent coasts in 1885.
Report Geological Survey of Canada, 1886, pp. B115-B121.

List of Plants collected by Dr. G. M. Dawson in the Yukon District and adjacent northern portion of British Columbia in 1887.
Ibid., 1887-88, pp. B215-B220.

Catalogue of Canadian Plants. Part IV. Endogens.
Geological and Natural History Survey of Canada, 1888, p. 1-248.

Catalogue of Canadian Plants. Part V. Acrogens.
Ibid., 1888, pp. 249-429. *Geological and Natural History of Canada.*

Macoun, John.—Continued.

Catalogue of Canadian Plants. Part VI. Musci.
Ibid., 1892, pp. 295. *Geological and Natural History of Canada.*

Notes on the flora of the Niagara Peninsula and shores of Lake Erie.
Journal and Proceedings of the Hamilton Association. Number IX., 1892-93. pp. 78-87.

The Forests of Canada and their distribution with notes on the more interesting species.
Transactions Royal Society of Canada, Vol. XII., Sec. II.

MacColl, Ewan.

Clàrsach nam Beann; or, Poems and Songs in Gaelic. Glasgow : Blackie & Sons, 1838.
12mo., pp. 200.

The Mountain Minstrel ; or, Poems and Songs in English. Glasgow : Blackie & Sons, 1838.
12mo. pp. 250. Has had six editions.

Poems and Songs. Chiefly written in Canada. Toronto : G. M. Rose & Co., 1883.
12mo., pp. 160.
Another Canadian edition, which bears the imprint of *The British Whip* office, Kingston, Ont., 1888, has a Biographical Sketch of the poet, by A. Mackenzie, F.S.A., Scotland. 12mo., pp. 232.

Macfarlane, Thomas.

On the Primitive Formations in Norway and Canada.
Canadian Naturalist, Vol. VII., Montreal, 1862, pp. 1, 113 and 161.

On the Extraction of Cobalt Oxide.
Ibid., Vol. VII., Montreal, 1862, p. 194.

On the various Theoretical Views regarding the Origin of the Primitive Formations. From the German of Naumann.
Ibid., Vol. VII., Montreal, 1862. p. 251.

Contributions to the History of the Acton Copper Mine.
Ibid., Vol. VII., Montreal, 1862, p. 447.

On a new Method of Preparing Chlorine, etc.
Ibid., Vol. VIII., Montreal, 1863, p. 39.

On the Origin of Eruptive and Primary Rocks.
Ibid., Vol. VIII., Montreal, 1863, pp. 295, 329 and 457.

On the Extraction of Copper from its Ores in the Humid Way.
Ibid., Vol. II., new series, Montreal. 1865, pp. 210-241.

Geological Sketch of the Neighbourhood of Rossie, N.Y.
Ibid., Vol. II., new series, Montreal. 1865, p. 257.

Geological Report on Hastings County.
Report of Progress of Geological Survey of Canada, from 1863 to 1866, Ottawa, 1866, p. 91.

Geological Report on Lake Superior.
Ibid., from 1863 to 1866, Ottawa, 1866, p. 115.

On the Rocks and Auriferous Beds of Portage Lake, Michigan.
Canadian Naturalist, Vol. VIII., new series, Montreal, 1863, p. 1.

On the Geological Formations of Lake Superior.
Ibid., Vol. III., new series, Montreal, 1863, pp. 177-244.

On the Extraction of Copper from its Ores in the Humid Way.
Ibid., Vol. III., new series, Montreal, 1868, p. 457.

Macfarlane, Thomas.—*Continued.*

On the Geology and Silver Ore of Woods Location, Lake Superior.
Canadian Naturalist, Vol. IV., new series. Montreal, 1869, pp. 37, 459.

On the Origin and Classification of Original or Crystalline Rocks.
Ibid., Vol. V., new series, 1870, pp. 47, 159–304 ; also Vol. VI., new series. Montreal, 1872, p. 259.

On the Classification of Original Rocks.
Transactions of the American Society of Mining Engineers, Vol. VIII., Easton, Pa., 1880, p. 63.

On the Use of Determining Slag Densities in Smelting.
Ibid., Vol. VIII., Easton, Pa., 1880, p. 71.

Silver Islet.
Ibid., Vol. VIII., Easton, Pa. 1880, p. 220.

Note on Zinc Sulphide.
Transactions of the Royal Society of Canada, Vol. I., Section 3, Montreal, 1883, p. 45.

On the Reduction of Sulphate of Soda by Carbon.
Ibid., Vol. I., Sec. 3, Montreal, 1883, p. 47.

Presidential Address before Section III.
Ibid., Vol. V., Sec. 3, Montreal, 1888, p. 1.

Remarks on the Use of Asbestos in Milk Analysis.
Ibid., Vol. V., Sec. 3, Montreal, 1888, p. 33.

Within the Empire; an Essay on Imperial Federation. Ottawa: James Hope & Co., 1891.

On the Use of Crysotile Fibre in Proximate Organic Analysis.
The Analyst, Vol. XVIII., London, 1893, p. 73.

MacGregor, J. G.

In the Transactions or Proceedings of the Royal Society of Edinburgh, viz.:

On the Electrical Conductivity of certain Saline Solutions. (In conjunction with J. A. Ewing.) Trans., 1873.

Note on the above. Proc., 1874-75.

On the Electrical Conductivity of Stretched Silver Wires. Proc., 1875-76.

On the Electrical Conductivity of Nickel. (In conjunction with C. M. Smith.) Proc., 1875-76.

On the Thermoelectric Properties of Cobalt. (In conjunction with C. G. Knott and C. M. Smith.) Proc., 1876-77.

On the Thermoelectric Properties of Charcoal and of certain Alloys, with a Supplementary Thermoelectric Diagram. (In conjunction with C. G. Knott. Trans., 1878.

On the Variation with Temperature of the Electrical Resistance of Wires of certain Alloys. (In conjunction with C. G. Knott.) Trans., 1880.

On the Absorption of low Radiant Heat by Gaseous Bodies. Proc., 1882.

In the Reports of the British Association, viz.:

Notes on the Volumes of Solutions. (In conjunction with J. A. Ewing.) 1877.

In the Transactions of the Royal Society of Canada:

On the measurement of the Resistance of Electrolytes by means of Wheatstone's Bridge. Vol. I., Sec. 3, 1882.

MacGregor, J. G.—*Continued.*

On Experiments showing the Electromotive Force of Polarization to be Independent of the Difference of Potential of the Electrodes. Vol. I., Sec. 3, 1883.

On the Transition Resistance to the Electric Current, etc. Vol. I., Sec. 3, 1883.

On the Density and Thermal Expansion of Solutions of Copper Sulphate. Vol. II., Sec. 3, 1884.

On the Density of Weak Aqueous Solutions of certain Salts. Vol. III., Sec. 3, 1885.

A Table of the Cubical Expansion of Solids. Vol. VI., Sec. 3, 1888.

On the Variation of the Density with the Concentration of Weak Aqueous Solutions of certain Salts. Vol. VII., Sec. 3, 1889.

On the Density of Weak Aqueous Solutions of certain Sulphates. Vol. VIII., Sec. 3, 1890.

On a Test of Ewing and MacGregor's method of measuring the Electric Resistance of Electrolytes. Vol. VIII., Sec. 3, 1890.

On the Density of Weak Aqueous Solutions of Nickel Sulphate. Vol. IX., Sec. 3, 1891.

On the Variation with Temperature and Concentration of the Absorption Spectra of Aqueous Solutions of Salts. Vol. IX., Sec. 3, 1891.

On the Fundamental Hypotheses of Abstract Dynamics. Vol., X., Sec. 3, 1892.

In the Transactions of the Nova Scotian Institute of Science, viz.:

On the Resistance to the passage of the Electric Current between Amalgamated Zinc Electrodes and Solutions of Zinc Sulphate. 1883.

On the Relative Bulk of certain Aqueous Solutions and their Constituent Water, 1886.

On the measurement of Temperature and Time. 1887.

On Carnot's Cycle in Thermodynamics. 1889.

On the Relative Bulk of Aqueous Solutions of certain Hydroxides, Vol., VII., p. 368.

On a Noteworthy Case of the Occurrence of Ice in non-Crystalline Columns, Vol. VIII., p. 377.

On some Lecture Experiments Illustrating Properties of Saline Solutions. Series 2, Vol. I., p. 71.

On the Graphical Treatment of the Inertia of the Connecting-Rod. Series 2, Vol. I., p. 193.

In the Philosophical Magazine, London, viz.:

Contact Action and the Conservation of Energy. February, 1893.

On the Hypotheses of Dynamics. September, 1893.

Pamphlets.

Technical Education at Home and Abroad. Halifax, N.S., 1882.

Address at the opening of the Twenty-Sixth Session of the Nova Scotian Institute of Natural Science. Halifax, N.S., 1888.

Address at the opening of the Twenty-Seventh Session of the Nova Scotian Institute of Natural Science. Halifax, N.S., 1890.

MacGregor, J. G.—*Continued.*

Calculus Dodging and other Educational Sins. St. John, N.B. 1890.

Book.

An Elementary Treatise on Kinematics and Dynamics. London and New York : Macmillan & Co. Crown. 8vo. pp. xvi+812, 1887.

Mair, Charles.

Frogs and their Kin.
British American Magazine, Toronto, 1863.

Twelvetrees : a Tale of the Ottawa.
Montreal Transcript, 1861.

Dreamland and other Poems. Ottawa, 1868. Crown 8vo.

The New Canada.
Canadian Monthly, Toronto, 1875.

Tecumseh. A Drama. Toronto and London, 1886. Crown 8vo., pp. 205.

The Ottawa Shiners.
The Week, Toronto, August, 1893.

The American Bison.
Transactions Royal Society of Canada, Vol. viii., Sec. 2, 1890.

MacKay, A. H.

Elementary Mathematics ; Method of Teaching.
Nova Scotia Educational Convention Report, 1874, pp. 16-28.

A Course of Study for the Schools of Nova Scotia.
Ibid., 1880.

Science Gossip for Beginners. A serial of twenty-two articles.
Standard, Pictou, 1880.

Botany of Disease. (Four thousand words.)
Ibid, 1880.

The Pictou Academy: an historical sketch. (Seven thousand words.)
Herald, Halifax, 1881.

Lichens of Nova Scotia.
Nova Scotian Institute of Science, Vol. v., Part III., 1881, pp. 299-307.

Successors of the Ghosts, Goblins, Ghouls, *et al.* (Five thousand words.)
Herald, Halifax, 1883.

Silicious Organic Remains in the Lacustrine Deposits of Nova Scotia.
Report British Association, pp. 742-783, 1884. ;

Among the Cryptogams. A monthly serial.
Acadian Science Monthly, 1883-84.

Vampire Plants and Strange Gardening. (Three thousand words.)
Standard, Pictou, 1885.

Organic Silicious Remains in the Lakes of Nova Scotia.
Canadian Record of Science, Vol. i., No. 4, Montreal, 1885, pp. 236-244.

Nova Scotia Fresh-water Sponges.
Nova Scotian Institute of Science, Vol. vi., Part III., 1885, pp. 233-240.

Mammalia of Nova Scotia : a Synopsis.
Academy, Vol. i., Nos. 2, 3, 4, 6, Pictou, 1885.

Spelling Reform.
Nova Scotia Educational Convention Report, 1885, pp. 16-28.

MacKay, A. H.—*Continued.*

Future of Our Education. (Two thousand words.)
Herald, Halifax, 1886.

New Fresh-water Sponges from Nova Scotia and Newfoundland.
Canadian Record of Science, Vol. ii., No. 1, Montreal, 1886, pp. 19-22.

Meteor of 15th September, 1887.
Educational Review, St. John, 1887.

Among the Water Nymphs ; a Popular View of our Diatomaceæ.
Herald, Halifax, 1887.

Algæ of Nova Scotia and New Brunswick, (Conjointly with Geo. U. Hay.)
Transactions Royal Society of Canada, Vol. v., Sec. 4, 1887, pp. 167-174.

Among the Constellations. Illustrated Serial on Uranography.
Educational Review, Vols. i.-ii., St. John, 1887-1889.

Ferndale School. Illustrated Serial on the Natural History of Eastern Canada for Schools.
Ibid., Vols. i.-iv., St. John, 1887-91.

Miscellaneous Educational and Scientific Articles.
Ibid., St. John, 1887-1889.

The Fresh-water Sponges of Canada and Newfoundland.
Transactions Royal Society of Canada, Vol. vii., Sec. 4, 1889.

Pictou Island ; with geological map of its environment.
Nova Scotian Institute of Science, 2nd Series, Vol. i., Part 1, Halifax, 1891, pp. 76-83.

Annual Reports on the Public Schools of Nova Scotia. (1) Of 1891, pp. 64 ; (2) of 1892, pp. 80 ; (3) of 1893, pp. 63.

Conspectus of Education in Nova Scotia ; for the World's Columbian Exposition. Halifax, 1893, pp. 18.

Journal of Education. Halifax. (1) April, 1893, pp. 100 ; (2) October, 1893, pp. 100 ; (3) April, 1894 ; pp. 50.

The True Scope and Function of the High School.
The Dominion Educational Association Report, 1892, pp. 63-67.

Explosive Gas Generated within the Hot Water Pipes of House Heating Apparatus.
Nova Scotian Institute of Science, 2nd Series Vol. i., Part 3, 1893, pp. 374-377.

Natural History Observations made at several stations in Nova Scotia during the year 1892.
Ibid., 2nd Series, Vol. i., Part 3, 1893, pp. 378-379.

Marchand, Felix G.

Fatenville. Comédie en un acte et en prose.
La Revue Canadienne Montréal, septembre 1869.

Erreur n'est pas compte. Vaudeville en deux actes et en prose. Montreal : Duvernay Frères. 1872.

Un bonheur en attire un autre. Comédie en un acte et en vers. Montréal : Gazette, 1884.
Mémoires de la Société royale du Canada, Tome i., Sec. 2, 1883.

Les Faux Brillants. Comédie en cinq actes et en vers. Montréal : L'Étendard, 1885.

8

Marchand, Felix G.—*Continued.*

Les Travers du Siècle.
Mémoires de la Société royale du Canada, Tome II, Sec. 1, 1884.

L'Aigle et la Marmotte.
Ibid., Tome III., Sec. 1, 1885.

Nos Gros Chagrins et nos Petits Malheurs.
Ibid., Tome VIII., Sec. 1, 1889.

Manuel et Formulaire Général et Complet du Notariat de la Province de Québec. Contenant : 1°, L'histoire du Notariat ; 2°, son organisation dans la Province de Québec ; 3°, un traité sur la responsabilité civile des Notaires ; 4°, un formulaire Français-Anglais des actes des Notaires. Montréal : A. Périard, 1892.

Marmette, Joseph.

François de Bienville. Roman Historique. 1ère édition, Québec : Léger Brousseau, 1870. 2ème édition, Montréal : Beauchemin & Valois, 1883. 12mo., pp. 440.

L'Intendant Bigot. Roman Historique. Montréal : Geo. Desbarats, 1872.

Le Chevalier de Mornac. Roman Historique. Montréal : Geo. Desbarats, 1873.

La Fiancée du Rebelle. Roman Historique.
La Revue Canadienne, Montréal, 1875.

Récits et Souvenirs. Québec : Darveau, 1881. 12mo., pp. 278.

Dans les Mémoires de la Société royale du Canada :

Une Promenade dans Paris. Impressions et Souvenirs, Tome II., Sec. 1, 1884.

Le Dernier Boulet. Nouvelle Historique, Tome III., Sec. 1, 1885.

Trois mois à Londres. Souvenirs de l'Exposition Coloniale. Fragments, Tome VII., Sec. 1, 1886. Aussi, le Canada Français, Vol. II., 1889, p. 114.

Matthew, George F.

Impressions of Cuba.
Canadian Naturalist, Vol. VII., Nos. 1 and 2, 1862, Montreal, 8vo., pp. 19-34 and pp. 76-85.

Observations on the Geology of St. John County, New Brunswick.
Canadian Naturalist and Geologist, Vol. VIII., August, 1863, Montreal. 8vo., pp. 241-260.

On the Azoic and Palæozoic Rocks of Southern New Brunswick.
Quarterly Journal of the Geological Society, 1865, London. 8vo., pp. 421-434.

Cupriferous Rocks of Southern New Brunswick—Notes on the Geology of Charlotte County—Dunsinane Coal.
Observations on the Geology of Southern New Brunswick, 1865, Fredericton, N.B. Royal 8vo., pp. 149-168.

In conjunction with Prof. L. W. Bailey. Preliminary Report on the Geology of Southern New Brunswick.
Report of Progress, Geological Survey of Canada, 1870-71, Ottawa, 1872. Royal 8vo., pp. 13-240.

On the Surface Geology of Southern New Brunswick.
Canadian Naturalist, Vol. VII., No. 8, 1871, Montreal. 8vo., pp. 431-454.

Matthew, George F.—*Continued.*

In conjunction with Prof. L. W. Bailey. Report on the Carboniferous System of New Brunswick.
Report of Progress, Geological Survey of Canada, 1872-3, Montreal, 1873. Royal 8vo., pp. 190-237.

Sur les Mollusques de la Formation Post-Pleiocene de l'Acadie.
Société Malacologique de Belgique, Annales, Tome IX., 1874, Bruxelles. 8vo., pp. 23, 1 plate.

On the Mollusca of the Post-Pleiocene Formation in Acadia.
Canadian Naturalist, Vol. VIII., No. 2, 1874, Montreal, 8vo., pp. 101-117.

In conjunction with Prof. L. W. Bailey. Summary Report of Geological Observations in New Brunswick.
Report of Progress, Geological Survey of Canada, 1874-5, Ottawa, 1876. Royal 8vo., pp. 84-83.

In conjunction with Prof. L. W. Bailey and Mr. R. W. Ells. Report of Geological Observations in Southern New Brunswick.
Ibid., 1875-6, Ottawa. 1877. Royal 8vo., pp. 318-368.

Report on the Geology of Charlotte County.
Ibid., 1876-77, Ottawa, 1878. Royal 8vo., pp. 321-326.

Report on the Upper Silurian and Kingston Series of Southern New Brunswick. Also, Report on the Superficial Geology of Southern New Brunswick.
Ibid., 1877-78, Montreal, 1879. Royal 8vo., pp. 1-6z and pp. 1-35xx.

Tidal Erosion in the Bay of Fundy.
Canadian Naturalist, Vol. IX., No. 6, August, 1880, Montreal. 8vo., pp. 368-373.

Illustrations of the Fauna of the St. John Group. No. I. The Paradoxides.
Transactions Royal Society of Canada. Vol. I., Sec. 4, 1883, Montreal. 4to., pp. 271-279, 2 plates.

Lacustrine Formation of Torryburn Valley.
Natural History Society of New Brunswick, Bulletin II., 1883, St. John, N.B. 8vo., pp. 3-20.

Illustrations of the Fauna of the St. John Group continued. On the Conocoryphea, etc.
Transactions Royal Society of Canada. Vol. II., Sec. 4, 1884, Montreal. 4to., pp. 99-124, 1 plate.

Discoveries at a Village of the Stone Age at Bocabec.
Natural History Society of New Brunswick, Bulletin III., 1884, St. John, N.B. 8vo., pp. 6-29.

The Geological Age of the Acadian Fauna.
Geological Magazine, N. S. III., Vol. I., October, 1884, London, G.B. 8vo., pp. 470-472.

Illustrations of the Fauna of the St. John Group. No. III. Descriptions of New Genera and Species.
Transactions Royal Society of Canada, Vol. III., Sec. 4, 1885, Montreal. 4to., pp. 29-84, 3 plates.

Note on the Genus Stenotheca.
Geological Magazine, N. S., Vol. II., September, 1885, London, G.B. 8vo., pp. 425-426.

Recent Discoveries in the St. John Group.
Natural History Society of New Brunswick, Bulletin IV., 1885, St. John, N.B. 8vo., pp. 97-102.

The Structural Features of Discotia Acadica (Hartt) of the St. John Group.
Canadian Record of Science, N. S., Vol. II., No. 1, January, 1885, Montreal. 8vo., pp. 9-11.

Matthew, George F.—Continued.

Synopsis of the Fauna of Division 1 of the St. John Group, etc.
Natural History Society of New Brunswick, Bulletin v., 1886, St. John, N.B. 8vo., pp. 25-31.

On the Cambrian Faunas of Cape Breton and Newfoundland.
Transactions Royal Society of Canada. Vol. IV., Sec. 4, 1886, Montreal. 4to., pp. 147-157, 11 figures.

Discovery of a Pteraspidian Fish in the Silurian Rocks of New Brunswick.
Canadian Record of Science, Vol. II., No. 4, October, 1886, Montreal. 8vo., pp. 2.

Additional Note on a Pteraspidian Fish found in New Brunswick.
Ibid., December, 1886, Montreal. 8vo., pp. 4.

A Preliminary Notice of a New Genus of Silurian Fishes.
Natural History Society of New Brunswick, Bulletin VI., 1887, St. John, N.B. 8vo., pp. 60-73.

Minerals of New Brunswick.
Board of Education Report, 1887, Fredericton. 8vo., pp. 14.

Sur le Développement des Premiers Trilobites.
Société royale Malacologique de Belgique. Tome XXIII., 1888. Bruxelles, 1889. 8vo., pp. 14, 10 figures.

The Great Acadian Paradoxides. Also, On the Kin of Paradoxides (Olenellus?), Kjerulfi.
American Journal of Science, 3rd Series, Vol. XXXIII., No. 197, May, 1887, New Haven. 8vo., pp. 380-392 1 figure.

Illustrations of the Fauna of the St. John Group. No. IV., Part I. Description of a New Species of Paradoxides. Part II. The Smaller Trilobites with Eyes.
Transactions Royal Society of Canada. Vol. V., Sec. 4, 1888, Montreal. 4to., pp. 115-166, 3 plates.

On the Classification of the Cambrian Rocks in Acadia.
Canadian Record of Science, Vol. III, No. 2, April, 1888, Montreal. 8vo., pp. 71-81 and pp. 303-315.

On Some Remarkable Organisms of the Silurian and Devonian Rocks of Southern New Brunswick.
Transactions Royal Society of Canada. Vol. VI., Sec. 4, 1889, Montreal. 4to., pp. 49-62, 1 plate.

Second Note on Stenotheca.
Geological Magazine, N. S. III., Vol. VI., May, 1889, London. 8vo., pp. 210-221.

On the Occurrence of Leptoplastus in Acadian Cambrian Rocks.
Canadian Record of Science, October, 1889, Montreal. 8vo., pp. 485-490.

How is the Cambrian Divided? A Plea for the Classification of Salter and Hicks.
American Geologist, September, 1889, Minneapolis. 8vo., pp. 138-148.

On Cambrian Organisms in Acadia.
Transactions Royal Society of Canada. Vol. VII., Sec. 4, 1890, Montreal. 4to., pp. 135-163, 5 plates, 3 cuts.

Sketch of the Life of Professor Charles Frederick Hartt.
Natural History Society of New Brunswick, Bulletin IX., 1890, St. John, N.B. 8vo., pp. 1-24, 1 plate.

Eozoon and other Low Organisms in Laurentian Rocks at St. John, N.B.
Ibid, pp. 36-41, 3 cuts.

Matthew, George F.—Continued.

On the Occurrence of Sponges in Laurentian Rocks at St. John, N.D.
Ibid., pp. 42-45.

On Some Causes which have Influenced the Spread of the Cambrian Faunas.
Canadian Record of Science, January, 1891, Montreal. 8vo., pp. 255-269.

Illustrations of the Fauna of the St. John Group. No. V.
Transactions Royal Society of Canada. Vol. VIII., Sec. 4, 1891, Montreal, 4to., pp. 123-169, 6 plates, 3 cuts.

President's Annual Address. On Palæozoic Insects, etc.
Natural History Society of New Brunswick, Bulletin IX., 1891, St. John, N.B. 8vo., pp. 25-33.

On a New Horizon in the St. John Group.
Canadian Record of Science, October, 1891, Montreal. 8vo., pp. 339-343.

Notes on Cambrian Faunas, 1. The Taconic Fauna of Emmons compared with the Cambrian Horizons of the St. John Group.
American Geologist, November, 1891, Minneapolis, 8vo., pp. 267-291.

Note on Leptoplastus.
Canadian Record of Science, December, 1891, Montreal. 8vo., pp. 461-462.

Illustrations of the Fauna of the St. John Group. No. VI.
Transactions Royal Society of Canada. Vol. IX., Sec. 4, 1892, Montreal. 4to., pp. 33-65, 2 plates.

Discoveries at a Village of the Stone Age at Bocabec. [Republication.]
Natural History Society, Bulletin X., 1892, St. John, N.B. 8vo., pp. 5-29, 1 plate, 2 cuts.

Protolenus, a New Genus of Cambrian Trilobites.
Ibid., 8vo., pp. 31-37.

List of Fossils found in the Cambrian Rocks in and near St. John.
Ibid. 8vo., pp. XI.-XXII.

Trematobolus, an Articulate Brachiopod of the Inarticulate Order.
Canadian Record of Science, January, 1893, Montreal. 8vo., pp. 276-279.

On the Diffusion and Sequence of the Cambrian Faunas.
Transactions Royal Society of Canada. Vol. X., Sec. 4, 1893, Ottawa. 4to., pp. 3-16, 2 cuts.

Illustrations of the Fauna of the St. John Group. No. VII.
Ibid. 4to., pp. 93-109, 1 plate.

The Climate of Acadia in the Earliest Times.
Natural History Society of New Brunswick, Bulletin XI., 1893, St. John, N.B. 8vo., pp. 1-18, 2 cuts.

Swedish Cambrian-Silurian Hyolithidæ and Con ulariidæ, by G. Holm. Review of this memoir.
Canadian Record of Science, July, 1893, Montreal, 8vo., pp. 433-440.

Illustrations of the Fauna of the St. John Group. No. VIII.
Transactions Royal Society of Canada. Vol. XI., Sec. 4, 1894, Montreal. 4to., pp. 85-129, 2 plates, 1 cut.

Mills, Wesley.

An examination of some controverted points of the Physiology of the Voice, especially the Registers of the Singing Voice and the Falsetto.
Journal of Physiology, Cambridge, England. Vol. IV.

Some observations on the Influence of the Vagus and Accelerator nerves of the Heart of the Sea-Turtle.
Ibid., Vol. v.

The secretion of Oxalic Acid in the Dog under a varying diet, (a modification of "Ueber die Ausscheidung der Oxalsaure durch den Harn")
Ibid., Vol. v.

The Innervation of the heart of the Slider Terrapin (Pseudemys Rugosa).
Ibid., Vol. vi.

The Heart of the Fish compared with that of Menobranchus, with Special Reference to Reflex Inhibition and Independent Cardiac Rhythm.
Ibid., Vol. vii.

Notes on the Urine of the Tortoise with Special Reference to Uric Acid and Urea.
Ibid., Vol. vii.

A Physiological basis of an Improved Cardiac Pathology.
Medical Record, New York. October, 1887.

Uric Acid,—(a) Its Medical Relations; (b) A Reliable Method of Quantitative Estimation.
Medical News, Philadelphia. June, 1885.

On the Physiology of the Heart of the Alligator.
Journal of Anatomy and Physiology, Edinburgh, Scotland.

The Rhythm and Innervation of the Heart of the Sea-Turtle.
Ibid., Vol. xxi.

Physiology of the Heart of the Snake.
Ibid., Vol. xxii.

The Causation of the Heart-beat and other Problems in Cardiac Physiology.
Canada Medical and Surgical Journal, Montreal, January, 1887.

Influence of the Nervous System on Cell Life.
Medical Journal, New York, December, 1883.

The Blood and Blood-vessels in Health and Disease.
Ibid., September, 1890.

Retention and Loss of Hair.
Canadian Record of Science, Montreal, July, 1887.

Life in the Bahamas.
Ibid., April, 1887.

Study of a Small and Isolated Community in the Bahama Islands.
American Naturalist, Philadelphia, Vol. xxi., October, 1887.

Comparative Psychology: Its Objects and Problems.
Popular Science Monthly, New York, March, 1887.

Reply to Criticism of the above.
Science, May, 1887.

The Habits and Intelligence of Squirrels.
Transactions Royal Society of Canada, Vol. v., Sec. 4, 1887.

Comparative Psychology,
Journal Comparative Medicine, January, 1888.

Mills, Wesley.—Continued.

The Psychic development of young animals and its physical correlation.
Transactions Royal Society of Canada, Vol. xI., Sec. 4, 1891.

Translation of Professor Hoppe Seyler's Address at the Celebration of the Opening of the Institute for Physiological Chemistry (Ueber die Entwickelung der Physiologischen Chemie und ihre Bedeutung fur die Medicin),
Medical Journal, New York, 1885.

Snake Poison from a Chemico-Physiological point of view.
Journal of Comparative Medicine and Surgery, Philadelphia, Vol. viii.

Elasticity as a Conservative Force in the Animal Organism.
Ibid.

Report of a Case of Poisoning from the Local Application of Ergotin.
British Medical Journal, London.

Some mistakes to be avoided in Dealing with the Diseases of the Nose and Throat.
Canadian Journal of Medical Science, Toronto.

Report of a Case of Congenital Ectopia of the Abdominal Organs.
Ibid.

Two Cases of Malignant Disease of the Stomach.
Ibid.

The Voice in Diagnosis and Prognosis.
Canada Medical and Surgical Journal, Montreal, May, 1882.

Fatality in Typhoid Fever.
Ibid., January, 1880.

Chronic Pyæmia following Urethral Dilatation.
Ibid., May, 1880.

Clinical Notes on Atropine Poisoning.
Ibid., August, 1880.

Obstetrics of the Hamilton City Hospital for Two Years.
Ibid., October, 1880.

On a Case of Thrombosis of the Left Ventricle.
Ibid., February, 1887.

Tonsillotomy and Uvulotomy.
Ibid., March, 1883.

Innervation of the Heart of the Slider Terrapin (Medical Aspects).
Ibid., December, 1885.

Physiological and Pathological Reversion.
Ibid., April, 1888.

Surgical Puncture of the Heart.
Medical News, Philadelphia, July, 1887.

A Case of Extreme Enlargement of the Tonsils causing Urgent Symptoms.
Archives of Laryngology.

Case of Lightning Shock with Recovery, with Drs. Buller and Paige.
Medical News, Philadelphia, August, 1883.

Valedictory Address to Graduate Class in Medicine of McGill University.
Medical Journal, Montreal, 1889.

Address delivered under the Auspices of the Associated Alumni Society of the University of New Brunswick. Fredericton, 1892.

Mills, Wesley.—*Continued.*

Articles in Buck's Handbook of the Medical Sciences, on Digestion, the Digestive Secretions, etc.

Hibernation and Allied States in Animals.
Transactions Royal Society of Canada. Vol. x. Sec. 4, 1892.

Natural or Scientific Method in Education.
Popular Science Monthly, New York, November, 1892.

The Action of Certain Drugs and Poisons on the Heart of the Fish.
Canadian Medical and Surgical Journal, Montreal, Mar b, 1886.

Hæmodynamics and Blood Pressure.
Ibid., 1887.

Clinical and Pathological Notes from a Breeding Station.
Journal of Comparative Medicine and Surgery, Philadelphia, July, 1889.

The Blood and Blood-forming Organs.
Canadian Medical and Surgical Journal, Montreal, December, 1886.

Ueber die Ausscheidung der Oxalsaure durch den Harn.
Virchow's Archives, Berlin, 1885.

Alterations of the Myocardium (G. Fantoni). Translation by Dr. Joseph Workman with notes by Dr. Wesley Mills.
Medical Journal, Montreal, June, 1889.

Heredity in Relation to Education.
Transactions Ontario Educational Association Toronto: and *Popular Science Monthly,* New York, 1894.

Books :—

Outlines of Lectures on Physiology (as delivered in McGill University). Montreal: W. Drysdale & Co., 1880.

A Text-book of Animal Physiology. New York: D. Appleton & Co., 1889.
Large 8vo., 700 pp.

A Text-book of Comparative Physiology. New York: D. Appleton & Co., 1890.
Small 8vo., pp. 689.

How to keep a Dog in the City. New York: Wm. R. Jenkins. Toronto: H. B. Donovan, 1891.

The Dog in Health and in Disease. New York: D. Appleton & Co., 1892.

Murray, George.

Verses and Versions. Contents; How Canada was saved; Grace Connell; Willie the Miner; The Madonna's Isle; The Neapolitans to Mozart, etc. Montreal: Foster Brown & Co., 1891.
12mo., pp. viii. + 403.

Murray, J. Clark.

Sir William Hamilton's Philosophy: an Exposition and Criticism.
Canadian Journal, Toronto, January and September and December, 1867.

Outline of Sir William Hamilton's Philosophy. A Text-book for Students. Boston: Gould & Lincoln, 1870.
Crown 8vo., pp. 287.

Murray, J. Clark.—*Continued.*

The Higher Education of Women. An address at the opening of Queen's College at Kingston, 1871.
Pamphlet, pp. 17.

The Ballads and Songs of Scotland, in view of their influence on the Character of the People. London: MacMillan & Co., 1874.
Crown 8vo., pp. 205.

Atomism and Theism.
Canadian Monthly, Toronto, January, 1875.

The Study of Political Philosophy. The annual University Lecture in McGill College, Montreal, 1877.
Pamphlet, pp. 16.

Dreams.
New Dominion Monthly, Montreal, June, 1877.

The First Ten Years of the Canadian Dominion.
British Quarterly Review, April, 1878.

The Scottish Philosophy.
MacMillan's Magazine, London, December, 1878.

Memoir of David Murray, late Provost of Paisley ; with sketches of local history in his time. Paisley: Alexander Gardner, 1881.
Crown 8vo., pp. 146.

Solomon Maimon.
British Quarterly Review, London, July, 1885.

A Handbook of Psychology. London: Alexander Gardner, 1885.
2nd ed., 1888; 3rd ed., 1890.
Crown 8vo., pp. 435.

Sir William Hamilton.
Scottish Review, Paisley, London and New York, July, 1886.

The Revived Study of Berkeley.
MacMillan's Magazine, London, July, 1887.

Solomon Maimon: an Autobiography. Translated from the German. London: Alexander Gardner, 1889.
Crown 8vo., pp. 307.

Christian Ethics.
Presbyterian College Journal, Montreal, March, 1889.

The Blind Deaf-mute, Helen Keller.
Scottish Review, Paisley, London and New York, October, 1890.

The Education of the Will.
Educational Review, New York, June, 1891.

An Introduction to Ethics. Boston: DeWolfe, Fiske & Co., 1891.
Crown 8vo., pp. 407.

A Summer School of Philosophy.
Scottish Review, Paisley, London and New York, January, 1892.

Christian and Unchristian Agnosticism. Sunday Afternoon Address in Queen's College, Kingston, April, 1892.

Psychology in Medicine.
Medical Journal, Montreal, June, 1892.

An Ancient Pessimist.
Philosophical Review, January, 1893.

The Faculty of Cramming: its Psychological Analysis and Practical Value.
Educational Review, New York, April, 1893.

Murray, J. Clark.—*Continued.*

The Poetry of the Columbian Celebration.
Presbyterian College Journal, Montreal, December, 1893.

Philosophy and Industrial Life. A Paper read at the Philosophical Congress in Chicago, August, 1893.
The Monist, Chicago, 1894.

O'Brien, Most Reverend Cornelius.

Philosophy of the Bible Vindicated. Charlottetown : Bremner Bros., 1870.
8vo., pp. 291,

Mater Admirabilis. Montreal : D. & J. Sadlier & Co., 1882.
18mo., pp. 248.

After Weary Years. Baltimore : John Murphy & Co., 1885.
8vo., pp. 433.

Saint Agnes, Virgin and Martyr. Halifax Printing Company, 1887.
13mo., pp. 90.

Aminta. A Modern Life Drama. New York : D. Appleton & Co., 1890.
8vo., pp. 187.

Memoirs of Right Reverend Edmund Burke, Bishop of Zion, first Vicar Apostolic of Nova Scotia. Ottawa : Thoburn & Co., 1894.
Crown 8vo., pp. 11. + 154, illustrated.

In pamphlet form :
Daniel O'Connell. A Lecture. Charlottetown, 1870.

Early Stages of Christianity in England. Charlottetown, 1880.

Pastoral Letters. Halifax, 1883-84-85-86-87-88-89, 1890-91-92-93-94.

Sermons :
The True Church.
St. John Telegraph, January 16, 1885.

The Hierarchy of the Church. Printed with Records of the Silver Jubilee Celebration of Bishops McIntyre and Rogers, Charlottetown : John Coombs.

The Prerogatives of the Roman Pontiff.
Halifax Herald, January 2, 1888.

Funeral Oration at the "Month's Mind" of late Bishop McIntyre.
Examiner, Charlottetown, June 5, 1891.

The Resurrection of the Dead.
Halifax Herald, April 18, 1892.

The Duties and Responsibilities of the Episcopate.
The Colonist, St. John's, Nfld., June 25, 1892.

Patterson, Rev. George.

A Brief Sketch of the Life and Labours of the Rev. John Keir, D.D., S.T.P. Reprinted from *Christian Instructor.* Pictou, N.S. : E. M. McDonald, 1859.
8vo., pp. 43.

The Present Truth. A Synod Sermon. Pictou, N.S., 1850.
8vo.

Memoir of the Rev. James MacGregor, D.D., Missionary of the Associate Synod of Scotland to Pictou, N.S., with notices of the colonization

Patterson, Rev. George.—*Continued.*

of the Lower Provinces of British North America, and of the social and religious condition of the early settlers. Philadelphia : J. M. Wilson ; Halifax : A. & W. McKinlay, 1859.
12mo., pp. 543.

Memoirs of Revds. S. F. Johnston and J. W. Matheson, and Mrs. Mary J. Matheson, with selections from their diaries and correspondence, and notices of the New Hebrides, their inhabitants, and missionary work among them. Philadelphia : William S. Martien. Pictou, N.S. : James Patterson, 1864.
12mo., pp. 504.

The Doctrine of the Trinity underlying the Revelation of Redemption. Edinburgh : Oliphant & Co., 1870.
12mo., pp. 244.

Prize Essay on the History of the County of Pictou, 1874.
In manuscript in Library of King's College, Windsor, N.S.

History of the County of Pictou. Montreal : Dawson Brothers, 1877.
8vo., pp. 471.

Jephthah's Vow.
British and Foreign Evangelical Review, London, 1875. 8vo., pp. 709-736.

Canadian Northwest and Manitoba College. Edinburgh, 1878.
8vo., pp. 16.

Canadian Northwest and the Gospel.
British and Foreign Evangelical Review, London, 1879. 8vo., pp. 709 718.

Missionary life among the Cannibals, being the life of the Rev. John Geddie, D.D., first missionary to the New Hebrides, with a history of the Nova Scotia Presbyterian Mission on that group. Toronto : James Campbell & Son ; Montreal : W. Drysdale & Co., 1882.
12mo., pp. 512.

The Teaching of Our Lord regarding the Sabbath and its Bearing on Christian Work.
Presbyterian Review, No. 13, 1893, New York. 8vo., pp. 1-19.

The Heathen World : its need of the gospel and the church's obligation to supply it. Toronto : Wm. Briggs, 1884.
12mo., pp. 293.

The Plague of Mice in Nova Scotia and Prince Edward Island.
Canadian Record of Science. 8vo., pp. 472-480.

Hon. Samuel Vetch, first English Governor of Nova Scotia.
Collections of Nova Scotia Historical Society, Halifax, 1885. 8vo., pp. 1-63.

Stone Age of Nova Scotia, as illustrated by a Collection of Relics presented to Dalhousie College.
Transactions of Nova Scotian Institute of Natural Science, Vol. VIII., 1888-89. 8vo., pp. 231-252.

Sketch of the Life and Labours of the Rev John Campbell. New Glasgow, N.S. : S. M. McKenzie, 1880.
8vo., pp. 37.

Penhallow, D. P.—_Continued._

Mechanism of Movement in Cucurbita, Vitis and Robinia.
Transactions Royal Society of Canada. Vol. IV., Sec. 4, 1886.

Additional Notes on Tendrils of Cucurbitaceæ.
Canadian Record of Science, II., 241.

Soil Temperature.
Agricultural Science, I., 75.

A Review of Canadian Botany from the First Settlement of New France to the 19th Century.
Transactions Royal Society of Canada. Vol. V., Sec. 4, 1887.

The Rearing of Bears and the Worship of Yoshit-suné by the Ainu of Yeso.
Canadian Record of Science, II., 481.

The Ainu. A Review.
Ibid., II., 438.

Notes on Shepherdia Canadensis.
Ibid., III., 360.

Notes on Nematophyton and a Laminated Fossil.
Transactions Royal Society of Canada. Vol. VI., Sec. 4, 1888.

The Food of Plants.
Canadian Record of Science, III., 333.

Notes on Erian Plants.
Ibid., IV., 242.

Gray's Scientific Papers. A Review.
Ibid., III., 503.

Text-Book on Botany. A Review.
Ibid., III., 501.

An Ancient Blaze.
Ibid., III., 500.

Pleistocene Flora of Canada.
Bulletin Geological Society of America, I., 311-344.

A New Botanical Laboratory.
Canadian Record of Science, IV., 86.

Note on a Peculiar Growth in Black Walnut.
Ibid., IV., 233.

Soil Temperature.
Ibid., IV., 229.

Sketch of the Life of Charles Gibb.
Ibid., IV., 183.

List of Botanical Gardens of the World.
Annals of Horticulture, New York, 1890, p. 217: 1891, p. 315; 1889, p. 165.

The Botanical Collector's Guide. Montreal: 1891, 10mo., p. 125.

Description of New Species of Fossil Plants in Paper by Sir J. W. Dawson on Fossil Plants from the Similkameen Valley, etc.
Transactions Royal Society of Canada. Vol. VIII., Sec. 4, 1890.

Notes on the Flora of Cacouna, P. Q.
Canadian Record of Science, IV., 432.

Notes on the Flora of St. Helen's Island, Montreal.
Ibid., IV., 389.

Notes on Specimens of Fossil Woods from the Erian (Devonian) of New York and Kentucky.
Ibid., IV., 242.

The Botany of Montreal. In Hand-Book for the Royal Society of Canada, Montreal Meeting, 1891.
12mo., p. 121.

Penhallow, D. P.—_Continued._

Notes on Post Glacial Plants from Illinois.
Transactions Royal Society of Canada, Vol. IX., Sec. 4, 1891.

Parka decipiens.
Ibid.

Additional Notes on Devonian Plants of Scotland.
Canadian Record of Science, V., I.

A New Species of Larix from the Interglacial of Manitoba.
American Geologist, IX., 6, 368.

Epitaphal Inscriptions.
Journal American Folk-lore Society, V., 305.

A Preliminary Examination of So-Called Cannel Coal from the Kootanie of British Columbia.
American Geologist, X., 331.

Notes on Erian (Devonian) Plants from New York and Pennsylvania.
Proceedings United States National Museum, XVI., 103.

Notes on Nemotophyton crassum.
Ibid., XVI., 115.

Poisson, Adolphe.

Mouvement de la Population Française dans les Cantons de l'Est.
Le Canada Français, Québec, Vol. I., 1888, p. 103.

Chants Canadiens. Québec: P. G. Delisle, 1880.

Heures Perdues. Québec: A. Côté et Cie, 1894.
12mo., pp. 254.

Reade, John

Has contributed to the following periodicals, newspapers, and collections of poems:

Montreal Literary Magazine (1856).
Montreal Gazette (1855-1894).
(1856-70, various contributions including poetry; 1870-94, editorial articles and book reviews).
British American Magazine (1863-1864).
Dewart's Selections from Canadian Poets (1864).
Stewart's Quarterly (1868-1870).
Illustrated Canadian News (1869-1880).
Dublin University Magazine (1870-1871).
Canadian Monthly (1872-1878).
Belford's Monthly Magazine (1876-1878.)
Rose-Belford's Canadian Monthly (1878-1882).
The Week (1884-1894).
Canadian Record of Science (1891).
Popular Science Monthly (1888).
Magazine of American History (1883-1890).
Dominion Illustrated (1888-1892).
Arcadia (1892-1893).
Memorial Diographies of the New England Historic Genealogical Society. Vol. V. (1894).
Canadian Birthday Book (1887).
Songs of the Great Dominion (1889).
Younger Poets of America (1890).
Poems of Places. Edited by H. W. Longfellow: Vol. V. (Ireland.) Two poems, "Devenish" and "Killynoogan," by John Reade.
Prophecy of Merlin and other Poems, Montreal, 1870.

Of contributions to the foregoing volumes or periodicals (poetry excepted), the following treat of subjects wholly or largely Canadian:

Our Canadian Village.
British American Magazine, February, March and April, 1864.

Rende, John.—*Continued.*

British Canada In the Last Century.
Dominion Monthly, August, September and October,
1873, and reproduced in "Picturesque Quebec," by
J. M. LeMoine, Esq.

The History In Canadian Geographical Names.
New Dominion Monthly, June, 1873.

Canadian Literature. Introductory Lecture of
Society of Canadian Literature.

Opportunities for the Study of Folk-lore In Canada.

Historics of Canada.
Canadiana, January, February and March, 1889.

The Early Interpreters.
Canadiana.

The Intermingling of Races.
Popular Science Monthly, January, 1888.

Thomas D'Arcy McGee, the Poet.

Sir L. H. LaFontaine, Bart.

In the Transactions of the Royal Society of Canada:

Language and Conquest. A Contribution to the
History of Civilization. Vol. 1., Sec. 2, 1882-83.

The Making of Canada. The Literary Faculty of
the Native Races of America. Vol. 11., Sec.
2, 1891.

The Half-breed. Vita Sine Literis. Vol. 111.,
Sec. 2, 1895.

Some Wabanaki Songs. Vol. v., Sec. 2, 1887.

Aboriginal American Poetry. *Ibid.*

The Basques In North America. Vol. v1., Sec.
2, 1888.

Roberts, Charles G. D.

Orion, and other Poems. Philadelphia : J. B.
Lippincott & Co., 1880.
Sq. 12mo., pp. 114.

In Divers Tones. Boston : D. Lathrop & Co. ;
Montreal : Dawson Bros., 1887.
12mo., pp. 134.

Poems of Wild Life. An Anthology. London :
Walter Scott ; Toronto : W. J. Gage & Co., 1888.
16mo., pp. 238.

The Canadians of Old. Translated from the
French of de Gaspé. New York : D. Appleton
& Co. ; Toronto : Hart & Riddell, 1890.

The Canadian Guide-book. Part I. New York :
D. Appleton & Co., 1891.
12mo., pp. 270.

Ave ; an Ode for the Shelley Centenary. Toronto :
Williamson Book Co., 1892.
Sq. 8vo., pp. 27.

Songs of the Common Day ; and Ave. London
and New York : Longmans, Green & Co. ; Toronto : William Briggs, 1893.
12mo., pp. 126.

Routhier, A. B.

Causeries du Dimanche (Critical Essays). Montréal : Beauchemin et Valois, 1871.
12mo., pp. 300.

Portraits et pastels littéraires. In 32o, Brousseau
Frères, 1872.

Routhier, A. B.—*Continued.*

A Travers l'Europe. 2 vols. Québec : A. M. Delisle, 1882-83.
8vo., pp. 412-409.

En Canot. Québec : O. Fréchette, 1881.
16mo., pp. 230.

Les Échos. (Poèmes.) Québec : A. M. Delisle, 1883.
12mo., pp. 312.

Lettre d'un Volontaire du 9ième Voltigeurs Campé
à Calgary.
Mémoires de la Société royale du Canada. Tome
111., Sec. 1, 1885.

A Travers l'Espagne. Québec : A. Côté, 1889.
8vo., pp. 406.

Les Grands Drames. Montréal : Beauchemin et
Fils, 1890.
12mo., pp. 450.

Discours à un concert de charité donné par Madame Albani.
12mo. A. Coté & Cie, 1890.

Conférences et Discours. Montréal : Beauchemin
et Fils, 1890.
8vo., pp. 417.

Le Comte de Paris à Québec. Introduction et
discours. Québec ; C. Darveau, 1891.

De Québec à Victoria. Québec : L. J. Demers, 1893.
8vo., pp. 300.

Christophe Colomb—Discours. Dans Les Fêtes
Colombiennes, In 8o. Québec : Léger Brousseau, 1893.

Dans Le Canada Français, Québec :

Introduction au *Répertoire National.* 1er vol.
Montréal : J. M. Valois et Cie, 1893.

Chronique de Paris. Vol. 1., 1888, p. 150.

La Question Romaine. *Ibid.,* p. 228.

Les Fêtes Jubilaires à Rome. *Ibid.,* p. 274.

Assemblée Générale des Catholiques de France.
Ibid., p. 471.

En Carriole. Vol. 11., 1889, p. 244.

Les Grands Drames. Vol. 111., 1890, p. 277.

L'honorable P. J.-O. Chauveau. *Ibid.,* p. 310.

Roy, Joseph-Edmond.

Le Premier Colon de Lévis, Guillaume Couture.
Lévis ; Mercier et Cie, 1884.
16mo., pp. 192.

Monseigneur Déziel. Sa Vie, ses Œuvres. Lévis :
Mercier et Cie, 1885.
12mo., pp. 182.

L'ordre de Malte en Amérique. Québec : A. Côté
et Cie, 1888.
12mo., pp. 68.

Voyage au Pays de Tadoussac. Québec : A. Côté
et Cie, 1890.
8vo., pp. 231.

De Quelques Coutumes Notariales.
La Revue Canadienne, Livraisons de mars, avril et
mai 1889.

Du Notariat et des Notaires au Canada avant 1663.
Le Canada Français, 1889, pp. 448, 505 ; 1890, p. 707.

La Justice Seigneuriale de Notre-Dame des Anges.
La Revue Canadienne, octobre 1890.

Roy, Joseph-Edmond.—*Continued.*

Claude Bermen de la Martinière. Lévis, 1901.
12mo., pp. 100.

Lettres du P. F.-X. Duplessis, de la Compagnie de
Jésus; accompagnées d'une notice biographique
et d'annotations. Lévis: Mercier et Cie, 1802.
8vo., pp. L-LXXXV., 1-803, 1 -XXX

Scène d'Hiver.
Le Canada Français, Vol. III., 1800, p. 229.

Notes sur le Greffe et les Greffiers de Québec.
Ibid., p. 707.

Royal, Joseph.

La vie de Sir Louis-H. Lafontaine,
La Revue Canadienne, Montréal, 1867.

Considérations sur l'union fédérale des provinces
anglaises de l'Amérique du Nord.
Ibid., 1867.

Le Capitaine Maillé.
Les Mémoires de la Société royale du Canada. Tome
XI., Sec. 1, 1893.

Le Canada : République ou Colonie. Montréal : E.
Sénécal et Fils, 1804.

The same in English, Montreal : E. Sénécal et Fils,
1804.
12mo., pp. 103.

Saint-Maurice, Faucher de.

A la Brunante.—Contes et Récits. Les Blessures
de la Vie.—Une Histoire de tous les jours. Montréal : Duvernay Frères et Dansereau, 1874.
1 vol., in-18 Jésus, p. VI + 347.

De Québec à Mexico.—Souvenirs de Voyage, de
Garnison, de Combat et de Bivouacs. Montréal : Duvernay Frères et Dansereau, 1874.
2 vol., in-18 jésus, pp. 236 et 271.

Choses et Autres.—Conférences, études, fragments. Montréal : Duvernay Frères et Dansereau, 1874.
1 vol., in-18 jésus, p. 291.

A la Veillée. Montréal : Duvernay Frères et
Dansereau.
1 vol., in-18 jésus. Ouvrage accepté par le minis-
tre de l'instruction publique de la province de Québec.

De Tribord à Babord.—Trois Croisières dans le
Golfe Saint-Laurent. Montréal : Duvernay
Frères et Dansereau, 1877.
1 vol., in 12mo., pp. 458.

Cours de Tactique. Québec, 1803.
1 vol., pp. 110.

L'Ennemi ! l'Ennemi ! Etude sur l'organisation
militaire du Canada. Québec, 1802.
1 vol., pp. 38.

Deux ans au Mexique, avec une notice par M.
Coquille, rédacteur du Journal *Le Monde* de
Paris. Québec : C. Darveau, 1878.
1 vol., 7 éd., in-18, pp. 222.

Promenades dans le Golfe Saint-Laurent. Les Iles,
Québec : C. Darveau, 1879.
1 vol., in-18, pp. 207. Avec préface par M. Marmier,
de l'Académie française, 1 vol., 7 éd., illustrée.

Promenades dans le Golfe Saint-Laurent. La Gas-
pésie. Montréal : Sénécal et Fils.
1 vol., in-8vo , 7 éd , illustrée, deuxième édition, C.
Darveau, 1880, 1 vol., 18mo., pp. 238.

Saint-Maurice, Faucher de.—*Continued.*

En Route.—Sept Jours dans les Provinces mari-
times. Québec : Côté et Cie, 1888.
1 vol., in 12mo., pp. 279.

A la Veillée, contes et récits.

Joies et Tristesses de la Mer. 1 vol., Montréal :
Cadieux et Dérome, 1888.
1 vol., 8vo., pp. 1885.

Loin du pays, Souvenirs d'Europe, d'Afrique et
d'Amérique. Québec : Côté et Cie, 1888.
2 vols., in 8vo., pp. (I). v + 411; (II). 555 + III.

L'Abbé Laverdière.—Etude biographique avec
portrait.
1 vol., s.l.n d., in 12mo., pp. 9.

Relation de ce qui s'est passé lors des fouilles
faites par ordre du gouvernement dans une
partie des fondations du collège des Jésuites de
Québec, précédée de certaines observations
accompagnées d'un plan par le capitaine Deville
et d'une photographie. Québec : C. Darveau, 1870.
1 vol. In-fol., pp. 48.

La Province de Québec et le Canada au troisième
Congrès international de Géographie à Venise,
1881. Lévis : Mercier et Cie, 1882.
In-8vo., pp. 43.

Notice sur Jean Vauquelin, de Dieppe, Lieutenant
de Vaisseau (1727-1764).
1 vol.
Aussi dans les *Mémoires de la Société royale du
Canada,* Tome, III., Sec. 1, 1845.

Les Canadiens-Français aux Etats-Unis.—Séance
de l'assemblée législative de Québec, du 28 mars
1883.
1 vol.

Notes pour servir à la construction du chemin de
fer projeté, le "Québec Oriental."
1 vol.

Discours d'inauguration ; à la première séance de
la première section de la littérature française de
la Société royale du Canada.
Mémoires de la Société royale du Canada, Tome I.,
Sec. 1, 1882.

L'Elément Etranger dans les Etats-Unis.
Ibid., Tome III., Sec. 1, 1883.

Procédures parlementaires : recueil des décisions
des Présidents de l'Assemblée Législative de
Québec, 1808-1885. Montréal : Imprimerie Générale, 1885.
1 vol., gr. 8vo., pp. 783.

Le Canada et les Canadiens-Français pendant la
guerre Franco-Prussienne, Québec : A. Côté et
Cie, 1888.
1 vol., 8vo., pp. 56.

Notes sur la formation du Franco-Normand et de
l'Anglo Saxon, Montréal : Eusèbe Sénécal et
Fils, 1802.
1 vol., in-18 pp. 85.

Maximilien, voyageur, écrivain, critique d'art,
poète, marin, observateur, philosophe, biblio-
phile et chrétien.
Mémoires de la Société royale du Canada. Tome
VII., Sec. 1, 1889.

Saint-Maurice, Faucher de.—*Continued.*

Notes pour servir à l'histoire de l'Empereur Maximilien d'après ses œuvres, les récits du capitaine d'artillerie Albert Hans, du médecin particulier de S. M., le docteur· Basch et des témoins oculaires de l'exécution. Québec: Côté et Cie, 1880.
> 1 vol. in 8vo., pp. 224. Avec un portrait de l'Empereur.

Notes pour servir à l'histoire du Général Richard Montgomery. Montréal: E. Sénécal et Fils, 1893.
> 18vo., pp. 96.
> *Mémoires de la Société royale du Canada.* Tome IX., Sec. 1, 1890.

L'Admiral Byng devant ses Juges et devant l'Histoire.
> *Ibid.,* Tome XI. Sec. 1, 1693. Aussi dans un vol., illustré.

Les Etats de Jersey et la Langue française, Exemple offert au Manitoba et au Nord-Ouest, Montréal: E. Sénécal et Fils, 1893.
> 1 vol., in-12mo., pp. 82.

✗ Saunders, William.

Insects Injurious to Fruits. Philadelphia: Lippincott & Co., 1883.
> 8vo., pp. 436, with 440 wood cuts. 2nd ed., 1892.

In the Transactions of Royal Society of Canada, viz. :

On the Importance of Economizing and Preserving our Forests. Vol. I., pp. 35-37.

On the Introduction and Dissemination of Noxious Insects. Vol. I., pp. 77-79.

On the Influence of Sex on Hybrids among Fruits. Vol. I., pp. 123-125.

Notes on the Occurrence of Certain Butterflies in Canada. Vol. II., pp. 233-235.

Catalogue of Canadian Butterflies, with notes on their distribution. Vol. III., pp. 85-100.

Observations on Early-ripening Cereals. Vol. VI., pp. 73-76.

The Yield of Spring Wheat, Barley and Oats Grown as Single Plants. Vol. VII., pp. 109-112.

In the Canadian Journal, viz.:

On the Occurrence of Vanessa Cœnia in Canada West. 1861, pp. 498-500.

List of Plants Collected Chiefly in the Neighbourhood of London, Ont. 1863, pp. 219-238.

Synopsis of Canadian Arctiidæ. 1863 pp. 340-377.

In the Canadian Entomologist, viz.:

Entomological Notes. Descriptions of Eggs and Larvæ of Canadian Butterflies. 1868, pp. 3-6;
1869, 53-57, 65-67, 73-77.

Notes of a Trip to the Saguenay. 1868, pp. 11-13.

Description of the Larva of Callimorpha Lecontei. 1868, pp. 20.

On the Larva of Pyramels Huntera. 1869, pp. 105-106.

Notes on Alaria Florida. 1869, pp. 6-7.

Notes and Experiments on Nematus ventricosus. 1869, pp. 13-17.

On a New Grape-seed Insect, Isosoma vitis. 1869, pp. 25-27.

Saunders, William.—*Continued.*

Notes on Hadena xylinoides. 1869, pp. 33-34.

On the Larva of Thecla Inorata. 1870, pp. 61-64.

On the Larva of some Lepidoptera. 1870, pp. 74-76.

An Insect Friend, Arma placidum. 1870, pp. 93-94.

Hints on Describing Caterpillars. 1870, p. 94.

Entomological Gleanings. 1870, pp. 111-113, 120-120, 140-140.

Notes on the Larva of Ophlusa bistriaria. 1870, p. 130.

On the Plum Curculio Conotrachelus nenuphar. 1870, pp. 137-139.

On Neonympha eurytris. 1870, pp. 130-142

On the Larva of Diphthera deridens. 1870, pp. , 145-146.

Hints to Fruit-growers. 1871, pp. 12-14, 25 27, 66-70, 149-155.

Entomological Gleanings. 1871, pp. 14-15.

On the Larva of the Peach-borer, Ægeria exitiosa. 1871, pp. 14-15.

Notes on Lepidopterous Larvæ. 1871, pp. 35-37, 225-227.

Report on the Colorado Potato Beetle. 1871, pp. 41-51.

On the Egg and Young Larva of Alaria Florida. 1871, p. 76.

On the Larva of Pricyela armataria. 1871, pp. 130-131.

On the Swarming of Danais archippus. 1871, pp. 150-157.

On the Larva of Halesidota maculata. 1871, p. 186.

On the Larva of Agrotis depressus. 1871, p. 103.

On the Larva of Hyperetis alienaria. 1871, pp. 209-210.

Notes on the Larva of Acronycta occidentalis. 1872, pp. 40-52.

Notes on Argynnis cybele. 1872, pp. 121-124.

Hints to Fruit-growers. 1872, pp. 133-136.

Blistering Beetles. 1872, p. 139.

On the Eggs and Young Larvæ of Melitæa Harrisii. 1872, pp. 161-163.

Osmia Canadensis. 1872, pp. 237-238.

On Danais archippus. 1873, pp. 4-8.

On the Larva of Plusia balluca. 1873, pp. 10-11.

The Isabella Tiger-moth, Spilosoma isabella. 1873, pp. 75-77.

The Grape-vine Plume-moth, Oxyptilus periscelidactylus. 1873, pp. 99-100.

On the Raspberry Saw-fly, Selandria rubi. 1873, pp. 101-103.

On the Bacon Beetle, Dermestes lardarius. 1873, pp. 171-172.

Notes on the Larva of Cosmia orina. 1873, p. 200.

On Colias philodice. 1873, pp. 221-223.

On the Tiger Swallow-tail Butterfly, Papilio turnus. 1874, pp. 2-5.

On Amphipyra pyramidoides. 1874, pp. 27-28.

On the Larva of Dearmia larvaria. 1874, pp. 32-33.

Saunders, William.—*Continued.*

On Limenitis disippus. 1874, pp. 46-49.

Notes on the Larva and Pupa of Saperda moesta. 1874, pp. 61-63.

On the Gooseberry Saw-fly, Nematus ventricosus. 1874, pp. 101-104.

On the Currant Geometer, Ellopia ribearia. 1874, pp. 134-139.

The Spotted Pelidnota, Pelidnota punctata. 1874, pp. 141-142.

On the Larva of Catocala ultronia. 1874, pp. 147-149.

The Mexican Honey Ant, Myrmecocystus Mexicanus. 1875, pp. 12-14.

On Eudryas grata. 1875, pp. 41-44.

On the Hellgrammite Fly, Corydalis cornutus. 1875, pp. 64-67.

On Delopeia bella. 1875, pp. 85-80.

On Drasteria crichtea. 1875, pp. 115-117.

List of Neuroptera, collected chiefly in the neighbourhood of London, Ont. 1875, pp. 152-154.

Notes on Catocalas. 1876, pp. 72-75.

On the Luna Moth, Actias luna. 1877, p. 33.

On Deilephila chamœnerii and D. lineata. 1877, pp. 63-67.

The Forest Tent Caterpillar, Clisiocampa sylvatica. 1877, pp. 158-159.

Notes on the Larva of Lycœna Scudderi. 1878, pp. 14-15.

Observations on the Eggs of Clisiocampa sylvatica and C. Americana. 1878, pp. 21-23.

The Achemon Sphinx, Philampelus achemon. 1878, pp. 101-103.

The Abbot Sphinx, Thyreus Abbotti. 1878, pp. 130-131.

Notes on a Winter Holiday. 1878, pp. 221-224.

The Goldsmith Beetle, Cotalpa lanigera. 1879, pp. 21-22.

Insect Powder. 1879, pp. 41-43.

Entomology for Beginners. No. 1, 1879, pp. 221-223. No. 2, 1880, pp. 4-6. No. 3, 1880, pp. 56-57.

On Two Mites. 1880, pp. 237-239.

The Indian Cetonia, Euryomia Inda. 1881, pp. 1-2.

The Satellite Sphinx, Philampelus satellitia. 1881, pp. 41-43.

The Legged Maple-borer, Ægeria acerni. 1881, pp. 66-70.

The Eyed Elator, Alaus oculatus. 1881, pp. 117-119.

On Notodonta concinna. 1881, pp. 138-140.

The Southern Cabbage Butterfly, Pieris protodice. 1882, pp. 1-2.

The Polyphemus Moth, Telea polyphemus. 1882, pp. 41-45.

The Leopard Moth, Ecpantheria scribonia. 1882, pp. 113-115.

The Grape Phylloxera, Phylloxera vastatrix. 1882, pp. 121-128.

On the Mouth of the Larva of Chrysopa. 1882, pp. 176-177.

Saunders, William.—*Continued.*

The Grape-berry Moth, Lobesia botrana. 1882, pp. 178-180.

The Poplar Dagger-moth, Acronycta lepusculina. 1882, pp. 221-223.

The Apple Leaf-crumpler, Phycita nebulo. 1883, pp. 1-2.

The Melon Moth, Eudioptis hyalinata. 1883, pp. 56-57.

The Apple-tree Aphis, Aphis mali. 1883, pp. 96-97.

The Promethea Moth, Callosamia promethea. 1883, pp. 231-233.

On Smerinthus exæcatus and S. myops. 1884, pp. 9-11.

Notes on a Trip to Point Pelee. 1884, pp. 50-53.

On Pulvinaria innumerabilis. 1884, pp, 141-143.

Description of the Larva of Agrotis decolorata. 1885, p. 32.

In Annual Reports of the Entomological Society of Ontario, viz. :

Insects Injurious to the Grape. 1870, pp. 30-53 ; 1871, pp. 17-21.

Insects Injurious to the Currant and Gooseberry. 1871, pp. 27-44.

Insects Injurious to the Grape. 1872, pp. 10-14.

Insects Injurious to the Strawberry. 1872, pp. 15-26.

On Some Innoxious Insects. 1872, pp. 51-58.

Insects Injurious to the Raspberry. 1873, pp. 7-17.

Insects Injurious to the Strawberry. 1873, pp. 18-19.

On Some Innoxious Insects. 1873, pp. 20-25.

Entomological Notes for 1873. 1874, pp. 17-21.

On Some of Our Common Insects. 1874, pp. 22-28.

On Some Injurious Insects. 1874, pp. 43-53.

On Canker Worms. 1875, pp. 23-28.

Notes of the Year. 1875, pp. 29-35.

On Some Common Insects. 1875, pp. 36-42.

Annual Address of President. 1876, pp. 6-10.

On Some Common Insects. 1876, pp. 35-38.

Notes of the Year. 1876, pp. 39-40.

Annual Address of President. 1877, pp. 4-6.

Aphides or Plant Lice. 1877, pp. 31-39.

Annual Address of President. 1878, pp. 4-8.

Notes of the Year. 1878, pp. 28-35.

On Papilio cresphontes. 1878, pp. 60-61.

Annual Address of President. 1879, pp. 4-9.

The Pea Weevil. 1879, pp. 63-65.

Notes on Various Insects. 1879, pp. 71-77.

Annual Address of President. 1880, pp. 5-9.

The Common Woolly Bear, Spilsoma virginica. 1880, pp. 21-22.

On Some Rare Insects Captured in Ontario in 1880. 1880, pp. 38-42.

On Mites. 1880, pp. 69-75.

Annual Address of President. 1881, pp. 5-9.

Saunders, William.—*Continued.*

Saunders, William.—*Continued.*

Saunders, William.—*Continued.*

Bulletin No. 18. Ladoga Wheat. February 7, 1893, pp. 14.

Report of the Director. Annual Report Experimental Farms. 1893, pp. 3-90.

Experimental Farm Notes, No. 1. The Germinating Power of Grain Grown in Canada during 1893. February, 1894, pp. 6.

Bulletin No. 20. Tuberculosis. Saunders and Robertson. February, 1894, pp. 30.

In Proceedings of the Society for the Promotion of Agricultural Science, viz. :

Notes on Wheats Grown as Single Plants at the Experimental Farm, Ottawa. 1890, pp. 59-61.

Annual Address of President. 1894, pp. 209-231.

Other Reports :

Reports on Adulteration of Food as Public Analyst for Windsor Division. 1883-1884, 1885-1886.

Report on the Progress of the Work in the Canadian Section of the World's Columbian Exposition. December, 1892, pp. 28.

Report on the Production and Manufacture of Beet Sugar. Prepared for the Canadian Government. February 7, 1892, pp. 47.

Schultz, His Honour John.

Botany of the Old River Trail and Red River Settlement.
    Transactions of Botanical Society of Canada, Kingston, 1861.

Chemistry of the Atmosphere and Prevailing Diseases of Red River Settlement.
    Institute of Rupert's Land, 1862.

A description of a journey from St. Paul to Fort Garry during the Sioux Massacre in Minnesota and Dakota, 1862.

Advocacy of Confederation of Canadian Provinces and the inclusion of the great Fertile Belt, 1864.

Evidence before Railroad Committee of United States Senate on the vast resources of Rupert's Land, 1866.

Opening of a Prehistoric Mound, 1874 and 1875.

In Reports of Debates of House of Commons in Library of Parliament, 1871-1882, viz :

Speeches in House of Commons on Indian Policy, Preservation of Buffalo, System of Surveys, Forest and Prairie Fires, Waterways of the Northwest, Railroad Communication, Survey and Lighting of Lake Winnipeg, First Red River Rebellion, Dawson Route, C. P. R., resources of the Northwest, preservation of sea animals of Hudson's Bay, Arctic research. Loyalty to the Empire, Unity of the Colonies, the Isotherms as affecting agricultural possibilities, and the resources of British Columbia.

Speeches in Senate on Manitoba and Northwest subjects.

Report upon Preservation of National Food Products and Resources of the Great Mackenzie Basin.

Later Phases of Indian Question.

Schultz, His Honour John.—*Continued.*

Development of Resources.

Means of Communication and Protection of Canadian Fisheries in Arctic Waters.
    In Senate Journals and Debates, 1882-1884.

Fostering of Loyalty and Patriotism among the children of our Common Schools. Dominion Day, 1892.
    In Pamphlet.

A Forgotten Northern Fortress.
    Transactions of Historical Society of Manitoba, 1893.

The old " Crow Wing Trail."
    Ibid., 1893.

Some very old Inhabitants. Speech on unveiling the monument commemorative of the Battle of Seven Oaks.
    Ibid., 1893.

The Innuits of our Arctic Coast.
    Transactions of the Royal Society of Canada, Vol. xi., Sec. 2, 1894.

Selwyn, Alfred R.C.

On the Geology of the Gold-fields of Victoria. (In a letter to Professor A. C. Ramsay, F.R.S., and F.G.S.)
    Quarterly Journal Geological Society, Vol. xiv'., p. 533. The author was at that time Geologist to the Colony of Victoria.

Report to Sir H. Barkly on permanence of auriferous veins in Victoria, Australia, in reply to Sir Roderick Murchison. Victoria Parl. P. No. 75, 12th July, 1858.

Note on the Geology of Victoria. (In a letter dated Geological Survey Office, Melbourne, 14th February, 1859, to Sir R. I. Murchison, F.R.S., F.G.S., etc.)
    Quarterly Journal Geological Society, Vol., xvi., p. 145.

On the Geology and Mineralogy of Mount Alexander and the Adjacent Country, lying between the Rivers Loddon and Campaspe.
    Ibid., Vol. x., p. 299.

By J. Beete Jukes and A. R. C. Selwyn. Sketch of the Structure of the country extending from Cader Idris to Moel Slabod in North Wales.
    Ibid., Vol., iv., p. 300.

Numerous Geological Maps and Reports on the Geology of Victoria, Australia, from 1852 to 1869, published in the Colony.

Various Notes on the Physical Geography, Geology and Mineralogy of Victoria, Australia. 1861 and 1866.

The Stratigraphy of the " Quebec Group " and the older Crystalline Rocks of Canada.
    Canadian Naturalist, Vol., ix., 1879.

Compendium of Geography and Travel: The Dominion of Canada and North America, Newfoundland, London : Stanford, 1883.

The Quebec Group in Geology.
    Transactions Royal Society of Canada, Vol. i. Sec. 4, 1882.

The Geology of Lake Superior.
    Ibid., 1883.

Descriptive Sketch of the Physical Geography and Geology of the Dominion of Canada, to accompany a new Geological Map. Montreal, 1884.

Selwyn, Alfred R. C.—_Continued._

Introductory or Summary Reports in the volumes of the _Reports of Progress_ of the Geological Survey of Canada from 1869 when he took the place of Sir William Logan, as Director of the Survey. See vols., from 1869-1881. Special Reports in the Reports of Progress as follows :

On the Gold-fields of Quebec and Nova Scotia, 1870-71.

On a Geological Reconnaissance from Lake Superior to Fort Garry, 1872-73.

Upon the Acadia Iron Ore deposits of Londonderry, Colchester Co., in Nova Scotia, 1772-73.

Observations in the Northwest Territory, from Fort Garry to Rocky Mountain House, 1873-74.

On Exploration in British Columbia, 1875-76.

Observations on the Stratigraphy of the Quebec Group, 1877-78.

On Boring Operations in the Souris River Valley, 1879-80.

On the Geological Nomenclature and the Colouring and Notation of Geological Maps, 1880-82.

On the Geology of the Southeastern portion of the Province of Quebec, 1880-82.

Stewart George.

Thomas D'Arcy McGee,

July, 1868, St. John, N.B. _Stewart's Quarterly._ This magazine was founded and edited by the author from April, 1867, to January, 1876 : 5 vols. printed. He also published and edited _The Stamp Collectors' Monthly Gazette_, St. John, N.B., June 1, 1865, to June 1, 1867, inclusive; 2 vols.

Halloween,

Ibid., October, 1868, St. John, N.B.

Charles Sangster and his Poetry,

Ibid., October, 1869, St. John, N.B.

Who is Enylla Allyne ?

Ibid., April, 1870, St. John, N.B.

E. L. Davenport, as Sir Giles Overreach.

Ibid., April, 1870, St. John, N.B.

Storm-stayed and the story which grew out of it,

Ibid., October, 1870, St. John, N.B.

Alexandre Davy Dumas,

Ibid., January, 1871, St. John, N.B.

Old and New Newspapers.

Ibid., January, 1871, St. John, N.D.

John Reade's Prophecy of Merlin.

Ibid., January, 1871, St. John, N.B.

Dialect Poets ; Bret Harte and John Hay.

Ibid., April, 1871, St. John, N.B.

Zozimus.

Appleton's Journal, New York.

Madame La Tour.

Ibid., New York.

Ballads of the Scaffold.

Canadian Monthly, Toronto. July, 1876.

Thomas Carlyle.

Belford's Magazine, Dec., 1876, Toronto.

Ralph Waldo Emerson.

Ibid., January, 1871, Toronto.

Oliver Wendell Holmes.

Ibid., February, 1877, Toronto.

Stewart, George.—_Continued._

James Russell Lowell.

Belford's Magazine, April, 1877, Toronto.

Henry W. Longfellow.

Ibid., June, 1877, Toronto.

John C. Whittier.

Ibid., October, 1877, Toronto.

William Cullen Bryant.

Ibid., November, 1877, Toronto.

How Five Little Midgets spent Christmas Eve.

Ibid., January, 1876, Toronto.

The Story of the Great Fire in St. John, N.B.

Toronto : Belford Bros., 1877.

8vo., pp. 292, with map and 31 plates.

Canada under the Administration of the Earl of Dufferin. Toronto : Rose-Belford Publishing Co., 1878.

 8vo., pp. 700, portrait.

Evenings in the Library. Toronto : Belford Bros., 1878.

8vo., pp. 254.

In the _Canadian Portrait Gallery_, Toronto, 1880-81, edited by J. C. Dent :—Sir S. L. Tilley, Sir A. G. Archibald, Hon. T. A. R. Laflamme, Hon. R. E. Caron, Hon. E. B. Chandler, Hon. Sir John C. Allan, Bishop Medley, Hon. C. E. B. De Boucherville, Hon. H. G. Joly, Mgr. Francois-Xavier Laval-Montmorency, Hon. Sir J. J. C. Abbott, Hon. Sir William Young, Hon. Timothy Warren Anglin.

R. W. Emerson, Alcott the Concord Mystic, Thomas Carlyle, Thoreau the Hermit of Walden, H. W. Longfellow.

Transactions Literary and Historical Society of Quebec.

James De Mille.

Souvenirs Personnels du Canada. Edited by the Count of Premio Real, Quebec, 1880.

The Beggar's Operation.

Ibid., Quebec, 1880.

Longfellow in Canada.

Literary World, Boston, Mass. 1881.

Frontenac's Will.

Magazine of American History, New York, June, 1883, p. 485.

Various Biographies, Twenty-five in Number, in Vols. IV., V., VI.

Appleton's Cyclopedia of American Biography, New York.

A Fatal New Year's Eve, being an account of Brig.-Gen. Richard Montgomery's Sword.

Mail, Toronto, December 22, 1883.

Frontenac and His times.

Winsor's Narrative and Critical History of America, Vol. IV., pp. 44, with 7 plates and autographs, 1884.

Sources of Early Canadian History.

Transactions Royal Society of Canada, Vol. III., Sec. 2, 1845.

Life and Times of Longfellow.

Scottish Review, London, Paisley and New York, No. 15, July, 1886, pp. 101-126,

Literature in Canada.

Canadian Leaves, Canadian Club of New York, edited by George M. Fairchild, jr., 1887.

Stewart, George.—*Continued.*

Emerson the Thinker.
Scottish Review, London, Paisley and New York, No.
22, April, 1888, pp. 288-307.

Nova Scotia and New Brunswick.
Encyclopædia Britannica, 9th edition, Vol. XVII.

Prince Edward Island.
Ibid., Vol. XIX.

Quebec Province and Quebec City.
Ibid., Vol. XX.

Simms, William Gilmore.
Ibid., Vol. XXII.

St. John, New Brunswick.
Ibid., Vol. XXI.

Three Rivers.
Ibid , Vol. XXIII.

Fifty Years of French Canadian Authorship.
The Critic, Halifax, N.S., June 18, 1887.

Letters in Canada.
The Week, Toronto, June 16, 1887.

Some French Canadian Books.
Ibid., Toronto, March, 1888.

A New Canadian Poet.
Ibid., Toronto, October 11, 1888.

Prominent Canadians. No. 10. Sir Samuel Leonard Tilley.
Ibid., Toronto, January 26, 1888.

The Fisheries Treaty. A Canadian View.
Magazine of American History, New York, May, 1888.

An Idyl of Dog Lane.
Saturday Night, Toronto, December, 1888.

Jottings by the Way.
The Week, Toronto, November 8, 1888.

Elizabeth Stuart Phelps and Her First Successful Book.
Ibid., Toronto, March 1, 1889.

French Canadian Books.
The Canadian Bibliographer, Hamilton, November, 1889.

A Half-forgotten Singer.
Trinity University Review, Toronto, December, 1889.

The Present Condition of Historical Studies in Canada.
Annual Papers of the American Historical Association, 1889.
Ibid., 1890.
Ibid., 1891.

Chapter "French Canadianisms," in "Slang, Jargon and Cant," edited by Charles G. Leland.
London : Whittaker & Co., 1890.
2 vols.

Literary Conditions in Canada.
The Independent, New York, March 6, 1890.

Some Canadian Writers.
Ibid., New York, March 13, 1890.

Literature in French Canada.
New England Magazine, Boston, September, 1890.

A Montmorency Adventure.
Dominion Illustrated, Montreal, February 15, 1890.

The Writings of W. H. H. Murray.
Belford's Monthly, New York, March, 1891.

Oliver Wendell Holmes.
The Arena, Boston, Vol. IV., No. II., July, 1891, pp. 129-141.

Stewart, George.—*Continued.*

St. Jean-Baptiste.
The Independent, New York, June 25, 1891.

James Russell Lowell.
The Arena, Boston, Vol. IV. No. V., October, 1891.
pp. 513-529.

John Greenleaf Whittier.
Ibid., Boston, Vol. V., No. I., December, 1891, pp. 36-49.

The Yellow Boy's Room.
The Independent, New York, December, 24, 1891.

The Legend of Crying Cove.
The Independent, New York, February, 18, 1892.

Fiction in the Court Room.
The Week, Toronto, March 11, 1892.

A Breakfast at Lord Houghton's.
The Lake Magazine, Toronto, October, 1892.

Some Famous Parrots.
Progress, St. John, N.B., March 12, 1892.

The Quebec Crisis.
The Speaker, London, March 5, 1892.

The Magdalen Islands.
The Pilot, Boston, April 9, 1892.

John Gilmary Shea.
Dominion Illustrated, Montreal, May, 1892.

The History of a Magazine.
Ibid., Montreal, August, 1892.

Sir Daniel Wilson.
Ibid., Montreal, November, 1892.

Canada's Destiny.
The Speaker, London, December 24, 1892.

Quebec City and Province.
Chamber's Encyclopædia, Vol. VIII., 1892.

Sir S. L. Tilley, K.C.M.G.
Men of the Day, edited by Louis H. Taché, Montreal, 1892.

Dr. John George Bourinot, C.M.G.
Ibid., Montreal, 1893.

Hon. A. G. Blair.
Ibid., Montreal, 1893.

Sir Joseph Hickson.
Ibid., Montreal, 1893.

Hon. William Stevens Fielding.
Ibid., Montreal, 1893.

Alfred, Lord Tennyson.
The Cosmopolitan, New York, December, 1892.

Songs of the French Canadian Children.
Dominion Illustrated, Montreal, February, 1893.

The Canadian Question.
The North American Review, New York, March, 1893.

Canada at the World's Fair.
Ibid., New York, May, 1893.

The First Steamer to Cross the Atlantic.
Chambers's Journal, Edinburgh, Scotland, June 17, 1893.

Essays from Reviews. Dawson & Co., 1st Series, Quebec, 1892.
16mo., 171 pp.

Essays from Reviews. Quebec : Dawson & Co., 2nd Series, 1893.
16mo., pp. 159.

Suite, Benjamin.—*Continued.*

Poutrincourt en Acadie.
Ibid., ii., Sec. 1, 1884, p. 31.

Le Golfe Saint-Laurent, 1000-1025.
Ibid., iv., Sec. 1, 1886, p. 7.

Le Golfe Saint-Laurent, 1625-1632.
Ibid., vii.. Sec. 1, 1889, p. 29.

Prétendues origines des Canadiens.
Ibid., iii., Sec. 1, 1882, p. 13.

La famille de Callières.
Ibid., viii., Sec. 1, 1890, p. 91.

Henry et Alphonse de Tonty.
Ibid., xi., Sec. 1, 1893, p. 3.

In The Citizen, Ottawa, viz. :
The name of the Ottawa, December 16, 1893.

How the Ottawa came to be River Ottawa, December 23, 1893.

Battle of Les Chats. December 30, 1893.

Jean Nicolet in Wisconsin, 1634-35.
Madison, Wisconsin, State Historical Society Proceedings, viii., 94, 188-194 ; ix.,107 ; x., 41, 292, 304, 372.

Les Laurentiennes, en vers. Montréal : Eusèbe Sénécal, 1870.
Pet. 12mo., pp. 208.

Histoire des Trois-Rivières. 1ᵉʳ livraison, Montréal : Eusèbe Sénécal, 1870. Cette brochure embrasse les années 1534-1637.
In 8vo., pp. 126 avec cartes.

Expédition militaire de Manitoba, 1870. Montréal ; Eusèbe Séuécal, 1871.
8vo., pp. 50.

Mélanges d'Histoire et de Littérature. Ottawa : Joseph Bureau, 1876.
12mo., pp. 500.

Le Coin du Feu. Québec ; Blumhart et Cie, 1877.
12mo., pp. 210.

Chronique Trifluvienne. Montréal : Compagnie d'Imprimerie Canadienne, 1879. Ce travail couvre les années 1637-1663.
8vo., pp. 237.

Les Chants Nouveaux, en vers. Ottawa : Imprimerie du Canada, 1880.
16mo., pp. 68.

La Poésie Française au Canada. Imprimerie du Courrier de Saint-Hyacinthe, 1881.

Album de l'Histoire des Trois-Rivières. Textes copieux. Années 1634-1721. Montréal : Geo. E. Desbarats, 1881.
14 × 19 pouces, 2 planches d'autographes.

Histoire des Canadiens-Français. Montréal : Wilson et Cie, 1882-84.
8 vols., 4to., pp. 160 chacun, avec 125 portraits, cartes et vues.

Situation de la Langue Française au Canada. Montréal : La Minerve, 1885.

Histoire de Saint-François-du-Lac. Montréal : Imprimerie de L'Etendard, 1886.
8vo., pp. 120.

Le Pays des Grands Lacs, 1603 à 1660.
Le Canada-Français, Québec, 1889-1890.

Pages d'Histoire du Canada. Montréal ; Granger Frères, 1891.
12mo., pp. 472.

Suite, Benjamin.—*Continued.*

Causons du Pays et de la Colonisation. Montréal: Granger Frères, 1891.
12m »., pp. 250.

Lower Canada during 1810-14.
Transactions of the Canadian Military Institute, Toronto, 1891-92.

De Machiche aux Trois-Rivières avant 1760. Un chapitre spécial à la fin du volume intitulé : "Histoire de la Paroisse d'Yamachiche." Trois-Rivières : P. V. Ayotte, 1892.

L'Emploi du Temps.
Le Manitoba, 20 septembre 1893.

Jeanne d'Arc Militaire.
Courrier du Canada, 16 avril 1894.

Tasse, Joseph.

La Vallée de l'Outaouais. 1873.

Les Canadiens de l'Ouest. Montréal : Cie d'Imprimerie Canadienne, 1878.
2 vols., 8vo., pp. (i.) xxxix. + 384 ; (ii.) 413.

Un Parallèle — Lord Beaconsfield et Sir John Macdonald. 1880.

Le 38ᵐᵉ Fauteuil ou Souvenirs Parlementaires. Montréal : E. Sénécal et Fils, 1891.
8vo., pp. 299. Avec portraits de MM. Mousseau, Masson, Royal et Girouard.

Voltaire, Madame de Pompadour et Quelques Arpents de Neige.
Dans les Mémoires de la Société royale du Canada.
Tome x., Sec. 1, 1892.

Discours de Sir Georges Cartier, baronnet. Accompagnés de notices. Montreal : Eusèbe Sénécal et Fils, 1893.
Gr. 8vo., pp. xii. + 817. Avec un portrait et fac simile d'une lettre de Sir G.-E. Cartier.

Tanguay, Mgr. Cyprien.

Relation du Voyage de l'Abbé J.-B.-Z. Bolduc autour de l'Amérique du Sud.
Rapports sur les Missions du Diocèse de Québec, juin 1843.

Répertoire du Clergé Canadien depuis la fondation de la Nouvelle-France jusqu'à nos Jours. Québec : C. Darveau, 1868.
8vo., pp. 321 + xxix.

Episode, voyage en France, Belgique, Prusse, Allemagne et Italie : Conférence.
Le Courrier d'Ottawa. 16mo ., pp. 20 1870.

Dictionnaire Généalogique des Familles Canadiennes depuis la Fondation de la Colonie jusqu'à nos Jours. 1ᵉʳ Vol. Montréal : Eusèbe Sénécal, 1871-1890.
4to., pp. 624.

Régistres de l'Etat des Personnes : Conférence.
Le Foyer Domestique, Ottawa. 16mo., pp. 19. 1878.

Monseigneur de l'Auberivière, 5ᵗᵐᵉ Évêque de Québec, 1739-40. Documents Annotés. Montréal : Eusèbe Sénécal, 1885.
12mo., pp. 169.

Répertoire Générale du Clergé Canadien par Ordre Chronologique. 2ᵉ édition. Montréal : F. Sénécal, 1893.
8vo., pp. 528 + 46.

Whitcaves, J. F.—*Continued.*

On the Land and Fresh-water Mollusca of Lower Canada. Parts I.-II.
Canadian Naturalist and Geologist, Vol. VIII., Series 1, 1868. 8vo., pp. 50-65 and 98-107, with 12 woodcuts.

Transatlantic Sketches. 1. On the Little Miami River, Wayuesville, Warren County, Ohio.
Zoologist, London, Vol. xxi., 1863, pp. 8419-8424.

On the Fossils of the Trenton Limestone of the Island of Montreal.
Canadian Naturalist and Geologist, Vol. II., New Series, 1865. 8vo., pp. 312-314.

On the Marine Mollusca of Eastern Canada.
Ibid., Vol. IV., New Series, 1869. 8vo., pp. 48-57.

On some results obtained by dredging in Gaspé and off Murray Bay.
Ibid., Vol. IV., New Series, 1869. 8vo., pp. 351-354.

Notes on some Canadian Birds.
Ibid., Vol. V., New Series, 1870. 8vo , pp. 103 and 230-231.

Report on a deep-sea Dredging Expedition to the Gulf of St. Lawrence.
Report of the Department of Marine and Fisheries, Ottawa, 1871. Large 8vo., pp. 12.

Report on a second deep-sea Dredging Expedition to the Gulf of St. Lawrence, with some remarks on the Marine Fisheries of the Province of Quebec.
Ibid., Ottawa, 1872. Large 8vo., pp. 22.

Deep-sea Dredging in the Gulf of St. Lawrence.
Canadian Naturalist and Geologist, Vol. VI., New Series, 1872. 8vo., pp. 351-354.

Notes on a deep-sea Dredging Expedition round the Island of Anticosti, in the Gulf of St. Lawrence.
Annals and Magazine of Natural History, Vol. x., Series 4, 1872, pp. 341-354. Reprinted, with some alterations and additions, in the *Canadian Naturalist and Geologist*, Vol. VII., New Series, 1875, pp. 86-100

Report on deep-sea Dredging Operations in the Gulf of St. Lawrence, with notes on the present condition of the Marine Fisheries and Oyster-beds of part of that region.
Report Department Marine and Fisheries, Ottawa, 1873. Large 8vo., pp. 29.

On recent deep-sea Dredging Operations in the Gulf of St. Lawrence.
American Journal of Science and Arts, Vol. VII., Series 3, pp. 210-219, March, 1874.

Notes on some Cretaceous Fossils collected by Mr. James Richardson at Vancouver and the adjacent Islands.
Report of Progress, Geological Survey of Canada, for 1873-74. Montreal, 1874. Large 8vo., pp. 260-264, with one plate.

On a collection of Himalayan birds recently presented to the Natural History Society by Major G. E. Bulger.
Canadian Naturalist and Geologist, Vol. VII., New Series, 1875. 8vo., pp. 394-400

Notes on the Marine Fisheries, and particularly on the Oyster-beds of the Gulf of St. Lawrence.
Ibid., Vol. VII., New Series, 1875. 8vo., pp. 336-349.

Geological Survey of Canada. Mesozoic Fossils, Vol. I., Part I. On some Invertebrata from the Coal-bearing rocks of the Queen Charlotte islands, collected by Mr. James Richardson in

Whitcaves, J. F.—*Continued.*

1872. Montreal, 1876. Large 8vo., pp. 92, with 10 plates and 0 woodcuts.

Critical notes on Fossils collected by A. R. C. Selwyn and Prof. Macoun in the valleys of the Peace, Athabasca and Clearwater rivers.
Ibid., Rep. Progr. 1875-76. Montreal, 1877. pp. 96-106.

On the Fossils of the Missinaibi and Moose rivers collected by Dr. R. Bell in 1875.
Ibid., 1875-76. Montreal, 1877. pp. 316-329.

Obituary Notice of Elkanah Billings, F.G.S., Palæontologist to the Geological Survey of Canada.
Canadian Naturalist and Geologist, Vol. VIII., New Series, Montreal, 1877. 8vo., pp. 251-241.

Preliminary Report on some supposed Jurassic Fossils collected by Dr. G. M. Dawson in the Coast Range of British Columbia.
Report of Progress, Geological Survey of Canada, 1876-77. Montreal, 1878. Large 8vo., pp. 150-159.

On some Marine Invertebrata from the West Coast of America. (Being a critical list of about 125 species from the Strait of Georgia, Burrard Inlet, etc., with description of a new Alcyonarian by Prof. A. E. Verrill, and of a supposed new Lamellibranchiate Bivalve by the writer.)
Canadian Naturalist and Geologist, Vol. VIII., Series 2, Montreal, 1878. 8vo., pp. 464-171.

On some Primordial Fossils from Southeastern Newfoundland. (With description of one new species.)
American Journal of Science, September, 1878. 8vo., pp. 224-226.

Geological Survey of Canada. Mesozoic Fossils, Vol. I., Part 2. On the Fossils of the Cretaceous rocks of Vancouver and adjacent islands in the Strait of Georgia. Montreal, 1879. Large 8vo., pp. 93, and 10 plates.

Provisional list of the Fossils collected by Dr. R. Bell in 1877, between the Long Portage of the Missinaibi River and York Factory.
Report of Progress, Geological Survey of Canada, 1877-78. Montreal, 1879. pp. 5 and 6c.

On some Marine Invertebrata from the Queen Charlotte Islands. Contains a list of 100 species, with descriptions of three new starfishes by Prof. A. E. Verrill, and of two new species of mollusca by the author.
Ibid., 1878-79. Montreal, 1880. Large 8vo., pp. 190a-205a.

On some remarkable Fossil Fishes from the Upper Devonian rocks at Scaumenac Bay, P.Q.
American Journal of Science and Arts, June, 1881, and reprinted in the *Annals and Magazine of Natural History* (London, England), August, 1881. 8vo., pp. 159-162.

On some Remarkable Fossil Fishes from the Devonian rocks of Scaumenac Bay, with descriptions of a new genus and three new species.
Canadian Naturalist and Geologist, Vol. x., New Series, Montreal, 1881. 8vo., pp. 27-35.

Description of a New Species of Psammodus from the Carboniferous rocks of the Island of Cape Breton.
Ibid., Vol. x., New Series, Montreal, 1881. 8vo., pp. 36.

Whiteaves, J. F.—*Continued.*

On some Fossil Fishes, Crustacea and Mollusca from the Devonian rocks of Campbellton, N.B., with descriptions of five new species.
Ibid., Vol. x., New Series, Montreal, 1881. 8vo., pp. 93-101.

List of Fossils collected by Dr. R. Bell in Manitoba during the season of 1880.
Report of Progress, Geological Survey of Canada, 1879-80. Large 8vo., pp. 57c-58c.

On the Lower Cretaceous rocks of British Columbia.
Transactions Royal Society of Canada. Vol. i. Sec. 4, 1882. 4to., pp. 81-80, with 3 woodcuts.

On some supposed Annelid tracks from the Gaspé Sandstones.
Ibid., Vol. i., Sec. 4, 1882. 4to, pp. 109-111, with 2 plates.

Note on the occurrence of Siphonotreta Scotica Davidson, in the Utica formation near Ottawa.
American Journal of Science and Arts, October, 1882. 8vo., pp. 278-279.

On a Recent Species of Heteropora from the Strait of Juan de Fuca.
Ibid., October, 1882. 8vo., pp. 279-280.

Recent Discoveries of Fossil Fishes in the Devonian rocks of Canada. Read before the Geological and Biological Section of the American Association for the Advancement of Science at the Montreal meeting in 1882.
American Naturalist, February, 1883. Large 8vo., pp. 158-164.

Geological Survey of Canada. Palæozoic Fossils, Vol. iii., Part 1. On some new, imperfectly characterized or previously unrecorded Species of Fossils from the Guelph formation of Ontario. Montreal, 1884.
Large 8vo. pp. 43, with 8 plates and 4 woodcuts.

Geological Survey of Canada. Mesozoic Fossils. Vol. i., Part 3. On the Fossils of the Coal-bearing deposits of the Queen Charlotte Islands collected by Dr. G. M. Dawson in 1878. Montreal, 1884.
Large 8vo., pp. 72, with 12 plates.

Note on a Decapod Crustacean from the Upper Cretaceous of Highwood River, Alberta, N.W.T.
Transactions Royal Society of Canada. Vol. ii., Sec 4, 1884. 4to., pp. 237-238.

Description of a New Species of Ammonite from the Cretaceous rocks of Fort St. John, on the Peace River.
Ibid., Vol. ii., Sec. 4, 1884. 4to., pp. 239-240.

Note on the Possible Age of some of the Mesozoic rocks of the Queen Charlotte Islands and British Columbia.
American Journal of Science and Arts, June, 1885. 8vo., pp. 441-419.

List of Marine Invertebrates from Hudson's Strait, collected by Dr. R. Bell in 1884.
Report of Progress, Geological Survey of Canada, 1882-3-4. Montreal, 1885. Large 8vo., pp. 58-60DD.

Contributions to Canadian Palæontology, Vol. i., Part i. (1) Report on the Invertebrata of the Laramie and Cretaceous rocks of the Vicinity of the Bow and Belly rivers and adjacent localities in the Northwest Territory.
Ibid., 1885. Large 8vo., pp. 89, and 11 plates.

Whiteaves, J. F.—*Continued.*

Colonial and Indian Exhibition. Catalogue of Canadian Pinnipedia, Cetacea, Fishes and Marine Invertebrata exhibited by the Department of Fisheries of the Dominion Government. Ottawa, 1886.
8vo., pp. 42.

Illustrations of the fossil fishes of the Devonian rocks of Canada. Part I.
Transactions Royal Society of Canada. Vol. iv., Sec. 4, 1886. 4to., pp. 101-110, with 5 plates.

On some Marine Invertebrata, dredged or otherwise collected by Dr. G. M. Dawson in 1885, on the coast of British Columbia; with a supplementary list of a few land and fresh water shells, fishes, birds, etc., from the same region.
Ibid., Vol. iv., Sec. 4, 1886, 4to., pp. 28, with 4 woodcuts.

Notes on some Mesozoic fossils from various localities on the coast of British Columbia, for the most part collected by Dr. G. M. Dawson in the summer of 1885.
Annual Report, Geological Survey of Canada, N. S., Vol. ii., Montreal, 1887. Large 8vo., pp. 108a-111a.

On some fossils from the Cretaceous and Laramie rocks of the Saskatchewan and its tributaries, collected by Mr. J. B. Tyrrell in 1885 and 1886.
Ibid., Vol. ii., Montreal, 1887. Large 8vo., pp. 153a-166a.

Illustrations of the fossil fishes of the Devonian rocks of Canada. Part 2.
Transactions Royal Society of Canada. Vol. vi., Sec. 4, 1888. 4to., pp. 77-96, with 6 plates.

Geological Survey of Canada. Contributions to Canadian Palæontology, Vol. i., Part ii. (2) On some fossils from the Hamilton formation of Ontario, with a list of the species at present known from that formation and province; (3) The fossils of the Triassic rocks of British Columbia; and (4) On some Cretaceous fossils from British Columbia, the Northwest Territories and Manitoba.
Montreal, 1889. Large 8vo., pp. 105, with 15 plates.

Descriptions of eight new species of fossils from the Cambro-Silurian rocks of Manitoba.
Transactions Royal Society of Canada. Vol. vii., Sec. 4, 1889. 4to, pp. 75-83, and 6 plates.

Descriptions of some new or previously unrecorded species of fossils from the Devonian rocks of Manitoba.
Ibid., Vol. viii., Sec. 4, 1890. 4to., pp. 93-110, with 7 plates.

Geological Survey of Canada. Contributions to Canadian Palæontology, Vol. i., Part iii. The fossils of the Devonian rocks of the Mackenzie River basin. Montreal, 1891.
Large 8vo., pp. 58, with 6 plates.

Descriptions of four new species of fossils from the Silurian rocks of the south-eastern portion of the District of Saskatchewan.
Canadian Record of Science, Vol. iv., Montreal, April, 1891. 8vo., pp. 293-303, with one plate.

Description of a new species of Panenka from the Corniferous Limestone of Ontario.
Ibid., Vol. iv., Montreal, October, 1891. 8vo., pp. 401-104, with 1 plate.

Whiteaves, J. F.—*Continued.*

Note on the occurrence of Paucispiral Opercula of Gasteropoda in the Guelph formation of Ontario.
Canadian Record of Science. Vol. IV., Montreal, October, 1891. 8vo., pp. 404-407.

The Orthoceratidæ of the Trenton Limestone of Manitoba.
Transactions Royal Society of Canada, Vol. IX., Sec. 4, 1891. 4to., pp. 77-90, with 7 plates.

Description of a new genus and species of Phyllocarid Crustacea from the Middle Cambrian of Mount Stephen, B.C.
Canadian Record of Science, Vol. v., Montreal October, 1892. 8vo., pp. 205-208.

Geological Survey of Canada. Contributions to Canadian Palæontology. Vol. I., Part IV. The fossils of the Devonian rocks of the islands, shores or immediate vicinity of Lakes Manitoba and Winnipegosis. Ottawa, 1892.
Large 8vo., pp. 106, with 15 plates.

Notes on the Ammonites of the Cretaceous rocks of the district of Athabasca, with descriptions of four new species.
Transactions Royal Society of Canada. Vol. X., Sec. 4, 1892. 4to., pp. 111-121, with 4 plates.

Notes on the Gasteropoda of the Trenton Limestone of Manitoba, with a description of one new species.
Canadian Record of Science, Vol. v., Montreal, April, 1893. 8vo., pp. 317-328, with 2 woodcuts.

Descriptions of two new species of Ammonites from the Cretaceous rocks of the Queen Charlotte Islands.
Canadian Record of Science, October, 1893, Vol. VI., pp. 441-446, with one full page plate.

The Cretaceous System in Canada. (Presidential Address in Section IV.)
Transactions Royal Society of Canada, Vol XI., Sec. 4, pp. 3-14.

The recent discovery of large Unio-like shells in the Coal-measures at the South Joggins, N.S.
Ibid., Vol. XI., Sec. 4, pp. 21-24, with one full page plate.

Notes on some Marine Invertebrata from the coast of British Columbia.
Ottawa Naturalist, Dec., 1893, Vol. VII., pp. 133-37, with four figures.

Williamson, Rev. James.

The Inland Seas of North America and the Natural and Industrial Productions of Canada, Kingston : John Duff, 1854.
8vo., pp. 78.

Observations at Kingston on the Transit of Venus.
In the Transactions of the Royal Society of Canada, Vol. I., Sec 3, 1883.

Withrow, W. H.

Catacombs of Rome, and their testimony relative to Primitive Christianity. London : Hodder & Stoughton, New York ; Hunt & Eaton.
12mo., cloth, pp. 560.

History of Canada, Boston and Toronto.
8vo., pp. 700. Illustrated.

Our Own Country, Toronto.
8vo., pp. 608. 360 Illustrations.

Withrow, W. H.—*Continued.*

A Canadian in Europe. Toronto: Hunter, Rose & Co.
12mo., cloth. Copiously illustrated.

Valeria ; The Martyr of the Catacombs, Toronto, London and New York.
12mo., cloth. Illustrated.

Barbara Heck. Toronto and London.
12mo., cloth.

Neville Trueman, the Pioneer Preacher. A tale of the War of 1812. Toronto and London.
12mo., cloth.

The King's Messenger ; or, Lawrence Temple's Probation. Toronto, London and New York.
12mo., cloth.

The Romance of Missions. Toronto.
12mo., cloth.

Worthies of early Methodism. Toronto.
12mo., cloth.

Men Worth Knowing ; or, Heroes of Christian Chivalry.
Methodist Magazine, 1881.

Missionary Heroes.
Ibid., 1882.

Wright, R. Ramsay.

Systematic Position of the Spongiadæ.
Canadian Journal, 1877, pp. 14.

Contributions to American Helminthology.
Proceedings Canadian Institute, N.S., Vol. I., 1879, pp. 1-24, 2 plates.

Notes on American Parasitic Copepoda.
Ibid., Vol. I., 1882. pp. 243-254, 2 plates.

On Demodex Phyllodes.
Ibid., 1883, pp. 275-281, 2 plates.

Trematode Parasites in American Crayfish.
American Naturalist, 1884, p. 429-30.

On the Organ of Jacobson in Ophidia.
Zoologischer Anzeiger, Vol. VII., 1884, p. 112.

On the Skin and Cutaneous Sense-Organs of Amiurus.
Proceedings Canadian Institute, N.S , Vol. II., 1884,

On the Nervous System and Sense-Organs of Amiurus.
Loc. cit., 1884, pp. 352-386, 3 plates.

On a Parasitic Copepod of the Clam.
American Naturalist, 1885, pp. 118-124, 1 plate.

On a Free Swimming Sporocyst.
Loc. cit., p. 310.

On the Hyomandibular Clefts and Pseudobranchs of Lepidosteus and Amia.
Journal Anatomy and Physiology, Vol. XIX., 1885, pp. 476-499, 1 plate.

On the Skull and Auditory organ of the Siluroid Hypophthalmus.
Transactions Royal Society of Canada, Vol. III., Sec. 4, 1885, pp. 107-118, 3 plates.

Introduction to Structure of Vertebrata.
In Standard Natural History, Boston : S. E. Cassino & Co., 1885, Vol. III., pp. 1-32, Imp. 8vo.

Account of Monotremes and Marsupials.
Ibid., Vol., v., pp. 11-45.

Of Ungulata.
Ibid., Vol. v., pp. 283-352.

Wright, R. Ramsay.—*Continued*.

Of Primates.
In Standard Natural History, Vol. v., pp. 430–528.

In conjunction with Dr. A. B. Macallum. Sphyranura. A contribution to American Helminthology.
Journal of Morphology, Boston, 1887, Vol. i., pp. 1–48, 1 plate.

Wright, R. Ramsay.—*Continued*.

An Introduction to Zoology for the use of Highschools. Toronto: Copp, Clark & Co., 1889. 12mo., pp. 314, with 194 figs.

Pathogenic Sporozoa.
Canadian Practitioner, Toronto, January, 1890.

Preliminary Report on the Fish and Fisheries of Ontario.
In Report of Ontario Fish and Game Commission, Toronto,1892,printed by order of Legislative Assembly, pp. 421–475, with 13 figs., text and 35 plates.